...ed as ...alist for *Time* ... a translator for the European Parliament. The preceding four novels in the Spike Sanguinetti series, *Shadow of the Rock, Sign of the Cross, Hollow Mountain* and *Sleeping Dogs* have all been published by Bloomsbury and to critical acclaim. He was shortlisted for the CWA Debut Dagger Award for best new crime writer of 2013. He is married and lives with his family in London.

thomasmogford.com
@ThomasMogford

A THOUSAND CUTS

Thomas Mogford

BLOOMSBURY

LONDON · OXFORD · NEW YORK · NEW DELHI · SYDNEY

BLOOMSBURY PUBLISHING
Bloomsbury Publishing Plc
50 Bedford Square, London, WC1B 3DP, UK

www.bloomsbury.com

BLOOMSBURY, BLOOMSBURY PUBLISHING and the Diana logo
are trademarks of Bloomsbury Publishing Plc

First published in Great Britain 2017
This paperback edition first published in 2018

British Library Cataloguing-in-Publication Data
A catalogue record for this book is available from the British Library.

ISBN: TPB: 978-1-4088-6850-8
        PB: 978-1-4088-6852-2
        ePub: 978-1-4088-6851-5

2 4 6 8 10 9 7 5 3 1

Typeset by Integra Software Services Pvt. Ltd.
Printed and bound in Great Britain by CPI Group (UK) Ltd, Croydon CR0 4YY

To find out more about our authors and books visit www.bloomsbury.com.
Here you will find extracts, author interviews, details of forthcoming
events and the option to sign up for our newsletters.

For Ali

PROLOGUE

Gibraltar, April 1940

'*Frightened*?' Harry looked across at his superior officer in surprise. He couldn't imagine Engineer Commander Arthur Baines being frightened of anything.

The older man stopped in the darkness of the road, reaching into his pocket for a pouch of tobacco. 'Poor choice of word, perhaps,' he said, as he packed the bowl of his pipe. 'But it is a daunting thing. To have a child. Suddenly, one finds one has so much to lose.'

As the match flared to life, Harry caught sight of Arthur's eyes and recognised, too late, the expression he'd seen on the night that the telegram had arrived. The telegram that had told him his eldest son had been killed by the Germans at Scapa Flow. Harry looked down at his feet, cursing himself for his thoughtlessness: he never should have shown Arthur the letter from Lizzie.

'But I'm pleased for you, Beck,' Arthur said, puffing rhythmically to draw the flame. 'It's what makes life worthwhile, after all.'

The two men continued down the coast road. The Rock loomed to their left, vast and sphinx-like against the night sky, swallowing up the moon. Beneath his boots, Harry felt the distant shudder of another reverberation. Ever since they'd arrived in this strange corner of the Mediterranean,

1

the sappers had been boring into the Rock, dynamiting its heart. Sometimes, in the early morning, Harry had seen them marching back through the Old Town, their faces white with limestone dust. The tunnels were meant to make people feel safe, but they had the opposite effect on Harry. It was as though the Army knew something that the Navy didn't.

As they passed the Dockyard, Harry felt the breeze on the nape of his neck, as warm as breath. Under the tobacco smoke, and the usual taint of bunker oil, he smelt a hint of something perfumed – pine resin, perhaps. A light caught his eye, and he turned towards the sea. 'The generator's off, Sir, isn't it?'

Arthur removed his pipe. 'I gave the order myself. Why?'

'I thought I saw something flash.'

They stopped outside the perimeter fence of the Dry Docks. Beyond the barbed wire, three iron gantry-cranes rose like sentinels. Lights sparkled on the Spanish side of the bay – 'non-belligerent' supposedly, but they all knew it to be colonised by German and Italian intelligence, just waiting for their chance to invade the Rock.

'Probably just the lighthouse at Algeciras,' Arthur reasoned. 'Sometimes they . . .' He broke off as they both saw the shaft of ghostly yellow light flash inside the Dry Dock graving. 'We'd better take a look,' Arthur said, pressing a penny piece into his pipe.

A wooden sentry box guarded the gateway. They approached the window, but found the hut empty save for a tin plate containing the remnants of dinner, the sandy floor littered with cigarette butts. 'Useless,' Arthur muttered. His contempt for the Dockyard Police was well known. 'Bloody amateurs' was the phrase he usually favoured, mouthed in silence by the rest of the Corps before he'd even had a chance to speak.

Harry stepped in front of him, suddenly protective of this upright, taciturn old man. On the gangway to their right, he made out the heavy machinery employed by those of his colleagues tasked with widening Dry Dock 1. There were rumours the *Ark Royal* was on her way to Gibraltar. It was only a matter of time before Hitler persuaded Mussolini to join the war, and then the Western Mediterranean would need a fleet.

The jagged silhouette of the fishing trawler reared above them. They'd sailed her in at first light, closed the gate and drained off the water until her fat, barnacled hull lay exposed, wedged on the bilge blocks. First Harry had fitted the Asdic, then the torpedo brackets. Within a month, he thought with a frisson of pride, the *Catalan Star* might be out hunting U-boats . . .

Feeling a hand on his shoulder, Harry spun round, but it was only Arthur, silhouetted in the half-light. Relief coursed through him: he wasn't cut out for combat, he'd realised; the adrenaline served only to muddy his mind. It takes courage to admit that you're afraid, Lizzie had told him the night before he'd left Portsmouth. And she should know: her father had emerged from the trenches at Passchendaele unscathed by the chlorine gas and shrapnel that had killed his brother and most of his friends. But the terror had never left him, Lizzie had said, the shame at having survived. And that night, safe in her warm embrace, Harry had let himself believe her comforting words. But he didn't feel so sure of them now.

'We need a light, man,' Arthur hissed. He jabbed a finger towards the gantry crane: 'Well, go on, Beck. Get a move on!'

Harry hurried over to the crane, crouching down and fumbling beneath its base until his hand found the solid heft of the torch. As his fist closed around the handle, he heard a scuffling noise behind him. He flicked on the switch and swung round, feeling his heart race as he circled the trawler, flashing the beam between the toolboxes and storage units that cluttered the platform.

But the only sound was the slop of the waves against the dock wall. Perhaps it *had* been a signal from across the water: they'd got through a few bottles of ale tonight, after all. Harry stumbled over something and dropped the torch. The beam went out and he cursed beneath his breath, falling to one knee and groping about in the darkness.

'Beck?' came Arthur's voice.

Harry's hand fell upon the torch. 'All's well, Sir,' he called back. Then he thumbed the switch back on, and stifled a scream.

Crouching on the walkway, just five yards in front of him, stood a young man with dark Andalusian skin. The Spaniard stared back at Harry, eyes narrowed beneath his thick black brows, then gave a slow shake of his head and pressed a finger to his lips.

Harry felt his stomach keel. The torch started to waver, and he heard his father's scathing voice in his head, remembered him jogging along the sidelines every Saturday afternoon, raincoat flapping, watching his short, scrawny son shiver in the mud, hanging back from the scrum, 'Get in there, boy!' Then the contemptuous shake of the head, 'Lord, *preserve* us . . .'

Just as Harry opened his mouth to call for Arthur, he saw the Spaniard point up at the hull of the trawler. Harry raised his shaking torch: one of the torpedo caps had been unscrewed. When he looked back at the Spaniard, their eyes locked, and Harry could see the terror in them.

A moment later there was a violent, ear-splitting boom, and a blinding cone of light blazed from the side of the trawler. And then Harry was soaring backwards, weightless, unanchored from time and reality.

A lifetime passed; Harry lay flat on his back, ears pulsating to the rhythm of his heart. His thighs felt damp, but it wasn't painful or sticky, and he realised with a sting of shame that he must have wet himself. He tried to take a breath, but something was wedged in the back of his throat. He forced his fingers between his teeth and found a wad of something soft. Tossing it aside in disgust, he felt the air seep into his lungs, sour with cordite, warmed by the flames that were flickering all around him now.

That was his war over, he thought – maybe his old man would even be proud of him. He knew Lizzie would be. He lowered an arm to haul himself up, then collapsed back onto the concrete. The arm was no longer there. He tried to breathe, but the thick coppery blood was filling his lungs. Perhaps he should just lie here for a while. Wait for Engineer Commander Arthur Baines to come and find him.

Lizzie's sweet face floated into his mind, and made him smile. She'd said in her letter that she believed it was a little girl she was carrying. Harry hoped he wouldn't be too much of a disappointment to his daughter. He'd love her like mad, that much he knew. So he closed his eyes, and waited for the ringing in his ears to fall silent.

PART ONE

GIBRALTAR, PRESENT DAY

1

Spike Sanguinetti walked alone up Engineer Road, scuffed leather briefcase swinging from one hand. His destination – Her Majesty's Prison, Windmill Hill – had replaced the old gaol at the Moorish Castle, a medieval fortress whose crumbling walls had proven a little too porous to criminals intent on escape. Though it was under a mile from Spike's office, most of the journey was uphill, and the levanter breeze, laden with moisture from its passage up the Mediterranean, brought the usual film of sweat to his high tanned brow.

The new facility was housed in an abandoned barracks at the southern tip of the Rock. As Spike reached the old army parade ground, now serving as prison car-park, he paused to catch his breath. The Windmill Hill plateau spread all around him, a curious microclimate of loose scree and thorn bushes – so similar, people said, to the mountains of Afghanistan that visiting troops still used it for training exercises. No sign of any squaddies today, Spike noted as he loosened his tie, just the metal-barred mouths of the Second World War defence tunnels, many of which now housed banks of computer servers owned by the online gaming companies that were the latest colonisers of the Rock.

A slight man waited by the gate, one hand shielding his eyes from the August glare. Spike recognised Danny Garcia at once by his dun-coloured suit and the oppressed slope of his shoulders. Garcia squinted in Spike's direction, then gave a wave of greeting and hurried over. 'Mr Sanguinetti,' he panted, clasping Spike's hand in both of his with a smile of relief. 'So good of you to come.' His small dark eyes widened. 'I thought perhaps you'd changed your mind.'

Spike retrieved his fingers from Garcia's damp grasp. 'Sorry I'm late, Danny.'

'No matter, no matter.' Garcia combed back the remains of his brown hair, then pressed the buzzer. 'You received the file, I hope?'

Spike nodded.

'Good, good.'

The gate swung open to reveal a large, sleepy-eyed prison warder. Garcia lowered his voice: 'I know you didn't have much time to prepare, but as I was saying to Laura only this morning . . .' He darted Spike an embarrassed glance, cheeks aflame with uxorious pride. 'My wife, Laura . . .'

Spike suppressed a smile. Good for you, Danny, he thought.

'If there's one lawyer on the Rock who can handle a tricky client, it's Spike Sanguinetti. Champion of the Underdog, that's what I told her.'

Spike winced a little: it was not a reputation to be cultivated. 'How bad is it?'

Garcia pressed his lips together. 'The prosecution case is strong. Mr Massetti is not what you might call a sympathetic defendant.'

The two lawyers walked down the breeze-block corridor, newly painted in an especially depressing shade of institutional mint. Most of the cells were empty, and through the open doors, Spike glimpsed padded bunk-beds and curved aluminium sinks. Not too bad, he concluded – better designed than most of the new-build flats his estate agent had taken him to view lately. 'And Massetti still hasn't said anything?'

'Other than to intimate that my services were no longer required, no.' Garcia held open his arms in defeat, looking for a moment like a conscientious social worker who knew that he'd failed his client. Then he forced himself to rally, and passed Spike a slim folder. 'My notes. They're a bit rough, but . . .'

The warder had stopped outside the interview room and was pulling out his keys.

'The trial's scheduled for 10 a.m. tomorrow,' Garcia said.

'In the Mags?'

Garcia nodded. 'The Attorney General's seeking prosecution under Section 94.'

'With Cassar on the bench?'

'Afraid so. You can reach me on my mobile . . .' Garcia trailed off, wringing his small hands.

'But?'

'I'll be out of town.' Garcia's blush deepened. 'Laura's persuaded me to take a surfing course. In Tarifa.'

Spike scratched one ear. If these days even Danny Garcia was getting fit, it might be time to reconsider hitting the gym. He held out a hand. 'You'll be doing three-sixties in no time, Danny.'

He watched Garcia scurry away, then turned to the warder. 'I'd like to be left alone with Mr Massetti.'

The warder let out a knowing chuckle. When he spoke, it was in *yanito*, the Gibraltarian patois of Italian, Hebrew, English and Spanish. '*Ese tio es waka.*'

Spike smiled. 'My clients usually are.' '*Waka*' was a swear word derived from the English. The 'N' preceding the 'K' had been lost over time, but the man's hand gesture had made the meaning clear enough.

The warder shrugged. 'You're the boss, Mr Sanguinetti.' Then he pulled open the door.

2

Christopher Massetti sat slumped in his plastic chair, heavy head lowered. He didn't flinch as the door clanged shut, so Spike just opened his briefcase in silence, taking an occasional glance at his prospective client as he laid out his notebook and prehistoric Dictaphone on the table. Massetti's physique was imposing for a man in his early seventies, he supposed, though his face was what Spike's father might have described as 'lived-in': broken nose striated with spider veins, bags like dried apricots beneath the eyes. His shoulder-length hair was squirrel-grey – silver, perhaps, when clean – and his mauve jumpsuit looked like it would need a high-temperature wash after a day spent pressed against his broad chest.

Spike placed the document file on the chair and his hands in his pockets. 'Mr Massetti?' Just as Garcia had warned him, the old man didn't react, so Spike raised his voice. 'My name is Spike Sanguinetti. Do you understand the charges being brought against you, Mr Massetti?'

A few seconds ticked past; Spike could hear Massetti's breathing, thick and hoarse. He rubbed his temple with a thumb and tried again. 'You've been charged with harassment under the Crimes Act 2011. If found guilty, you run the risk of a custodial sentence. At the very least, you'll be subject to a restraining order preventing you from making any further contact with Eloise Capurro.'

At the sound of his alleged victim's name, Massetti opened his eyes but didn't lift them, just focused on a spot on the floor somewhere near Spike's feet. At least he's not asleep, Spike reasoned, then looked down again at Danny Garcia's notes. 'You've been refused bail due to concerns that you might interfere with prosecution witnesses. The maximum sentence that the court can confer is twelve months, and under these circumstances, I must advise you that's the probable outcome.'

Massetti shifted slightly in his chair, but then he just closed his eyes again. Fighting a surge of frustration, Spike glanced up at the clock. He was going to be late for dinner. He placed both hands on the table and willed the man to look at him. 'We're due in court tomorrow morning, Mr Massetti. At least tell me how you intend to plead.'

But the old man kept his counsel, and Spike silently conceded defeat. He started to gather his things together, then caught sight of Massetti's hands. The wrinkled skin was mottled with old scars and fresh scabs, but it was the fingers that disturbed Spike, working in and out of each other, like muscular worms seeking purchase in stony ground. Massetti must have sensed his gaze as he interlaced them, trying to control the tremors. Withdrawal symptoms: Spike had seen them before. He reached out a hand. 'You know you have a right to see a doctor, Mr Massetti.' But as soon as Spike touched Massetti's shoulder, the old man raised an arm and smacked the back of his hand across Spike's face.

Spike stumbled backwards, astonished at the man's strength. His chair overturned, scattering Garcia's carefully drafted notes across the floor. Hearing footsteps outside,

Spike pulled his hand away from his eye and was strangely shocked to see a smear of red on his fingertips.

The door flew open, and the warder's face hardened as he sized up the situation. He took out his radio with a wearied shake of the head.

But Spike was already on his feet. He caught the warder's cuff. 'It's fine,' he said, gesturing at the documents on the ground. 'I just tripped.' At the edge of his vision, Spike saw Massetti raise his head in surprise. 'I'll be back tomorrow,' he added, as he wiped the blood out of his eye with one thumb. 'We'll talk more then.'

3

Spike hesitated outside the restaurant, fingering the hastily applied Steri-Strips that criss-crossed his left eyebrow. Then he straightened his tie and walked inside, hearing the small brass bell above the door give its familiar tinkle.

The restaurant was busy for a Tuesday. And tonight, each table gave a fair representation of the castes that made up modern Gibraltarian society. Even in the wake of Britain's vote to leave the EU, the Rock's appeal as a financial centre endured. Spike recognised at a glance the sweating recruits for the online gaming companies, so fresh off the plane from London that they hadn't had time to adjust their wardrobes to the climate. The tax lawyers, liquoring up non-doms, their raucous laughter failing to conceal that telltale sharpness behind the eye. The insurance brokers – yesterday's boom industry – in their sensible suits with a touch of the idiosyncratic thrown in: the spotted bow-tie, the statement jewellery. There was even the odd bored-looking Russian or Italian, ignoring his surgically enhanced wife, here under sufferance to see out his required period of tax residency. The only soldiers and sailors these days were frozen in time, immortalised in the sepia photographs on the walls – the *Ark Royal* at anchor, her cheering crew unaware that just a few weeks later she'd be cut in two by a German U-boat.

Ignoring the barrage of glances at his damaged face, Spike sought out Jessica and found her sitting at their usual table, tanned arms folded across her narrow chest, giving no hint of the baby bump hidden below. If she'd heard the bell she didn't look up, just stared at the empty ceramic jar on the table in front of her. Spike knew what that meant. He wasn't just late, he was six breadsticks late.

Sensing his presence, Jessica turned, and he tried to gauge how much trouble he was in from the expression in her dark eyes. Fearing the worst, he raised a hand to his wound in mitigation. She conceded a small smile. 'One of your better excuses, I suppose.'

'Sorry.' Spike leant in to kiss her, catching a hint of the citrus scent she knew that he liked. The restaurant chatter ramped up around them as Spike squeezed onto the cracked red banquette opposite her, the sad low croak of Nina Simone just audible beneath the babble.

Jessica reached up and twisted his chin to get a better view of his injury. Not especially gently, he thought.

'Well?' She flicked up her eyes to meet his. He was about to tell her all about it, when Marcela Peralta appeared at his shoulder with a starched white napkin filled with ice. As ever, Spike couldn't help but be impressed by the restaurateur's efficacy and discretion. 'Thanks, Marcela,' he said, as he gingerly dabbed the cold compress against his eye.

Marcela just arched a blackened eyebrow and placed two leather menus embossed with her name on the table. Then she glided away, brittle bird-like body swamped by the flowing silk robes that she favoured for evening service. No one knew her real age: the more vicious members of her circle hinted that she was over ninety, but Spike had never dared ask.

17

Jessica sighed. 'That'll keep tongues wagging in the Old Town for a few days.'

'I'm sure Marcela has more juicy things to gossip about,' Spike replied, distracted by the pinkish hue that had come away on the napkin. The cut was deep: maybe he should have got it stitched.

'Here.' Jessica snatched the ice from him in exasperation. He flinched as she pressed it into the socket. He was going to have an impressive shiner; he wondered how that would play out in court tomorrow. 'Shall we order?'

Marcela had her back to them, perching at the counter on her swivel stool, scribbling away as usual. As if by telepathy, she raised a hanging wing of silk, and one of her devoted Spaniards jumped to her silent command and approached their table.

Orders despatched to the kitchen, Spike covered Jessica's hands with his. 'So how was the viewing?'

She took a sip of iced water, then let slip a grimace of heartburn. 'Same as the last one. Great view, crappy flat.'

'We could always do up Dad's place. Get a bigger mortgage.'

'I see little enough of you as it is.'

It was a circular discussion they'd been having for months, so they were both grateful when the food arrived. Marcela's chef had outdone herself tonight, Spike thought, feeling his mouth water as he admired the whole sea bass recumbent on its bed of grilled cherry tomatoes, the wilted beetroot greens he knew would have been picked that day from the restaurant's kitchen garden. He waved away the waiter, hearing his father's voice in his head as he scored the point of the knife down the lateral line and eased the white flesh away from the bone: '*Genoese migrants, son – we know our way round a piece of fish.*'

'How was work?' Spike asked.

'They're benching me.' Jessica suddenly looked weary. 'Despite the fact I don't start maternity leave for another six weeks. Highlight of my day was an ID parade.' She tipped up the fish with her knife, considered the veined green discs of fennel beneath, then wrinkled her nose and pushed the plate away. Raging hunger which dissipated after two mouthfuls: another of the gods' many and varied ways to torment the pregnant. 'So who was it?' she asked.

'My new client.' That surprised her. 'Christopher Massetti.'

Jessica made an 'Ouch' expression, suggesting that the name was not unknown to the police. Spike was about to enquire further when Marcela reappeared, her shrewd green eyes roving over the debris, checking that glasses had been refilled, appetites sated. Beneath Marcela's cropped silver hair, her face was indented with hundreds of tiny lines, but soft as a peach, Spike knew, having been engulfed into her rose-water-scented embrace many times as a boy. Somehow, somewhere, the cupid's bow of crimson lipstick had been carefully reapplied. 'So?' She glowered down at them like an ageing film star demanding affirmation of her genius.

Spike stifled a smile. He knew what Marcela expected of her customers. 'The fennel was particularly delicious.' And it was true. He could still taste a hint of aniseed on his tongue.

But Marcela had already turned her attention to his companion. 'I hear it can be helpful for those in *your* condition.' To Spike's surprise, Jessica blushed. Having achieved the desired effect, Marcela looked back at Spike. 'And how is your father? Health still troubling him?' She pressed her scarlet lips together in sympathy. 'We've missed him at our bridge nights.'

Spike grinned back, knowing from a recent conversation with Rufus that the sentiment was not reciprocated: '*These women, son. It's like Orestes being pursued by the Furies.*' 'Dad's on great form. He's been helping out with Charlie. Says it's given him a new lease of life.'

A look of confusion crossed Marcela's face.

'Charlie lives with us now,' Spike explained. 'We made it official.' He felt Jessica squeeze his hand. 'We've adopted him.'

Marcela reached down to ruffle Spike's dark hair. 'I remember you coming here as a little boy. You were always a favourite, even then. And now you have a child at home,' she continued, as the plates vanished around them. 'And a baby on the way.' She picked up Jessica's left hand to study the small daisy-shaped engagement ring, its petals comprised of yellow and white diamonds. 'At least there's a ring, I suppose. But you young people do make a habit of putting the cart before the horse, don't you?'

Spike gave a sheepish smile. 'It's all happened pretty fast.' He saw Jessica flash him a look across the table. When it came to Marcela Peralta, his fiancée and father were of one mind: a little went a long way.

'We should get the bill,' Jessica said firmly, as she pushed back her chair. 'I'll just be a minute.'

Spike helped her up, watching her wend her way as gracefully as possible between the tables towards the lavatories. Marcela patted Spike's arm. 'She's lovely, Spike. You're a lucky man.' Then she glided away to the next table.

4

When they got back to Chicardo's Passage, the house was already in darkness. The state-of-the-art baby monitor had been left on the kitchen table beside the incinerated remains of an M&S steak-and-kidney pie, and through its tiny speakers, Spike could just make out the gentle rhythm of Charlie's breathing.

Jessica looked exhausted. Spike could tell that the heartburn was troubling her again, so he sent her up to bed while he heated some milk. But by the time he made it up to their room, she was already asleep, a pillow wedged between her knees and an as-yet unopened copy of *What to Expect When You're Expecting* on the mattress beside her.

Resisting the temptation to lie down next to her, Spike switched off the light and crept back downstairs. His briefcase was just where he'd left it, discarded by the front door in the dark hallway. He carried it through the bead curtain to the kitchen, then pulled out the grey Lever Arch file marked 'R v Massetti' and braced himself for the task ahead.

It took him more than an hour to wade through the witness statements and supporting documentation. From a defence counsel's perspective, it made for depressing reading. The complainant, Dr Eloise Capurro, had provided a detailed dossier evidencing what appeared to be a sustained campaign of harassment by Christopher Massetti. If the prosecution needed just two instances when Dr Capurro had felt under threat of violence to make their case, they were spoilt for choice. Behind the next divider, Spike found a photocopy of Massetti's criminal record. Amongst the panoply of alcohol-related minor convictions he might have expected, there was one that gave genuine cause for concern. Four years ago, Massetti had been convicted of ABH. The sentence had been suspended, but it meant that when it came to violence, the man had form.

Spike pushed the file away and tucked his hands behind his head, wondering once again what had possessed him to take the case. His business partner, Peter Galliano, would not approve, that much he knew. So far, Peter had been prepared to indulge Spike's occasional forays back into the unprofitable world of criminal defence law where he'd begun his career – as long as such enterprises didn't impact upon Peter's grand plan to transform their two-man firm into a tax-advisory monolith. But the compromise was wearing thin, and as Peter's ambitions intensified, so did Spike's frustrations with corporate tax work. He'd never been particularly moved by money, and had always found criminal defence law rewarding, even if it came with its moments of wretchedness. He knew that Jessica understood that, despite the fact that he invariably found himself on the opposite side of the police.

It was one of the many things he admired about her, Spike thought as he gazed around the kitchen, finding everywhere the evidence of how she'd taken the Sanguinetti family in hand since he'd finally persuaded her to move in. At first, Jessica had been content to illuminate previously esoteric rituals, such as why the fridge needed to be cleaned, and what to do with fabric conditioner. But little by little, she'd made her presence felt in other more subtle ways. Rufus's watercolour kit and prescription medicines, neatly tidied away into the wicker baskets she'd found in a thrift shop on Main Street. The alphabet magnets she'd known Charlie would love stuck to the fridge.

Hearing the click of the bead curtain, Spike turned to see his father hovering in the doorway. Over his striped pyjamas, Rufus Sanguinetti wore a grey cashmere cardigan that Spike suspected pre-dated his own birth. In any event, it had sustained so many generations of hungry moths that it looked as though Rufus had been peppered by machine-gun fire, yet had by some miracle survived.

'Can't sleep?' Spike asked.

Rufus gave a stoic wave of the hand and lowered his gangly body into a wooden chair. 'Thought I heard the boy cry out. That's all.'

Spike stared at his father in wonderment. He had no memory of such solicitude during his own childhood. Maybe it came with old age.

Rufus laid his hands on the tabletop, which Spike recognised as a silent command for tea. So he got to his feet and flipped on the new electric kettle that Jessica had bought for them.

'I wondered if the boy might fancy an egg for his breakfast,' Rufus called out in that abrupt way he had when slightly embarrassed.

Spike turned in alarm. His father's culinary skills were legend for all the wrong reasons. 'There's really no need, Dad. I can see to Charlie tomorrow.'

'I'd say you've enough on your plate already.' Rufus pulled the client file towards him and felt for his spectacles. 'As in *Christopher* Massetti?' he asked, looking up with a frown.

Spike nodded; he'd long since abandoned fears over client confidentiality when it came to his father. Turning back to the counter, he poured the boiling water into the blue enamel teapot, waiting for the leaves to infuse, thinking that the tea never tasted quite as good as it had from their whistling old cast-iron kettle.

'I overlapped with Christopher for a year at the Christian Brothers,' Rufus began behind him. 'He had a sharp mind. Particularly proficient at chess.' Spike set down a chipped mug in front of his father and waited for more. 'There was an incident with some of the boys in his year. Bullying in schools is not uncommon, of course, but the campaign against Christopher was particularly vicious. In those days, there was still an assembly each morning, and during prayers, the boys at the front of the balcony would take it in turns to spit onto Christopher's head.' Rufus cupped the tea in his hands and blew on it. 'Looking back, I suppose the masters must have known what was going on, but received wisdom then was that children should be left to sort these things out between themselves. Let the natural order prevail, that kind of nonsense. And I suppose it did, in a way. There was a fight, and Christopher shattered another boy's cheekbone. He was big for his age, even then. The boy lost the hearing in one ear, and Christopher was expelled. We lost touch after that, but I don't think Christopher ever really got over it. Never settled into anything.' Rufus shot Spike one of the disappointed looks that had proved invaluable over a teaching career which had spanned five decades. 'I *had* heard he was volunteering at the Gibraltar Museum, but the demon drink . . .' He peered over the rims of his half-moons and tapped his eyebrow. Spike scowled back like a teenager: 'It's not a beer injury, Dad. But thanks for asking.'

His father pushed himself to his feet. 'Nice cuppa, son. Heaps better.'

Once he was gone, Spike spent another twenty unproductive minutes on Massetti's file before his eyelids started to droop. He was just about to switch out the light when a thought struck him. It took him a quarter of an hour to find what he was looking for amongst his father's crowded bookshelves, and then he climbed the steep creaking staircase and joined his fiancée in bed.

5

Whether it was Marcela's fennel, or his decision not to drink alone at supper, Spike slept well that night, and found himself in buoyant mood the next morning as he once again made the steep climb up Engineer Road. The sun was high in the sky, but not yet strong enough to be oppressive, and on such a glorious day a person could believe that almost anything was possible – perhaps even the successful defence of an indefensible client, Spike thought as he walked into the interview room.

At first glance, things appeared to have improved overnight. Some kindly prison officer must have taken Massetti in hand, as his hair had been washed and combed, and he'd been provided with a serviceable blue suit for his court appearance.

'Our case has been bumped to midday, Mr Massetti,' Spike said. 'So we have some time.'

Once again, Massetti made no reply, but today Spike had come prepared. He clicked open his briefcase and placed his father's copy of Bronstein's *The Chess Struggle in Practice* on the table between them. Massetti inched forward for a better look, and for the first time Spike caught a spark of interest in his expression. 'I don't play myself. But I understand you're fond of the game.'

Massetti laid a hand on the cover and drew the book towards him. He looked as though he'd dried out a little,

Spike thought, the tremors less obvious. Then he spoke for the first time, his voice low and gruff. 'Thank you.'

Spike delved back into his briefcase, fearing that if he stopped to acknowledge this minor breakthrough then he risked his client clamming up again. He pulled out a photocopy of Massetti's criminal record and passed it to him. 'You have a previous conviction for a violent crime, Christopher. That increases the chances of a prison term.'

'Prison's not so bad,' Massetti replied.

Spike hesitated. For men like Massetti, he knew there could be some truth in that. He'd defended enough alcoholics to know that a clean bed and three meals a day might well trump hanging around a public park scrounging for loose change. But that kind of talk wasn't going to help Massetti today. 'You're on remand, Christopher. General lock-up won't be like this.' Seeing Massetti drop his eyes to his feet again, Spike snapped his fingers in his face. 'Come on, Christopher. This is serious!'

Massetti looked up, grey eyes unexpectedly challenging and alert. 'I find that people usually let me down.'

A few years ago, Spike might have agreed. But things had changed. So he sat back and waited as his client drummed his thick fingers on the dust jacket of the book. Then, just as Spike was about to give up, Massetti sat forward and clasped his hands together. 'All right, Mr Sanguinetti. What is it that you want to know?'

Spike reached for his Dictaphone with a grin.

6

As was his custom before a difficult case, Spike arrived promptly, and was relieved to find the street outside the New Law Courts empty of the usual rabble of harassed briefs and anxious petty criminals. Savouring his last few moments of solitude, he leant back against the side wall of the courthouse and closed his eyes, trying to ignore the flutterings in his stomach. However many years he practised, however many cases he notched up, the first day of trial never got any easier.

'Topping up your tan, Sanguinetti?'

Instantly recognising his oldest friend's sardonic drawl, Spike opened his eyes to see Drew Stanford-Trench striding towards him. Drew's English accent had grown more clipped since he'd hit his thirties, Spike realised. Like most of Gibraltar's elite, Drew had been sent to public school in the UK. On his return to the Rock, he'd elected to tone down his accent to fit in with his colleagues, modifying his vowels towards that soft Latino lilt – neither Spanish nor Italian, but somewhere in between. But as the years had passed, and Drew's practice had prospered, he'd reverted to type.

They shook hands, and Drew leant back against the wall next to Spike. 'Thought I'd be locking horns with Garcia.' An arch sideways glance: 'Pity. I was looking forward to a relaxing few days.'

'You obviously haven't seen Danny in action for a while,' Spike retorted. 'He's a very able advocate.'

Safe in the knowledge that Danny Garcia was unlikely to be rivalling him in the 'Rising Stars' section of the *Legal 500* in the near future, Drew made no effort to conceal his scepticism. He was looking a little jowlier these days, Spike was pleased to note, though his patrician, blond good looks still ensured he was rarely short of female company.

'I'm surprised to see you slumming it in the Mags,' Spike said. And he meant it: Drew had taken silk in the last round of appointments and was proving adept at focusing his talents on a more lucrative class of client. 'I thought you'd have passed this one on to a junior.'

'Oh, you know me,' Drew replied, toying nonchalantly with a cufflink. 'I like to keep my hand in.' He caught sight of Spike's black eye and inclined his head.

'Slight misunderstanding with my client.'

'And he's pleading *not* guilty?' Drew pursed his lips in amusement, each one surrounded by a line of freckles, an indelible reminder that the pale settled on the Rock at their own peril.

'Innocent until proven guilty,' Spike sing-songed.

'You still buy that crap? Well, there's always one, I suppose.' Drew's ringtone erupted in his pocket, and Spike recognised Gibraltar's national anthem, 'Gibraltar, Gibraltar, the Rock on which I stand . . .'

Sliding out his smartphone like a sheriff, Drew squinted at the screen. 'When this is over, we should catch up. My old man would love to see you.' He was already at the courthouse door when he glanced over one shoulder, phone pressed to his ear. 'You got engaged, right?'

Spike nodded, and Drew tossed back his head in silent laughter and disappeared inside. Turning back to the sun, Spike allowed himself one last moment to clear his mind. Then he ran a hand through his thick dark hair and followed his opponent into the courthouse.

7

Eloquent preamble delivered, Drew Stanford-Trench turned to the bench. 'The Crown calls Dr Eloise Capurro.'

The courtroom watched in silence as an elegant woman in her sixties made her way to the stand. In her long black dress and muted Hermès scarf, she was perfectly attired for the role she was about to play. Had she been wearing widow's weeds and a veil, she could hardly have looked more appropriate.

Drew lunged forward to help his key witness up to the witness box. Pre-rehearsed, Spike suspected, as the woman looked sturdy enough on her feet.

'When you're *quite* ready, Mr Stanford-Trench,' the stipendiary magistrate barked, sharp-eyed as ever. Alan Cassar was a notoriously irascible QC; a practising Methodist, he liked to commit to a few months' magistracy a year to atone for the piles of cash he made advising hedge funds the rest of the time. It was one of the fringe benefits of Gibraltar's fused legal profession, in which both solicitor and barrister work were available – money could flow from one, conscience be salved by the other.

'Dr Capurro,' Drew began. 'Can you tell the court when you first met the accused?' He gestured towards the dock, where Massetti was staring into nowhere as a fat young prison officer stood guard behind him.

Eloise gazed at her counsel, small sharp chin raised in determination. She'd not looked at Massetti at all, Spike noted. The tension was clear in the way she held her neck. 'Three months ago,' she replied, her accent a neutral English, a hint of the Estuary in the vowels perhaps, long suppressed.

'On the ninth of May this year?' Drew read, then glanced up for her confirmation.

Eloise nodded. 'Five days before my husband died.'

'And under what circumstances did you meet Mr Massetti?'

'I was sitting with John at the hospital . . .'

'John Capurro?' Drew was guiding her. 'Your late husband?'

'Yes.' Eloise swallowed. 'It was about seven p.m. A nurse came in and said John had a visitor.'

'Christopher Massetti? The man in the dock?'

As one, the court turned to look at Massetti, and Spike saw his client as they must. Large, sweaty man in a cheap suit, striped shirt straining around his gut. *Guilty*.

As Eloise forced herself to follow their gaze, Spike saw an ugly red flush rise on her cheeks beneath the thick layer of face powder. 'Yes,' she said. 'That's him.' She turned back to Drew, drinking in the encouragement from his reassuring brown eyes.

'Thank you, Dr Capurro. And then what happened?'

'I told the nurse that I'd never heard of the man. But John said it would be all right.'

'And was it?'

'Well, in he came.' Her voice sharpened, and Spike found himself wondering if that was how she'd used to address her late husband. He knew a bit about her from the witness statements – how she'd spent most of her career at a family practice in Kent, until she'd met John Capurro in her fifties, on holiday in Spain. They'd returned to Gib together, where she'd worked as a locum at a surgery on Rosia Road. Serving that type of community, she'd have to be tougher than she looked.

'John asked me to step outside,' Eloise continued. 'He said he wanted to speak to Mr Massetti alone.' She cleared her throat, and Drew indicated to the clerk, who approached with a glass of water.

'Were you surprised when John asked you to leave?' Drew asked.

'I was unaware John even knew the man. I couldn't imagine what they had in common. But John was reasonably bright that day, so I did as I was asked. I only left them for a moment to get a cup of coffee.'

Spike watched the care with which she set down her glass.

'When I came back, I heard raised voices.'

'Where were the hospital staff?' Drew asked.

'Summer hours, probably,' Eloise muttered, referring to the fact that between June and September, office hours on the Rock ran from eight a.m. until two-thirty p.m. 'Not something I bother with myself,' she added. Her accent suddenly sounded more English than ever, and she made no effort to temper the disdain in it. Even Cassar, from the Olympus of his bench, looked slightly uncomfortable.

'So you went in.' Drew was beside the witness box now, one hand on the wooden rail, the better to offer his fullest support. 'And what happened next?'

'Mr Massetti' – she hissed the double 's' – 'had his hands around John's neck. He was shaking him.'

Drew turned to the court and raised his blond eyebrows. 'Violently?'

'Yes,' Eloise said. 'Shaking him and shouting.' Her voice caught, and Drew allowed her a moment to collect herself, face expertly composed into an expression of indignation and concern. Then his eyes found Spike's, and he gave the flicker of a grin.

Drew swung back round to face his witness. 'And what did you do then, Dr Capurro, when you found the accused throttling your terminally ill husband?'

'Your Worship,' Spike interjected, 'my learned friend is testifying on behalf of the witness.'

Cassar weighed this, then gestured for Eloise to continue.

'I screamed at him to stop. But he didn't even seem to realise I was there. So I pulled the emergency cord.'

'And?'

'I tried to drag him off. But he pushed me away.'

'Did you feel in danger, Dr Capurro?'

'Yes. Yes, I did.'

Drew opened his mouth for his next question, but Eloise interrupted him. 'Then Anthony arrived, thank God . . .'

Drew cocked his head, and Eloise glanced up at Cassar, as though fearing she'd made a misstep. Spike rifled through the witness list – there was no mention of any 'Anthony'.

'Anthony?' Drew echoed.

'Sir Anthony Stanford,' Eloise said. 'Your father,' she added for the benefit of those too slow to make the connection.

Seeing the look of shock on Drew's face, Spike resisted the temptation to laugh.

'Did you know about this?' Cassar called over from the bench.

'Certainly not, Your Worship,' Drew replied.

The magistrate swivelled his eyes to Spike, who shrugged his shoulders with a smirk that suggested it was news to him, but that he was rather enjoying his opponent's discomfort. Cassar glared back, and Spike straightened his face.

'Then for your sake, Mr Stanford-Trench, let's hope that Sir Anthony is peripheral to the evidence,' Cassar said. 'Because I'll not have a case of mine overturned on the basis of a conflict that should have been obvious to Crown Counsel from the outset.' The magistrate waved a hand as though swatting away a couple of irritating wasps. 'We'll review the matter in my chambers at close of session.'

As Spike sat back down, he saw an unmarked white envelope lying on his seat. He looked over his shoulder, but whoever had delivered it had gone.

'Please continue, Dr Capurro,' Drew said.

Eloise paused to regain her thread, and Spike tore open the envelope and examined the papers inside. It took him a moment to realise their value, then he grabbed a highlighter pen and started marking them up.

'Ah, perhaps you could tell us what happened after Sir Anthony arrived, Dr Capurro,' Drew urged, throwing a searching glance in Spike's direction, trying to work out what he was doing.

'A male nurse came in,' Eloise said. 'Between the two of them, they managed to get Mr Massetti out of the room. But by then, of course, John's BP was through the roof.'

'BP?'

Eloise gave a stiff smile. 'My husband's blood pressure, Mr Stanford-Trench. When the doctor finally arrived, I advised her to sedate him.'

'And where was Mr Massetti at this point?'

'I believe he was being escorted from the hospital by security.'

'Did your husband recover, Dr Capurro?'

'John had Grade Three pancreatic cancer, Mr Stanford-Trench.' Eloise narrowed her gaze. 'There's no recovering from that.'

Drew bit his lip. 'Apologies, Dr Capurro. I meant did your husband regain consciousness after Mr Massetti's assault?'

Spike got to his feet, highlighter in hand. 'Your Worship, Mr Massetti has not been charged with assault.'

'Quite right. Rephrase, Counsel.'

'After your husband's altercation with the defendant,' Drew corrected.

'No. John deteriorated rapidly after that. He died the following Wednesday.'

'A more rapid deterioration than might have been the case without the defendant's involvement?'

'Your Worship,' Spike called out, 'Dr Capurro is not an expert witness.'

'The complainant is a doctor of some forty years' standing,' Drew retorted.

But Cassar didn't seem in the least concerned by the point of law. 'Let's move *on*, Mr Stanford-Trench.'

There was a steel in Drew's eyes now. 'When did you see Mr Massetti next, Dr Capurro?'

'The day my husband died.' Eloise gave a strange smile, as though she still couldn't quite believe it. 'Mr Massetti came to the house. When I saw who it was, I didn't want to let him in, but he put his foot in the door.'

'You must have been frightened.'

'I was. If my nephew hadn't arrived when he did, I don't know what might have happened.'

'But even then Mr Massetti didn't leave you alone, did he?'

'No. He stood out on the street all night.' Eloise's voice fell, her eyes focusing on her hands. 'I could see him from my bedroom window.'

'Take your time, Dr Capurro.' Drew was back at her side. 'I know this must be painful for you.'

'Every night thereafter, I would see Mr Massetti outside our house on Governor's Street. My nephew insisted that we install a CCTV camera, but it was unreliable. So I kept a diary.'

Drew waited for Cassar to shuffle through the prosecution bundle until he found his copy. 'And when did you see the defendant last?'

'At my husband's funeral,' Eloise said.

A hush fell across the courtroom, and Spike could sense the audience settling into their seats as though for a bedtime story. Each case had its moments of tedium and of titillation, he knew, and the public gallery had remarkable antennae for which was which.

'The service was at the Cathedral of St Mary the Crowned,' Eloise began. 'John had spent a great deal of time selecting the music, choosing his favourite readings. He wanted it to be a quiet ceremony, a time to reflect.'

Eloise's smile fell. 'As we got out of the car, I saw Mr Massetti standing outside the church.' Everyone turned again to look at the dishevelled man in the dock. 'The last reading was from Luke, Chapter Six – "*But I say unto you which hear, love your enemies, do good to them which hate you.*"' Eloise looked up at Cassar, who nodded his approval. 'It seemed . . .' She swallowed. 'It seemed as though John was asking me to give Mr Massetti the benefit of the doubt. I thought maybe John's death had disturbed him in a way I didn't understand. Silly, really.' She took a sip of water and recomposed herself. 'John's casket was lying beneath the altar. We'd covered it in madonna lilies. But when we started singing the last hymn, "As the Green Blade Riseth", Massetti got to his feet and walked up the aisle. As soon he reached the coffin, he started pulling off the flowers, shouting like a madman. Then he stamped on them.'

Hearing the collective intake of breath from the court-room, Spike fought an urge to roll his eyes. Desecrating the dead's floral arrangements appeared to be a more shocking crime than terrorising the living.

'And what happened then, Dr Capurro?' Drew said, steepled fingertips nestling in the neat cleft of his chin.

'Anthony called the police.'

Another reference to Sir Anthony: now even Cassar began to look perturbed. For a moment Spike thought he was going to adjourn, but then he changed his mind and waved Drew on.

'And when the police arrived?' Drew asked.

'One of them tried to take Mr Massetti by the arm, but he lashed out.'

Spike's hand climbed unthinkingly to his eyebrow.

'The defendant *struck* a police officer?' Drew said, turning again to the court, face aghast with righteous disbelief. 'At your husband's *funeral*?'

Spike let out a snort: Drew never could resist the chaser.

'Yes.' Eloise dared another glance at Massetti, contempt mixing now with something like triumph.

'Assault charges against Mr Massetti were dropped,' the magistrate explained to the court, 'when it became apparent that Dr Capurro had chosen to pursue a harassment charge.'

Drew waited for complete silence before continuing. 'You must have been very frightened, Dr Capurro. Do you consider the accused to be a violent man?'

Spike was already on his feet. 'Your Worship, this is inadmissible evidence!'

Cassar glared back with an intensity that made Spike wonder if his stomach was starting to rumble.

'The question of whether or not Mr Massetti is violent amounts to bad character evidence,' Spike went on. 'An application is required for that, and the Crown has made none.'

Cassar gave a grunt. 'Rephrase, Mr Stanford-Trench.'

Drew sighed. 'Dr Capurro. Did you fear for your *physical safety* in the presence of the defendant?'

Finally, the tears found a path down Eloise's powdery cheeks. 'Yes,' she replied with a strangled sob, and the courtroom inhaled en masse in satisfaction.

'No further questions.' Drew's eyes met Spike's, glittering like those of a poker player who'd just presented his opponent with a royal flush.

'Would you like me to call a recess?' Cassar asked gently. But Eloise just pursed her thin lips and shook her head, stubborn as a little girl.

'Very well. Mr Sanguinetti, your witness.'

8

Eloise Capurro stared back at Spike from the witness box with wary but determined eyes. Given the ordeal of her testimony, it seemed brutal to subject her to further questioning. But then Spike thought of what Peter Galliano liked to say when scruples began to gnaw at his conscience – 'Why don't we just let the Law take care of itself, eh, Sanguinetti?' Best get started then. 'Dr Capurro,' Spike said. 'You told the court that you first met Christopher Massetti on the night of the ninth of May. Is that correct?'

'Yes.'

'But that's a lie, Dr Capurro. Isn't it?'

Eloise jerked up her chin in shock. Drew was already on his feet, 'Your Worship!'

Cassar motioned for him to sit back down. 'Let's find out what we're objecting to, shall we, Mr Stanford-Trench?'

'You have in fact met Mr Massetti on several occasions over the past three years, haven't you, Dr Capurro?' Spike said, keeping his voice curt and authoritative. 'Most recently on the 1st of November of last year.'

'You are mistaken, sir,' Eloise replied, eyes flashing.

'You're an educated woman, Dr Capurro,' Spike continued. 'A *professional*. So you must know that it's an extremely serious offence to perjure yourself in court.'

Drew was still on his feet. 'My learned friend is harassing the witness, Your Worship.'

But Cassar waved Spike on, so he reached down and picked up a sheaf of photocopied documents. He set one bundle on Drew's table, another on the bench, then turned and walked to the witness box. 'Could you tell me what this is, please, Dr Capurro?' he asked, placing the document in front of her.

Eloise put on her spectacles, then looked up in disbelief. 'But this means nothing,' she said, seeking affirmation from Drew, but he had his head down, speed-reading the new evidence.

'Answer the question, please, Dr Capurro,' Spike urged. 'Describe to the court what this is.'

'It's an excerpt from medical notes.'

'And who is the patient?'

'Christopher Massetti.'

The court let out a murmur, the sweetest of melodies to Spike's ears. Good old Danny Garcia – he must have told a paralegal to drop off the notes as soon as they'd arrived. Spike pointed to a particular paragraph he'd highlighted in fluorescent yellow. 'Could you read this extract for the court, please, Dr Capurro?'

'*November first*,' Eloise read in an icy, staccato voice. '*Mr Massetti presented with a two-day history of epigastric pain. No change in bowel habit or vomiting associated. Suspected gastritis. Referred for blood tests and given a prescription for antacids.*' She glanced up.

'Who wrote these words, Dr Capurro?'

To her credit, she didn't flinch. 'I did.'

Another gratifying murmur.

'So you *had* met Mr Massetti before the ninth of May, hadn't you, Dr Capurro?'

'It would appear so, but . . .'

'In fact,' Spike cut her off, 'you had treated Mr Massetti on no fewer than three occasions over the last three years, hadn't you?'

'If that's what the notes say, I suppose I must have done.'

'So why did you lie to the court, Dr Capurro?'

'I didn't *lie*.' She practically spat out the word. 'I simply didn't remember. I see up to twenty patients per session. That's thousands of patients a year. No GP could possibly remember everyone they treat.'

'Have you told any other lies on the stand today?' Spike asked, counting down the seconds before Drew would make his presence felt. But the interjection was almost instantaneous:

'Your Worship, Dr Capurro has already provided an explanation for . . .'

'Perjuring herself,' Spike completed.

Cassar threw Spike a warning glance, and he bowed his head. 'I'll rephrase, Your Worship.' He turned back to Eloise. 'Your testimony is that you "simply" forgot the fact that you treated Mr Massetti on several occasions over the last three years, is it not, Dr Capurro?'

She gave a stiff nod, and Spike leant forward and cupped one hand behind his ear. 'Speak up, please.'

'*Yes.*'

'How old are you, Dr Capurro?'

'Sixty-six.'

'Do you often have trouble with your memory?'

Pre-empting Drew's objection, Spike addressed Cassar. 'If Dr Capurro's defence for lying to the court is that she "simply didn't remember", then the line of questioning is entirely appropriate.'

Cassar nodded, but he was knocking on sixty himself, and the set of his mouth suggested it was not a tactic of which he much approved.

'I'll repeat the question, Dr Capurro,' Spike went on, throwing her a sympathetic smile. 'Just in case you've already forgotten it.'

Eloise clenched her jaw, trying to hold her temper.

'Do you often have trouble with your memory?'

'No.'

'But you did on this occasion?'

'It would appear so.'

'So it's possible that if you have trouble remembering treating Mr Massetti on the days of the first of November and the seventh of June of last year, and on the eighteenth of August of the previous one, then you might also have trouble accurately recalling the events that took place on the ninth of May of this year?'

'No.' Eloise removed her spectacles, hands shaking. 'Absolutely not.'

'Nothing further, Your Worship,' Spike said, feeling the eyes of the court upon him as he strolled back to his table.

Cassar peered down at Eloise, trying to ascertain her condition. 'We'd better leave it for today. My chambers,' he repeated to counsel as he stood up. The courtroom followed him to their feet, and Spike watched as Massetti shuffled out of the dock. Then he turned to the witness box, where Eloise sat motionless, eyes downcast. Drew was busy making notes, so Spike stepped forward to help her up, unsure of his reception. But a small bird-like figure beat him to it. The elderly woman threw Spike a scathing look as she passed, and he was surprised to recognise Marcela Peralta, resplendent in a red silk Chinese coat buttoned to the neck. 'Can I help?' Spike asked.

The restaurateur turned her head just a fraction. 'I think you've done quite enough for one day, Spike Sanguinetti.' Then she took Eloise by the arm and led her out of the courtroom. Spike stared after them, trying to shake the sting of shame. Rough-handling a witness was an integral part of the job, but it wasn't one in which he took any pleasure. His duty may have been to defend his client by whatever means possible, but when that involved undermining the credibility of an aged widow, it didn't fill him with much enthusiasm.

Drew got to his feet. 'What larks!' he hissed into his Spike's ear. Then he modulated his voice into a slow Texan drawl, 'After you, Counsellor.'

9

The New Law Courts had been opened by the Minister of Justice some years ago, and to Spike's unpractised eye, the building shared unfortunate aesthetic similarities with Gibraltar's modern prison. Too much Government money allocated to the project, not enough taste. Just around the corner on Main Street stood the original Georgian court-house, with its cool stone portico and its beds of orange orchids. It was still in use for larger trials, where counsel would seek shade beneath the same gracious date palms as their forebears had during the *Mary Celeste* 'ghost ship' trial of 1872. By contrast, the occupiers of the modern court complex had to content themselves with standard-issue yucca plants and cheap wall-mounted plasma screens, and Cassar's temporary chambers occupied a styrofoam-ceilinged office on the second floor.

'Oh, sit down, would you?' Cassar barked as Spike and Drew walked in. He'd already loosened his tie, and a dark ruff of curly chest hair sprung forth behind his undone top button. He looked hungry and irritable, traditionally a volatile combination, Spike knew.

'So.' Cassar knitted his knuckles and looked Drew up and down with his fierce eyes. 'Your father. Sir Anthony Stanford.'

'I had no idea he was a party to the evidence,' Drew replied.

'But you must have *known* he was a friend of the Capurros.'

'Of course. It's the only reason I agreed to take the case.'

That caught Cassar by surprise, and he gave a frown of disapproval. But if he expected Drew to cower for mercy, he was to be disappointed. Drew just stared back at him, as though daring him to question the judgment of a QC who'd agreed to represent a family friend.

It was a common enough problem on the Rock, Spike knew. In a population of 30,000, issues of conflict of interest arose daily. The most pressing was finding a jury without any connection to the accused. As a result, judges in Gibraltar enjoyed a far greater discretion to try cases without juries than their UK counterparts.

Spike watched Cassar chew the inside of his cheek, as he often did when weighing up how best to proceed. Drew must have seen it too, as he decided to help him along. 'This *is* Gibraltar,' he coaxed in his honeyed tones. 'Where everybody knows . . .'

'Everybody,' Cassar murmured.

Spike couldn't help himself. 'Especially when it comes to Sir Anthony Stanford.'

'In that case,' Cassar snapped, 'I imagine even Counsel for the Defence has an acquaintance with the man in question?'

'Oh, I wouldn't describe it as an acquaintance, Your Worship,' Drew threw in. 'Mr Sanguinetti is a close friend of the family.'

Cassar looked from one lawyer to the other, as though trying to decide which of them was lower in his estimation.

'Your Worship,' Drew resumed, his tone suggesting that he was tiring of the topic. 'Of course I'll withdraw if you insist. But if I do, perhaps Mr Sanguinetti should do the same. No doubt a delay in proceedings will ensue, at an inevitable cost to the Attorney General's Office, but . . .' Drew held his arms out wide, his face a picture of reason and regret.

Cassar mopped his brow with his handkerchief and darted a look of raw hatred at the rattling air-conditioning unit. 'Are you planning to call your father as a witness?'

'Not at present,' Drew said. 'But I will need to take a statement. I can have a junior do it, if you like.'

'Sir Anthony *is* available, I presume?'

'He's in London today. On business.'

'Naturally,' Cassar muttered, failing to hide the note of bitterness in his voice. Despite his age, Sir Anthony Stanford had accrued a portfolio of juicy non-executive directorships in Gibraltar and abroad that was the envy of men thirty years his junior. 'We'll resume tomorrow at ten a.m.,' Cassar concluded. 'Speak to your father, Mr Stanford-Trench. I want to have his testimony before we begin.'

'Very well, Your Worship.'

As Cassar pulled a Tupperware sandwich box from his desk drawer, Spike saw Drew suppress a smirk, and not for the first time felt a little ashamed of him. Out in the hallway, they passed another group of lawyers. 'Nice work on the EasyBet opinion,' one well-fed QC called over to Drew, and the two men fell into step, leaving Spike to watch his old friend choose just the right expression as he passed through the revolving doors.

Not sorry to be deserted, Spike slowed his stride to let them pull away. He felt a sudden, powerful desire to see Jessica. But then another of his business partner's irritating maxims came to mind – 'Crime doesn't pay' – so he turned onto Town Range, preparing himself for another long afternoon of tax-advisory work.

10

Balancing a cardboard tray of coffees in one hand and his briefcase in the other, Spike shouldered open the door into the black-and-white tiled reception of Galliano & Sanguinetti.

Ana Lopes glanced up from her computer screen with one of her more unsettling smiles, her bare feet curled beneath her in the ergonomic swivel chair she'd demanded. As usual when employing someone new, Spike knew more about her than was decent – she was thirty-two, recently divorced and entirely overqualified for the role of receptionist-cum-personal assistant at a two-man law firm. Over the course of the job interview, she'd seemed impervious to Spike's gentle probing as to why a First-Class English and Philosophy graduate from Bristol University would want the position, but in the end Peter had persuaded him that it would be churlish to look a gift horse in the mouth.

'You seem preoccupied,' Ana observed as she sugared her double espresso, almond eyes glinting up at Spike from behind her spectacles.

'Do I?' Spike looked at her with suspicion. He was never quite sure if she was being serious. But Ana already seemed to have lost interest. Her headset was back on and he could see her face contorting as she struggled to decipher another of Peter Galliano's interminable dictated notes. Spike made a half-hearted check of his in tray. 'Any calls?'

Ana paused the tape. 'Some woman from Bonanza Gaming. Congratulating you on the work you did on the SPV.'

As if on cue, Spike heard a lusty baritone rise from the office opposite and caught a snippet of Gilbert and Sullivan's 'When I Was a Lad'.

Ana raised a well-tended eyebrow. 'I may have mentioned it to Peter.'

'So I can hear.'

The song had reached its murderous peak by the time Spike pushed open his business partner's door. 'Young Sanguinetti!' Peter stood up from his leather-topped desk, and Spike saw a manila file dancing in his hands. Emblazoned on the front in Peter's beautiful slanting penmanship, he read the words, 'Bonanza Gaming, Quarter 1'.

'Don't you just love that name? Such . . .' Peter paused to light a Silk Cut Ultra and wave away the smoke. '*Possibility*.'

'Ana said they were pleased.'

Peter widened his long-lashed eyes and sat back down. 'The CFO had no *idea* how much money they could save by registering the company in Gib. And circumventing the point of consumption tax? Now that was a stroke of genius.'

Spike flinched: if there was genius in him, it was distressing to think it might lie in the field of corporate tax law. When he looked back, Peter was eyeing him through a smoke ring, a smile hovering at the edge of his red lips. 'You don't look as happy as you might, Spike.'

'It's been a long day.'

Peter leant forward, soft belly spilling over his desk. 'This is exactly the sort of client we should be targeting. The kind where we can get in on the ground floor and help them grow. When Bonanza enters the Russian market, we should do very nicely, thank you – particularly if they can be persuaded to give us part of our fee in equity.' Peter rapped a hairy knuckle on the file. 'We need to think about the future, Spike. Especially now you're a family man.'

'I'd better get on.'

'Still tied up with that harassment trial?' Peter kept his expression neutral, but Spike could sense his disapproval from the way he stubbed out his half-smoked cigarette, mashing it into one of the tiny square Cartier ashtrays he liked to nestle in the palm of his hand as he perambulated around his office, bellowing into his speakerphone. 'Finishing any time soon?' he asked innocently, fingertips caressing the cover of the 'Bonanza' file.

Spike thought of the diminished figure of Eloise Capurro in the witness box, and turned away. 'Tomorrow, I expect.'

'The sooner the better, *maestro*.'

Spike felt Ana Lopes's inquisitive eyes follow him as he crossed the hallway to his office. Hearing Peter's triumphant humming restart behind him, he closed the door in relief. Then he tugged on the tropical ceiling fan – installed by a visiting Sea Lord in the Second World War and still working well – and took out his list of questions for Christopher Massetti.

11

Having successfully dodged Peter's entreaties to join him for a swift half at the Rock Hotel 'to discuss firm strategy', Spike decided to knock off early. GBC weather had predicted 65 per cent humidity, and by the time Spike got home to Chicardo's Passage, his shirt was plastered to his back.

As soon as Charlie heard the click of the bead curtain, he scrambled to his feet and threw his arms around Spike's legs. When the little boy finally released him, Spike saw that his mouth was wreathed with chocolate. Rufus had been feeding him Nutella again, in flagrant disregard of one of Jessica's strictest diktats. Spike couldn't muster the energy to start an argument, so he just dampened a square of kitchen roll under the tap and rubbed off the evidence.

'Shame,' Rufus called over from the table. 'I thought he looked rather splendid. Like a conquistador.'

'I am cookin',' Charlie announced, kneeling in front of a rust-fringed colander filled with spoons. He scanned the cork-tile floor, assessing all options, then selected a pepper grinder to add to his pile. 'Spoon soup,' he said, holding out the colander for his grandfather's approval. Spike could see the muscles in his arms quiver beneath the weight of the steel. But he held fast: he was growing stronger, taller every week.

'You mean soup spoon,' Spike corrected.

'No, no, spoon soup,' Rufus said, as he tipped up the colander to his mouth. 'Delicious.'

Spike found a pint of milk in the fridge and took a long gulp. Knowing this was also *verboten* under the new house rules, Charlie glanced up at his father with respect, and Spike smiled. 'How was nursery?' he asked, watching Charlie pad back to his station beneath the kitchen table.

'Oh, fine,' Rufus said. 'He pushed a teacher, apparently. They made me sign a book.'

The boy's guilt-ridden eyes flicked from Spike to Rufus. 'It was accident,' he murmured.

'We've talked about it, haven't we?' Rufus said.

Charlie gave a fast nod, mouth turned down at the corners.

'If you're going to push someone, you make sure they don't get up again,' Rufus added, and Spike closed his eyes in irritation. When he opened them, he saw his father watching him, mouth twitching. 'Just a joke, son. Where's your sense of humour these days?' Rufus gave Charlie a wink, then turned back to Spike. 'Jessica's upstairs. Looking a little peaky, I thought.'

Spike walked over to Charlie and kissed the dark curls on the top of his head, drawing in the wild-flower fragrance that was an uncomfortable reminder of the boy's late mother. He hoped Jessica didn't feel the same. Charlie made no reaction, just drew a baking tray of folded tea towels from under the table.

'Cloth cake!' Rufus said. 'My favourite.'

12

Jessica's decision to prepare a family supper of couscous and roasted vegetables had always seemed to Spike a risky one, and, after watching Rufus and Charlie push the food around their plates for half an hour, even she conceded defeat and let Spike order an eighteen-inch Americano from Rocky's Pizza. Once he'd finished the washing-up, Spike forced himself back to the kitchen table, leaden-eyed with carbohydrate, leaving the three of them slumped on the mustard-coloured sofa, watching *Peter Pan* for what surely must have been the twentieth time.

Spike hadn't made much progress with his examination-in-chief, and was still undecided as to whether to let Massetti take the stand. Though he'd succeeded in making his client talk, Massetti was still proving frustratingly reticent about many aspects of the case. It wasn't easy to put together a persuasive defence for a client who couldn't – or wouldn't – explain what exactly it was he'd wanted from the Capurros.

So it was after midnight when Spike finally made his way up the narrow staircase to the room he now shared with Jessica, steeling himself as he sat down heavily on the futon. She'd bought it to replace the childhood bed he'd still found himself sleeping in aged thirty-nine, and he couldn't bring himself to tell her that he hated it. Tonight, she lay curled in the foetal position, and in the moonlight, Spike had time to study her wide mouth, the smooth tanned skin with the hint of a freckle. How had he got so lucky? She'd given him not just a second chance, but a third and a fourth. You weren't supposed to get those odds.

Stretching out beside her, he stared up at the familiar stains and shadows on the ceiling. Number 12 Chicardo's Passage was still as dilapidated as it had been when Spike's mother had killed herself twenty years ago. Somehow the house had felt temporary ever since, as though both father and son had been waiting for someone or something to come along and make them change it.

Spike rolled over, trying to shake the feeling that this was all too good to last. To be given one healthy child and have another on the way. To have found a woman who loved him and was prepared to put up with his father; to have a chance to leave this damp terraced house that had been clinging – like the Sanguinetti family that inhabited it – to the Rock for nearly two centuries. How could that be allowed?

Because it can't, you fool, a small stubborn voice hissed in his head, an echo of all the people he'd let down over the years.

Willing himself to ignore it, Spike drew Jessica close, feeling a faint wing-beat of movement from their unborn child. Just let things stay as they are, he whispered to himself like a mantra. Then he closed his eyes.

13

The next morning, Spike braved the queue of shrieking toddlers and exhausted mothers at Little Rock Nursery, and plunged into the maze of the Old Town with some relief. He gave a hearty 'Good morning' to Old Man Levy and his wife as he passed them on Cannon Lane, off as usual to buy their morning bagels from Idan's. Five decades of marriage and still holding hands. Spike was still smiling to himself as he reached the New Law Courts, but then he saw Drew Stanford-Trench standing outside, locked in what appeared to be hostile dialogue with Alan Cassar.

Still smarting from his ticking-off in Cassar's chambers the day before, Spike hung back and watched with interest as the stipendiary magistrate glared at Drew, then shouldered past him through the revolving doors. Drew stared after him, rubbing the bridge of his nose between finger and thumb. Then he tugged down the tails of his navy worsted suit in one brisk movement, and followed Cassar into the courthouse.

Spike waited another moment, then jogged up the stairs to the first floor in a state of mild apprehension. Through the glass panel in the door to Cassar's courtroom, he made out Eloise Capurro sitting in the third row of the public gallery, the shrunken form of Marcela Peralta perching beside her. Strange, he thought as he reached for the door handle – he didn't remember seeing the Capurro family dining at Marcela's, yet now the two women seemed inseparable.

'There's been a development.'

Drew was at Spike's elbow, cramming a file into his overflowing briefcase. He was trying to look relaxed but Spike knew him better than that. 'What is it?'

Drew snapped closed his briefcase. 'You'll see.'

They entered the courtroom as the door to the cells opened, and Christopher Massetti stepped into the dock, wearing the same suit and expression of defiant indifference as the day before, Spike was depressed to note. Cassar bristled past him, bald pate gleaming, trailed by his clerk, whose anxious expression gave him the air of a courtier who'd just discovered that his status with his monarch was unexpectedly on the wane.

'Could the defendant please stand?' Cassar asked.

Massetti either didn't hear, or pretended not to.

'Mr Massetti!' Cassar raised his voice, and the police guard rapped Massetti hard enough on the shoulder to make him jump to his feet.

'It has just been brought to my attention' – Cassar glowered at Drew – 'at extremely late notice, that the complainant has altered her position.'

Spike was loath to turn and stare, but circumstances trumped etiquette. Eloise Capurro's eyes were lowered, hands clamped between the knees of her trouser suit.

'The complainant has informed Crown Counsel that she has withdrawn her support for Mr Massetti's prosecution, and has no further evidence to offer.'

Spike looked round at Massetti and saw his Adam's apple slide up and down his bristly throat.

'The court notes that Mr Stanford-Trench has phrased Dr Capurro's "change of heart" extremely carefully. No doubt because he is aware that his client has now left herself open to a charge of giving false evidence.'

Eloise was crying now, and perhaps it was that which made Cassar rein in his tone. 'The Attorney General will consider whether to charge Dr Capurro for wasting police time, but under the circumstances, there may be a case for leniency. As for Mr Massetti' – the magistrate's distaste was evident – 'I have no choice but to dismiss the charges against him.'

The only sound now was the urgent tip-tap of the steno-type machine as the clerk strained to catch up with his master.

'Now this court has a busy schedule,' Cassar went on, 'so if counsel would kindly clear their tables for two lawyers who are here to argue a legitimate case, and we can return to the docket . . .' Cassar turned to the guard: 'Get on with it, Sergeant!', and the officer unlocked the gate to the dock and pushed Massetti into the courtroom.

Eloise Capurro looked up. As she met Massetti's eye, Spike saw the last bit of colour drain from her face. Then, as smoothly as if she were ejecting an undesirable from her restaurant, Marcela Peralta took her friend's elbow and eased her towards the exit.

14

Spike found his client standing on the corner of Town Range, shoulders hunched, blinking in the midday sun. At his feet lay a sun-bleached Morrisons shopping bag containing, Spike assumed, his prison effects. Tourists bustled past him, laughing and chatting, oblivious to the small drama that had just played out in the courthouse above them.

'Christopher?'

Massetti glanced up. It seemed to take him a moment to remember who Spike was. He cleared his throat and extended his slab of a hand. '*Tenkiù*,' he mumbled in *yanito*.

Spike shook it. The palm was callused and dry. 'You're a lucky man, Christopher.'

Massetti gave a lopsided grin. 'Not often.'

'Well, you were today. But now you have to stay away from Eloise Capurro.' Spike's eyes searched the old man's face. 'Because if you end up back in court, they will throw the book at you.'

Massetti reached slowly for his plastic bag.

'So you'll keep away from the Capurro family?'

'Sorry about your eye,' Massetti said in his gruff voice. 'And thanks for this.' Massetti held out Rufus's chess book; Spike took it, then watched his client shuffle away, feeling a small but resilient sense of foreboding.

Hearing the courthouse doors rotate behind him, Spike turned and saw Drew Stanford-Trench striding towards him. Over Drew's shoulder, Gibraltar's Swiss-built cable car was inching its way up the Rock, no bigger than a matchbox.

They walked together along Main Street. For a man whose case had just fallen apart, Drew seemed surprisingly chipper. 'Epic waste of time, of course,' he drawled, stifling a yawn. 'But my clerk will be pleased to have my diary freed up.'

For something more lucrative, Spike thought, but didn't say.

'Got you off the hook too.' Drew shot Spike another of his sideways glances. 'Can't imagine you were looking forward to putting that client of yours on the stand. Dog of a defence case, but then I expect you and Galliano have to take what you can get these days, right?' The corner of Drew's mouth curled, and – perhaps because Spike knew he was right – he fought an overwhelming urge to give his old friend a punch on the shoulder, something he would have done without thinking five years ago.

Drew stopped. 'I almost forgot. My old man wants you to come to supper. He's very curious to meet the future Mrs Sanguinetti.'

Spike rolled his eyes, but secretly he was pleased. He hadn't seen Sir Anthony Stanford for so long that he'd been starting to wonder if he'd fallen out of favour at Dragon Trees. 'Send me through some dates,' he said.

Drew gave a mock salute, then turned towards Irish Town, no doubt heading for the HQ of the Liberal Party, the latest political group that was rumoured to be courting him. The levanter breeze had stilled, and Spike could hear the pulse of the cicadas in the mimosa trees. His mood was just starting to lift when he passed an off-licence and saw Christopher Massetti standing by the till. Racked on the counter in front of him were three dark bottles of spirits. Spike averted his eyes and kept walking.

PART TWO

15

The evening of the dinner with Sir Anthony came around quickly, one of the hottest Augusts on record passing in a blur of late nights at the office, antenatal appointments and unfathomably expensive trips to Mothercare. So it was early September by the time that Spike led Jessica up the steep road that twisted around the western flank of the Rock. He had so much on at work that he'd been tempted to cancel, but Jessica had been keen to see Dragon Trees, the house where Spike had spent so many summers during his teenage years, and he felt a strange desire to introduce her to the old man who'd acted *in loco parentis* when his own father had proven unequal to the task.

The evening sky was clear, the mountains of Morocco on the far side of the Straits streaked with purple in the setting sun. At moments like this, seeing the shipping freight pass from Atlantic to Mediterranean, Mediterranean to Atlantic, Spike felt as though they might be living at the very centre of the globe. He turned to Jessica with a smile. She looked very beautiful tonight, and he hoped she knew it. Whatever the evening ahead might hold, right now he felt a tremendous sense of contentment.

'Here's trouble,' Jessica said, pointing to a Barbary macaque crouching on an outcrop above the road. Thick grey fur bulked the monkey's square jaw; her yellow-brown eyes gleamed with intelligence. Sitting at her feet was a smaller male, his dextrous fingers twining through his mate's pelt, searching for fleas and flecks of limestone.

'She's got the right idea.' Jessica gave Spike a playful nudge, and he pulled a face. His future wife wasn't the first Gibraltarian woman to relish the fact that Barbary macaque society was a matriarchal one.

A hiss came from the crags above as a younger female appeared. The matriarch turned, repelling her rival with a mere look. Last year, the more antisocial Rock Apes had been rounded up and deported to a safari park in Stirling. How Scotland felt about becoming a Botany Bay for Gibraltar's primates was unclear, but a new pecking order had emerged within the colonies, a new set of females taking charge. Not unlike the current regime at Chicardo's, Spike thought with a rueful smile as they continued along the dusty road.

They reached the fences marking the perimeters of Gibraltar's mansions. Most were empty – investments by the super rich, inhabited only when the taxman demanded it. Through thick wire mesh entwined with evening jasmine, Spike could just make out the red clay of a tennis court, its expensive surface cratered by the seeds and suckers blown down by the swirling winds of the Rock. Then the wire ceded to the intricate wrought-iron that Sir Anthony preferred, and Spike lowered his six-foot-three frame to the security camera. He glanced over at Jessica, then held down the button and awaited their summons.

16

'*Pish pine*!' Spike exclaimed in *yanito*, feeling his stomach keel as he caught his first glimpse of the huge plate-glass cube protruding from the back of the house. A chuckle rang out behind him: 'A lifetime on the Rock and the man still has no head for heights.' It was Drew, of course, but then Spike heard Sir Anthony's deep, reassuring voice, 'It's perfectly safe, Spike. The glass we used for the floor is 12mm thick.'

Spike took a tentative step forward, forcing himself to look down. Under his feet, he made out the jagged canopies of the ancient dragon trees that gave the house its name. The only sense of substance came from the four heavy steel joists that supported each corner of the cube, their bases sunk deep into the terrace beneath.

Spike edged back onto solid ground. 'I knew you were engaged in building work, Anthony, but this is something else.'

Their host allowed himself a modest smile as he tore a strip of lead from the neck of a champagne bottle. 'A man must never stand still, Spike.'

Sir Anthony looked well tonight, Spike thought, taking in the bright crow-like eyes, the well-cut silver hair that was surely still as lustrous as it had been in his youth. The man had fifteen years on Rufus, yet the comparison was not one from which Spike's father emerged with credit. It was hard to imagine Sir Anthony being troubled by any of the things that bothered other people, like ill health, or mortgages. He seemed insulated, protected by his excellent genes and limitless self-confidence.

'You always were a jammy sod, Spike,' Drew murmured. He was leaning against the kitchen door-frame, watching Jessica with undisguised admiration as she sauntered fearlessly around the cube.

Hearing a muted pop behind him as Sir Anthony eased out the cork, Spike went over to help him pour, tipping each glass by its fine crystal stem the way the old man had taught him all those years ago. He held out a half-glass to Jessica, and she hesitated.

'In my day,' Sir Anthony called out, 'expectant mothers were encouraged to relax with the occasional drink.'

'In your day,' Drew countered, 'the dinosaurs still ruled the earth.' Spike suspected that Jessica agreed, but she accepted the glass anyway, and they all repaired to a trio of deep sofas.

Spike sipped his champagne, glancing around at the minimalist surroundings – the whitewashed walls glowing amber in the last rays of the sunset, the coconut lounge chairs which surely no one would ever really want to sit in, let alone a man who'd quietly had both hips replaced. It was certainly impressive, but part of Spike missed the old Dragon Trees, the sprawling bohemian mansion cluttered with frayed Moroccan rugs and chipped vases, walls hung with the black-and-white photos that Drew's mother had lovingly collected over the years.

Sir Anthony got to his feet and raised his glass. 'To an old and loyal friend, whose escapades have kept me entertained ever since he was a boy, and whose integrity and intelligence I have always admired.' Spike turned away, surprised to feel his cheeks burning. 'And to Jessica. I fear you may have a challenging job on your hands, my dear, but it should come as some consolation to learn that in all the years I've known Spike, I've never seen him look so happy.' Sir Anthony turned back to Spike, and his craggy face softened. 'Your mother would be proud of you, son. To Jessica and Spike – and the newest member of the Sanguinetti family.'

Spike stared at the bubbles corkscrewing up through his champagne flute. Then his eyes found Jessica's, and she smiled. From somewhere deep inside the Bulthaup kitchen came a thin, irritating beep. 'Drew,' Sir Anthony said, and his son stood up with a long-suffering shake of the head.

17

The candlelit table had been positioned in the very centre of the glass cube, and as they took their seats, Spike had the unwelcome impression that they were levitating. So he focused on his food, forking up another crisp leaf of cos lettuce. Supper had been simple but delicious, the main event a *salade niçoise* in the French rather than British style – fresh tuna instead of tinned, no boiled potatoes.

'How's that law firm of yours, Spike?' Sir Anthony asked. 'You took up with that chap who had the car accident. The big one with the little beard . . .' He waved an impatient hand at his son. 'Oh, what's his name, Drew?'

'Peter Galliano,' Drew supplied.

Sir Anthony took another sip of Sancerre. 'Brave decision, I always thought . . .'

Spike braced himself.

'Leaving a firm like Ruggles & Mistry to go it alone. Especially with . . .' Sir Anthony caught Spike's expression and peered across the table. 'Well, I suppose you must know what you're doing.' He paused. 'We have a little announcement of our own.'

Spike saw Drew shift in his seat. 'Not tonight, Dad.'

'Why not?' Sir Anthony said, and Drew conceded defeat with a small shake of the head.

'The Liberals have asked Drew to stand.'

'For Parliament?' Jessica said.

'For Chief Minister.'

Spike half-expected Drew's face to crease up, but he just cast his eyes downwards, focusing on realigning his cutlery. A few years' graft were usually needed before one of Gibraltar's three main parties would put up a candidate for the top job. To be parachuted in as Party Leader was unheard of. Perhaps Drew felt the same, as a sprinkling of colour had leached into his cheeks. It must be embarrassing to be run by your father, Spike imagined, but then Sir Anthony was a man used to getting what he wanted. Like most people on the Rock, Spike knew those parts of Sir Anthony's background which he had considered salient to reveal – how he'd overcome an impoverished childhood in Gibraltar to build a career in the British Diplomatic Service, culminating in an appointment as Her Majesty's Ambassador to Portugal. Most men in his position would have accepted their knighthood and retired gracefully to the golf course, but Sir Anthony had had other plans. Even at ninety, his reputation cast a long shadow over the Rock.

Jessica laid a hand on Drew's. 'Congratulations.'

'The election will be called early next year,' Sir Anthony said. 'It's the start of a long, hard road.'

Spike tilted the wooden salad bowl towards his host, but the old man's hand darted out like a lizard's claw to decline. Sir Anthony's appetite, like everything else in his life, was kept in careful check. He dabbed at his lips with a napkin. He looked relieved somehow, as though he'd just tested the concept on a focus group.

'Spike was up against Drew in court the other day,' Jessica said. 'Seems our future Chief Minister gave him a run for his money.'

Spike appreciated the gesture, but Jessica's choice of topic could hardly have been worse, as he saw Sir Anthony's wrinkled mouth tighten. 'Poor, dear Eloise.'

Spike glanced across the table. If Drew didn't think they should discuss the Massetti case, then Spike was more than happy to comply. But in the end it was Jessica who forced the issue, turning to Sir Anthony with her most charming smile. 'So what *did* happen that night at the hospital?'

Vanity expertly stoked, Sir Anthony folded his napkin on his lap and readied himself to hold court again.

18

'Of course I've known John Capurro all my life,' Sir Anthony declared as he shaved off a slice of lemon tart with his fork and let it dissolve on his tongue. He pushed his plate away with a sigh. 'Eloise had called me to say John might not last the night. But when I got to the hospital, the ward was deserted. It reminded me of that seventies film.' He snapped his fingers at his son. 'You know . . .'

'*The Godfather*,' Drew said, and Sir Anthony nodded in surprise, as though it were a little-known art-house flick his son had done well to remember.

'When I got to John's room, I thought he must have had a seizure, or a heart attack, as there was someone leaning over him. A doctor, I naturally presumed.' Sir Anthony frowned at the memory. 'But something about the man wasn't right. The hands, I think; fingernails bitten down. And his clothes. Like a vagrant.'

Spike crossed his arms, suddenly protective of a former client who wasn't there to defend himself.

'He was rambling. Shouting.' Sir Anthony inclined his head to Jessica in consideration of her feminine sensibilities. 'Well, the language wasn't pretty, my dear.'

'What was it that Massetti wanted to know?' Jessica asked with customary directness.

'The very question I put to Eloise. She had no idea. But the *way* he was asking – so desperate. Thankfully, a male nurse heard the commotion. Together we got Massetti out of the room, but John never really recovered after that.'

Spike turned to Drew. 'So why did Dr Capurro drop the case?'

Before Drew could answer, his father had raised his voice, 'Well it's obvious, isn't it? Massetti intimidated her. Forced her to drop the charges.' Sir Anthony knitted his grey-tufted eyebrows. 'I'd put money on it.'

'But Massetti was still in custody the night Eloise made her decision,' Jessica said in that soft voice she used when managing Charlie out of one of his more challenging tantrums.

'Then perhaps she'd just had enough of it all,' Sir Anthony retorted, turning back to Spike and fixing him with his shiny black eyes. 'I spoke to Eloise's nephew after the trial. He told me you'd been extremely rough with her in the witness box.' Sir Anthony reached for a ceramic bowl on the sideboard. 'Maybe she couldn't stomach any more of it.'

Spike looked away. He felt like a teenager again, the prodigal son who'd fallen short of Sir Anthony's exacting standards. Then, beneath the table, he felt Jessica's hand take hold of his. 'Spike was just doing his job.'

'If that's what you call it,' Sir Anthony said, delving into the bowl.

Spike felt a sudden stir of anger. 'Marcela Peralta was at the hearing. You know her, of course,' he said, watching Sir Anthony position a pair of walnuts in his right hand and squeeze.

'A little,' Sir Anthony replied. They all heard the dry, dusty crack, and the old man opened his fist. 'It's easier than you might imagine,' he said to Jessica, pleased to have won her attention. 'I'm sure even you could manage it.'

Best behaviour or not, Jessica couldn't let pass such a blatant display of chauvinism, so she pursed her lips and reached into the bowl. A moment later, she'd cracked a nut in the same way, and everyone laughed. The awkward moment had passed.

'What were you saying?' Sir Anthony asked.

'Marcela Peralta. I didn't know she and Eloise were friends.'

Sir Anthony gathered up the small, brain-like fragments of nut with his fingertips. 'They're not. John might have known Marcela a little from the old days. But Eloise keeps a different circle.'

Silence fell around the table, and Spike saw Jessica arch her back in her chair. 'We should call a cab.' Spike stood up and held out a hand to Sir Anthony. 'Thank you for a wonderful evening.'

19

The next day, an impromptu air-traffic-control strike in France left the management team of Bonanza Gaming stranded in Paris, and Spike grateful to find himself with an empty diary. Ever the opportunist, Jessica persuaded him to take the morning off, and he was just considering crawling back into bed when she handed him a coffee and told him to prepare himself for a morning of back-to-back viewings with their estate agent, Juan Felipe. The idea filled Spike with dread, and the fact that he was nursing a low-level hangover had done little to improve his mood by the time Juan Felipe threw open the door to Flat 40B, Atlantic Heights, and ushered them inside.

'So this is what £550,000 gets you,' Spike muttered in disbelief as he took in the modest dimensions of the apartment. It shouldn't really have come as a surprise. The property boom in Gibraltar was relentless – owning a piece of real estate on the Rock, however shoddy, was the best way to qualify for the tax breaks. Most of the locals had been priced out decades ago.

The estate agent adjusted the fat Windsor knot of his tie and pressed on, undeterred. 'I think you've got a real opportunity here, Mr Sanguinetti. All these clean lines. The sort of starter home a young couple could put their stamp on. Make their own.'

Spike choked back a laugh, then felt Jessica's hand of warning on his wrist. So he cast another sceptical look around the flat, taking in the poorly fitted window locks, inhaling the depressing scent of factory-fresh MDF.

Juan Felipe must have been blessed with an optimistic disposition, as he mistook Spike's silence for approbation and steered them into the box room that he'd designated as the 'master bedroom'. 'Fabulous storage,' he said, yanking open the only cupboard to reveal shelves crammed with tabloid newspapers and used tea-bags. He pushed it closed with no hint of self-consciousness, and even Spike found himself impressed by the young man's chutzpah. 'And as for the vista . . .' he continued with an extravagant sweep of the arm towards the sliding doors.

Spike stepped out onto the balcony and stared at the view across the Europort. 'Vista?' he echoed as he took in row upon row of stark apartment blocks, obscuring the Straits like iron bars. He slipped a hand between the plastic panels that protected the balcony from the six-storey drop to the car-park below, wondering how long it would take Charlie to work out how to open the sliding doors.

'I'm sure those can be adjusted,' Juan Felipe improvised.

'*Very* reassuring,' Spike said, feeling a pang of remorse as he saw the young man's open face fall.

'Might I have a word in private with my fiancé?' Jessica asked, giving Juan Felipe one of the tight smiles that Spike knew meant she'd reached the limits of her patience. The estate agent must have picked up on it too, as he flashed Spike a look of solidarity and headed back inside.

'*Vale*,' Jessica murmured, and Spike readied himself. 'You don't want to live in the Old Town. And this place isn't good enough for you – you've made that crystal clear.' She sucked her teeth. 'But this is what we can afford, Spike. You'd know that if you'd bothered to turn up to any of the other viewings.'

Spike felt Juan Felipe's keen eyes watching them through the glass. 'It's not been deliberate, Jess,' he said. 'We're trying to build the business back up, and Peter still can't work at full capacity.'

'Is that because of the accident or the Rioja?'

They glared at each other, until Jessica backed down with a sigh, probably, Spike thought, because she knew that he agreed with her, but didn't know how to make any of it better. 'Well, you're here now,' she resumed. 'So let's talk about what you *do* want. You want a house, right?'

Spike hadn't really thought about it, but now that he did . . . 'I suppose so. Yes.'

'By the sea?'

He nodded. 'With a terrace overlooking the beach.'

Jessica raised her eyes skywards. 'Then we need to have a serious discussion with the bank.' From the set of her face Spike knew she was having one of her silent debates. She must have reached some conclusion, as she spoke again. 'There is another option. Your father could sell Chicardo's Passage and move in with us.'

'*Permanently*?' They both heard the edge in Spike's voice, and Jessica had just opened her mouth to reply when his mobile rang. He turned away gratefully to answer it.

'Mr Sanguinetti?' came a voice.

'Yes.'

'This is Dr Martinez. From St Bernard's Hospital.'

Spike felt his breathing accelerate.

'I'm afraid there's been an accident.'

20

Spike paced around the hospital waiting room, phone clamped to one ear. This was it, he realised, the day he'd been dreading all these years since his father had first been diagnosed with Marfan syndrome. Macabre scenarios played through his head as he listened to the landline ring out. Flashing blue lights as the paramedics stretchered Rufus out of the house; defibrillators firing as they attempted to resuscitate him in the back of the ambulance . . .

Jessica had looked aghast when Spike had told her he had to leave the viewing – Juan Felipe had just been getting back into his stride. Reasoning that it was better not to worry a heavily pregnant woman until he knew how serious it was, it had seemed better to lie to Jessica, tell her it was work again. A decision he would be paying for later, he suspected.

He leant over the reception desk again until the nurse was obliged to raise his head. Taking in the breadth of his neck, Spike wondered if it had been he who'd intervened on Eloise Capurro's behalf. 'Like I said,' the nurse muttered, Gibraltarian accent thickening in irritation. 'The doctor is with a patient. She'll be with you as soon as she can.'

'Mr Sanguinetti?'

Spike spun round to see a tall woman in green scrubs standing behind him. She extended a slender hand. 'I'm Dr Martinez. Would you come this way?'

'It's my father, isn't it?'

'The patient wasn't carrying a wallet.' Dr Martinez glanced at her watch. 'We had no way of identifying him.'

But the hospital had still known to call me, Spike thought grimly. He was only too aware of his father's tendency to head out into the Old Town armed only with a set of house keys and a few loose coins.

Dr Martinez walked so quickly Spike had to increase his stride to keep up with her. They reached the ward and she led him towards a bed shrouded in pale green curtains. The air was thick with disinfectant and other more organic aromas, a smell that took Spike back to the year before last, to all the nights he'd sat in vigil over Peter, never expecting him to wake up after the hit-and-run that had left him in a coma.

'You should prepare yourself, Mr Sanguinetti,' Dr Martinez said. 'The patient fell against a plinth in the Alameda Gardens. He's sustained some nasty facial abrasions. Fortunately, most of the injuries are superficial, but what really worries us are his . . .'

Spike already knew what she was going to say, 'Underlying health issues.'

Dr Martinez didn't disagree, just drew back the curtains.

Spike stared down at the old man in the bed. His eyelids were purple, the sockets shiny and swollen with fluid. The skin of his face was yellow, his dry upper lip stuck rodent-like to his gums. 'It's Massetti,' Spike exhaled in relief. 'Christopher Massetti.'

Dr Martinez was staring at him strangely. 'How do you spell that?' she asked, picking up the chart at the end of the bed.

Spike spelled out the name.

'Are you a family member?'

'His lawyer.'

'That makes sense – your business card was in his pocket.' Dr Martinez reached up and adjusted Massetti's drip. 'I'm afraid that Mr Massetti is in the early stages of liver failure. We found a dangerously high quantity of alcohol in his blood.'

'I see.'

'If he doesn't stop drinking, he'll most likely be dead within the year.' Dr Martinez glanced round, and Spike saw the crow's feet fan out around her tired eyes. 'Mr Massetti will have ongoing health and social care needs. I'd be uncomfortable discharging him without someone to keep an eye on him. Get him settled at home at the very least.' She held Spike's gaze. 'Does he have family? Close friends?'

Recognising the subtext, Spike fought an urge to run for the door. 'None that I know of,' he replied carefully. 'When will he be well enough to leave?'

Dr Martinez's bleeper went off and she checked the screen. 'We need the bed. Tomorrow, all being well.' Mind already on her next case, she offered Spike a distracted handshake, and then she was gone.

Spike turned back to Massetti, seeing his swollen face loll to one side. Then he stood up and walked away, determined that for once he wouldn't let himself get involved.

21

But then, of course, the email follow-up from Dr Martinez had landed in Spike's in-box, a carefully worded message which already seemed to assume an obligation on his behalf. Over the course of a broken night, Spike had drafted a polite response in his head, suggesting that the doctor explore alternative arrangements for Massetti's care. But after breakfast, just as he'd been about to hit send, she'd called him on his mobile – number withheld. The conversation had been brief and entirely one-sided. Dr Martinez was between shifts, she'd briskly informed him, and only had a moment to talk. Mr Massetti would be ready for discharge into Spike's care at 10 a.m. that morning. She'd hung up before Spike had had a chance to voice any of his objections, and he was left reflecting that he'd just been swindled by a practised and very capable grifter.

So two hours later, he found himself back outside the hospital, awaiting his appointed assignation. He'd arrived early, so he sat down on the steps to take another look through the *Gibraltar Chronicle*.

'*Liberals Choose Their Man*,' the front page screamed, '*Drew Stanford-Trench QC To Run*'. The centre pages featured an enormous colour photograph of Drew at his chambers, surrounded by law books and seated, for some reason, on the corner of his desk, as though a mere chair could not contain a man of such purpose and dynamism. '"*It's a firetrap*," *Stanford-Trench says of Gibraltar's Old Town. "We need a comprehensive programme of redevelopment to protect our people and safeguard our heritage. The locals have been overlooked for too long. I want a Gibraltar for Gibraltarians . . .*"' A litter bin stamped with the Rock's coat-of-arms was within bowling distance; Spike screwed up the newspaper and pitched it inside with satisfying accuracy. He checked the time. Still fifteen minutes to the hour. Little Rock was just around the corner. Might as well stretch his legs.

As Spike approached the nursery, it sounded as though a massacre was going on. He placed both arms flat along the fence and looked over. One tribe of children was pushing plastic wheelbarrows around the coloured safety surface. Another was based in the sandpit, toddlers furiously digging with sticks and spades, as a solid little girl in blue-rimmed spectacles issued commands.

Spike looked for Charlie and found him sitting alone in the corner, brown legs crossed like a miniature Buddha as he gathered together a pile of palm seeds that had fallen from an overhanging tree. A little girl with a wheelbarrow thundered past him and knocked over his pile, but Charlie didn't even look up, just shrunk his head down into his shoulders and started to rebuild. Seeing the boy whispering to himself, Spike felt a sudden clutch at his heart. To lose a father at two, then be orphaned at three: it was barbaric. He needed to do more for the boy, find some way to help him regain his confidence.

At last one of the teachers glanced round, but it was only to glare at Spike – this tall suited stranger staring into a playground. So he turned away and headed back to the hospital.

Just as Dr Martinez had promised, Massetti was waiting in reception. Spike dropped to his hunkers, nose protesting at the smell of stale sweat and booze emanating from Massetti's shirt. 'Do you think you can stand up, Christopher?'

As Massetti glanced round, Spike was shocked again by the lurid bruising around his eyes. He swung an arm around his neck and heaved him up, still not sure if the old man even knew who he was.

As they made their way towards the front of the taxi rank, Spike saw the driver glance in his rear-view mirror, take in Massetti's condition and recalculate his fare.

Spike was sweating heavily by the time he'd manoeuvred Massetti into the back of the cab. 'What's the address, Christopher? Christopher?'

Again there was no response, and Spike felt his temper rise – he didn't have the patience for another round of Massetti's deaf-and-dumb routine, particularly not pro bono. But then he saw Massetti's lips quiver. 'Governor's Meadow Estate,' he mumbled.

'You heard the man,' Spike called through, and the driver put the cab in gear and pulled away in the direction of the Commercial Dockyard.

22

The taxi came to a halt on Rosia Road, and Spike looked up through the passenger window at the cracked-concrete face of the tower block that Christopher Massetti called home. Governor's Meadow had been one of the first housing estates to be built in Gibraltar after the Second World War. Most of the civilian population had been evacuated in 1940, and when they'd returned, they'd found a very different Rock from the one they'd left behind. Buildings had been destroyed by bombing raids from Vichy France and from Italian forces, but the main devastation had come from the conversion of residential homes into military facilities. Money in the fifties had been tight, and the quality of accommodation built to house the returning locals was notoriously poor.

Spike paid the fare and walked around to the other side of the cab. Once again, the driver did nothing but watch in silence as Spike heaved Massetti out, so he couldn't resist a sarcastic 'Thanks for all your help, *compa*', as he slammed closed the door. Then the taxi hurtled off, wheels spinning on the hot tarmac, both man and machine relieved to escape what Spike was starting to think of as 'the Massetti effect'.

Spike took Christopher's elbow, and the old man leant heavily against him, hand gripping his wrist so tightly it made him wince. In the hallway, the flaking paint and anti-Spanish graffiti made him reappraise Flat 40B, Atlantic Heights. 'Which floor are you on?' he asked, noting with some apprehension the cramped, cage-fronted lift, its steel doors dented and warped.

'Five,' Massetti grunted, then limped past the lift to the stairwell.

They set off up the stairs, Spike keeping close by Massetti's heels, carrying his hospital bag like a dutiful squire. Just as he was starting to think his presence unnecessary, Massetti leant a thick forearm on the landing wall, and Spike saw that his shoulder-length hair was slick with perspiration, his face grey. 'Want to rest for a bit?' he asked.

Massetti managed a shake of the head, blowing bursts of air through his bared teeth like a horse. The door to the flat opposite opened just a fraction, and Spike saw a curious eye peer out from the gloom, perhaps lamenting the fact that Massetti had returned. Spike stared back and the door quietly closed.

At last they reached the fifth floor, and Massetti groped above the lintel until he found a key. An important safety measure, Spike supposed, for someone liable to lose their wits and possessions of an evening. Massetti's fingers shook as he tried to insert it into the lock.

'Let me,' Spike said irritably, then shoved open the door.

At first Spike wondered if they'd broken into someone else's flat. The place was immaculate – the armchairs worn but clean, the cheap pine coffee-table polished to a high gloss, chess game still in play. Spike set down Massetti's bag and walked over to the floor-to-ceiling bookcases. The spine of each book had been carefully aligned by height: Dante's *Divina Commedia* in the original Italian, *My 60 Memorable*

Games by Bobby Fischer, *Force H: The Royal Navy's Gibraltar-based Fleet*. Poetry, chess, militaria: it was like a more orderly version of Rufus's study. A desk piled with papers faced an enormous picture window, and even Spike was struck by the panoramic view of the Bay of Gibraltar. Then he turned and saw Massetti slumped on the sofa, and noted the pallor of his face. 'I'll get you a glass of water.'

The first cupboard Spike opened in the kitchenette confirmed they were at least in the right flat, shelves crammed with half-drunk bottles of spirits. He closed it quietly, then tried another, where he found a collection of pint glasses, most of them liberated from Gibraltar's hundred-odd pubs. As Spike filled one with tap water, his eye was caught by a portable stove on the work surface. The built-in cooker had been disconnected; perhaps Massetti couldn't afford to fix it.

Hearing the unmistakable sound of retching, he turned and saw Massetti's head lolling, a dark pool of sick glistening on the carpet below. 'Christ,' Spike muttered, as he reached for his phone.

But Massetti held out a hand. 'It's old blood,' he gasped, 'it happens sometimes.' He forced himself to his feet, swaying a little as he tried to pull an arm out of his vomit-covered coat. Spike caught him before he fell, then helped him into the bathroom, fighting off a wave of nausea as he twisted on the shower.

The old man let himself be undressed like an obedient toddler. The skin of his body sagged at the buttocks and waist, and there were bruises on his hips and ribs, some black and new, others dating from an earlier fight or fall. Averting his eyes, Spike grabbed a bar of Imperial Leather from the sink and held it out. 'Can you . . . ?'

Massetti nodded, and Spike drew the shower curtain and gratefully retreated.

Ten minutes later, Spike somehow managed to manoeuvre Massetti out of the shower and into bed. He fell asleep almost immediately, so Spike pulled to the bedroom door and set to work cleaning up the mess.

It wasn't the first time Spike had cleared up after a drunk, and just as he remembered, it was the smell that bothered him most. He walked over to the picture window and shunted open the top panel, hearing a herring gull scream as it soared on the thermals of the Rock. The papers on Massetti's desk began to rustle in the breeze, so he headed for the bookcase and placed one of the weightier tomes on top of a pile of photocopied newspaper articles.

Curiosity piqued, he looked closer. '*Gibraltar Dockyard Bomb: Man Executed*', one headline read. *Manchester Guardian*, 31 October 1940. '*Gibraltar Dockyard Explosion*', *The Times*. Every article was of a similar vintage, and all on the same theme: '*Spanish Saboteur Hanged in Gib*' – the *Daily Sketch*, the *Gibraltar Chronicle* . . .

Hearing the sound of snoring from the bedroom, Spike picked up the top article, folded it into his suit pocket and left.

23

Re-emerging onto Rosia Road, Spike checked the time. The entire morning had now been lost, but at least there was an email from Peter, attaching a press release which announced that the Gibraltar regulator had finally agreed to grant a gambling licence to Bonanza Gaming. That should keep Peter humming for a while, Spike thought. No doubt he was humming his way to Jury's Wine Bar already.

Spike walked on towards the striped awning of Marcela's. As soon as he heard the bell, the headwaiter pointed up at the clock and shook his head.

'It's all right, Guillermo,' came Marcela's clipped voice, 'I'll see to Mr Sanguinetti.'

Registering the wintry expression on the old woman's face, Spike found himself wondering how his day could get much worse. He tried what he hoped was a meek yet charming smile, but there was no mercy in Marcela's haughty green eyes as she offered him a cool cheek to kiss. 'Still *persona non grata*, Marcela?' he asked.

'I thought better of you, that's all.'

Spike looked away, feeling, he imagined, a little like Charlie when placed on what Jessica had dubbed 'the thinking chair'. 'Have you seen Dr Capurro since the trial?' he asked, for want of anything better to say.

'She's been brought very low,' Marcela snapped back. '*Very* low. Her nephew says she's barely left the house.'

'It's my job, Marcela. You know that.'

'Then you should exercise better judgment when selecting your clients. Guillermo!' The Spaniard jumped to attention as Marcela swept majestically back to the counter, teal caftan swishing.

Guillermo took Spike's takeaway order with his usual precision and speed, then returned with an espresso and a shot glass of limoncello. '*Cortesía de la casa.*'

'*Mano de santo,*' Spike replied in his increasingly rusty Spanish, and Guillermo bowed his grey head.

The coffee tasted sweet and strong; Spike considered the limoncello for a moment, then decided against and pulled out the newspaper article he'd taken from Massetti's flat.

31 October 1940 – The Colonial Office confirmed this morning that the execution of a Spanish national took place yesterday in Gibraltar. Esteban Alejandro Reyes, aged twenty-one, was found guilty of offences under the Gibraltar Defence Regulations after a three-day trial before the Chief Justice of Gibraltar.

A native of La Línea who lived and worked on the Rock, Reyes was recruited by a Spanish agent working for the German Secret Service and exhorted to commit sabotage in Gibraltar. On 9 April this year, he succeeded in smuggling a bomb over the border to Gibraltar and planting it in the Dry Docks of HM Dockyard. The explosion on 10 April caused the deaths of two Royal Naval Engineers, Engineer Commander Arthur Baines, aged fifty-four, and Engineer Lieutenant Harold Beck, aged twenty-two. Reyes himself was injured in the blast, but recovered in time to attend his trial. He is survived by a wife.

Set above the text was a black-and-white photograph of a handsome, dark-skinned youth being escorted towards an official-looking building by a member of the Gibraltar Security Police. His hands were tightly cuffed behind his back, his head lowered.

'Another case?' Marcela was standing at Spike's shoulder, the curve of her flamingo-painted lips suggesting she might have brought herself to forgive him. Spike passed her the newspaper article and she slipped on the horn-rimmed reading glasses that hung from a black ribbon around her neck. With her pixie-cut white hair, she suddenly looked like the very ancient curator of a London fashion college.

'Do you remember this?' Spike asked, realising as soon as he said it that the assumption that Marcela was old enough to do so might offend her. If it did, she didn't say, just made a series of soft clicking sounds with her tongue as she squinted at the smudged print. When she'd finished reading, she pulled off her spectacles and started polishing them on the silk of her caftan. 'It was a terrible thing,' she said without looking up. 'An act of treachery in a time of war.'

'Did you know him?'

'Who?'

'The saboteur. Esteban Reyes.'

'I knew *of* him. We all did.'

Guillermo appeared with Spike's order. It had been a long time since breakfast, and just the aroma of garlic and rosemary was enough to make Spike's mouth water. He gave Marcela her money and leant in for a kiss of thanks. 'What you need to remember,' she whispered in his ear, 'is that everyone was so young.'

Spike waited for more, but Marcela just tucked the cash into a leather pouch and turned back to the counter. It wasn't until he was nearing Massetti's flat that he realised she hadn't asked him where he'd found the article.

24

Spike was perspiring heavily by the time he reached the fifth floor, the plastic bags he'd loaded with milk and orange juice cutting into his palms. He found the key he had replaced on the lintel, then pushed open the door with a sense of familiarity that troubled him. This wasn't a trip he wished to be making on a regular basis.

After restocking Massetti's fridge, he stood back, hand on the open door, considering whether he could just leave the old man to it. He knew what Peter would say – that Spike had already exceeded any fiduciary or moral duties that bound him – but years of operating as unofficial carer for his father had taught him better, so he took out the box of rice and chicken stew and addressed himself to the portable stove. Knowing that what talents he possessed lay more in the cerebral than the practical, he eyed the device with suspicion. A pot of clear gel squatted in a metal drawer beneath the single hob; Spike lit the wick with a cigarette lighter from the kitchen shelf and it provided a surprisingly efficient circular flame. Once he'd tipped the food into an oblong steel pan, he surveyed his work with a sense of satisfaction, then prepared himself to tackle Massetti's stash of booze. Job done, he checked on the patient.

Massetti was lying on his back, the only movement the laboured rise and fall of his chest. Spike edged towards his desk and had just slipped the article back on top of the pile when he heard a surly voice call out behind him, 'Get away from there! Those papers are private.'

Spike turned and saw Massetti pushing himself up into a sitting position, face contorting with the effort. The bruises had formed a strangely beautiful rainbow around his eyes.

'Hungry?' Spike asked. 'I am.'

To his surprise, Massetti nodded, so Spike returned with two plates and pulled up a chair by the bed. The stew was delicious, slow-cooked for hours, Spike suspected.

Massetti peered at the food. 'You make this?'

'Bought it from Marcela's. Ever been in?'

'Not my kind of place.' Massetti raised the fork to his mouth. The tremors were back, Spike saw, his right hand shaking so violently that Spike wondered if it might be easier to feed him himself. 'Who's Esteban Reyes, Christopher?'

'My father,' Massetti replied.

Spike looked up sharply, but Massetti didn't seem to notice. 'My mother was pregnant when Esteban was arrested,' Massetti went on. 'After they executed him, she was evacuated to a refugee camp in Jamaica. She died of septicaemia a few months after I was born. Childbed fever, they used to call it.' He wiped his mouth with his sleeve. 'There was another couple at the camp. Mark and Josephine Massetti. They'd lost a baby of their own on the journey. It wasn't uncommon. Conditions on the evacuation boats were very primitive. After the war, they returned to Gib and raised me as their own.'

'When did you find out Esteban was your father?' Spike asked, as he chased the last few grains of rice around his plate.

'I always knew I was adopted. But I didn't know about Esteban till I was a teenager. That was when the taunts began. Traitor's bastard. Son of a whore. That kind of thing.' Massetti pushed his plate away and leant back against his pillow. 'Then Franco closed the border with Spain, and people found other things to gossip about.'

Spike picked up their plates and set them on the desk. He remembered the tail end of that strange time – 1969–1985, sixteen years in which Gibraltar had been sealed off from the rest of the world. If the Second World War evacuation had hardened the Gibraltarians into a people, the border closure had forged them into a unit.

'Josephine told me to leave well alone,' Massetti continued. '*There's no point raking up the past*, she used to say. Jo was a lovely woman. Too good for this world.' Massetti gave a fond smile which softened his bruised face. 'We lost her a long while back, then Mark died in the late nineties. That was when I started looking into the case against Esteban. At first there wasn't much. But then some of the files were declassified. You know the National Archives at Kew?'

Spike nodded.

'Anyone can order documents from there. And now, of course, there's the internet.'

'What was it that you hoped to find? That your father was innocent?'

Massetti tilted his large head.

'I'd be the same,' Spike said, and he felt Massetti's grey eyes searching his face for a hint of scorn or judgment.

Finding none, Massetti continued. 'I suppose I hoped Esteban might have been falsely accused. There was another man mentioned in the official reports. A poet. Raúl de Herrera?'

Spike shook his head: Spanish literature had never been his forte.

'He was a big noise once. Even decorated by Franco.'

'I didn't think Franco liked anything that didn't involve guns.'

Massetti's eyes creased with amusement. 'That's why de Herrera's work appealed. His poetry is full of violence. The imagery of blood sacrifice. People called him the Spanish Yeats.'

Spike realised he was getting out of his depth in a conversation with Christopher Massetti. He was starting to see what Rufus had found to admire in him.

'At the trial,' Massetti went on, 'the Gibraltar Security Police claimed that Raúl de Herrera had been working with the *Abwehr*. The German Secret Service. That he gave my father the bomb.'

Seeing Massetti grimace as he lowered an arm beneath the bed, Spike crouched down and found a box file beneath the metal frame. He placed it on Massetti's lap, and the old man started rifling through: 'Here.' He passed Spike a black-and-white photograph. At the bottom of the mount, Spike read in faded curling script, '*La Línea, diciembre 1939*'. The camera had captured three young men sitting around a table in a smoke-filled café. To the right, Spike recognised a handsome, dark face. 'That's your father?'

Massetti nodded.

'And the poet?' Spike asked, momentarily forgetting the name as he pointed at the man sitting in the middle.

'Raúl de Herrera,' Massetti supplied.

De Herrera looked to be the oldest of the group, his small, humourless eyes boring into Esteban's face, black moustache waxed into pointed ends like a cut-price Dalí. 'What happened to him?' Spike asked.

'After Esteban was convicted, de Herrera was arrested by the junta. But it was just to placate the British government. Twenty-four hours later, he was released.'

'Bet that went down well.'

'He was killed six months later. A bar brawl, allegedly.' Massetti tapped the side of his bent nose. 'But the British got their man in the end, I think.'

Spike looked back at the photograph. A third figure sat in profile, the sunlight flooding through the café window obscuring his features. Dangling from the open neck of his shirt was a pendant. Its teardrop shape caught the light. 'Who's this?'

Massetti shrugged. 'I think the picture was taken in secret. See how no one is looking at the camera?'

Spike did. 'Where did you find it?'

'At the Isthmus Museum in La Línea. They've got a section on local writers and artists.' Massetti gave a low chuckle. 'Not a very large section.'

The photograph didn't look like a copy. 'Is this the original?' Spike asked.

'It's not like anyone'll miss it. It's hardly the Prado.' There was a churlishness to Massetti's tone now, and when Spike looked up, he saw him staring at the door. In the direction of his booze stash. It must have been forty-eight hours since he'd last had a drink, Spike realised. The withdrawal symptoms could be savage: he was surprised Dr Martinez hadn't found a way to keep him in hospital a little longer. 'So this photograph proves that your father was in contact with de Herrera just before the bomb went off,' Spike said, more as a means to distract the man than anything else. 'You must have been disappointed.'

'It's hardly conclusive,' Massetti retorted. 'But no, it wasn't what I'd hoped to find. Although . . .' He seemed to be weighing up whether or not to trust Spike. Decision made, he dipped back into the box and passed him an envelope. It was addressed to 'Christopher Massetti, c/o The Gibraltar Museum'.

'May I?' Spike said.

Massetti nodded, and Spike pulled out a small square of notepaper headed 'GHA': Gibraltar Health Authority. Spike read aloud the three lines handwritten in shaky biro: *'There's something I need to tell you. It's about your father. Please come. JC.* John Capurro wrote to you?' he asked.

Massetti nodded. 'He spent a lot of time at the museum. After he got ill. We got to know each other a little.'

'And you think he knew your father, Esteban?' Spike picked up the photograph again: could John Capurro be the third man at the table?

'They would have been about the same age,' Massetti replied.

'So that was why you were at the hospital that night? Because John Capurro asked you to come?'

'But when I got there John wouldn't tell me anything. Said he'd made a mistake.'

Massetti was looking worryingly pale; Spike hoped he wasn't going to be sick again. 'Why didn't you tell me about this before the trial, Christopher? It would have helped your case.'

The old man gave no answer, and Spike felt his frustration return. 'And why harass Eloise?'

'Because she *knew*,' Massetti snapped. 'She was his *wife*. You didn't see how they were together. Whatever John knew about Esteban, you can be sure she did too.' Massetti grabbed Spike's wrist, eyes burning. 'I thought maybe Eloise might talk to you. Tell *you* what her husband knew.'

Alarm bells started to ring, and Spike gently detached himself and got to his feet. 'I'm sorry, Christopher. I can't help you with this.'

Massetti pushed the box file away from him. 'Take it then. And the papers on the desk. I don't want them any more. Chuck them out. Just like you did with my drink.'

At the bedroom door, Spike turned. 'There's more food in the fridge, Christopher. Make sure you eat it.' He tried an encouraging smile. 'Dr Martinez said a health visitor would come this week. As soon as they tell you you're well enough, you should go back to the Gibraltar Museum. Ask for your old job back. I could put in a good word for you, if you like.'

But Massetti didn't smile back. Ignoring the quiet insistent voice of warning in his head, Spike picked up the box of papers and left.

25

Spike had never been a fan of surprise parties, and as he looked around the patio garden of the Royal Calpe pub, he questioned once again why he'd let Ana Lopes persuade him that this would be a good idea. The chocolate icing on the enormous cake she'd ordered, emblazoned with Jessica's name and a baby rattle, was already melting in the evening sun, while most of Jessica's colleagues were at least three pints down, no doubt seeking Dutch courage for what Spike suspected must be their first experience of a baby-shower-cum-maternity-leave party.

Jessica was the only woman in the unit, and her colleagues all wore plain-clothes suits, their eyes starting to glaze as Detective Inspector George Isola held forth. Isola boasted a wide repertoire of bawdy anecdotes, Spike knew, and he liked his subordinates to laugh in all the right places. The fact that the Woman of Honour was not amongst them must have irked him, as he flashed Spike a look that wasn't hard to decipher. *Can't even get this right* was the most benign interpretation.

'Late for her own party,' Peter Galliano muttered.

'That's always the danger with surprises.' Rufus took a prim sip of Prosecco, like an old maid savouring her glass of sherry after church. 'What did you tell her, Spike? That you were meeting for a quiet drink?'

Spike shrugged.

'What you're really saying,' Peter chimed in, 'is that date night with Spike is insufficient to bring Jessica in on time.'

'Precisely,' Rufus replied, and Spike gave a weary smile. He supposed he ought to be happy that the two men were getting along. It wasn't as though they had much in common – Peter the bon viveur, and Rufus almost Presbyterian in his tastes. The only thing that brought them together was Spike. For his sake they had forged some sort of half-hearted modus vivendi, and for that he was grateful.

'Another round?' Peter asked.

Spike watched his business partner limp away towards the bar, then turned to his father. 'What do you know about Christopher Massetti's parents?'

Two policemen glanced around at the sound of the name.

'Mark and Josephine Massetti?' Rufus confirmed, the skin of his forehead pleating like a concertina as he considered the best way to describe the pair. 'They used to run the cash and carry on Devil's Tower Road. Typical Genoese sailing stock – same as us.' Rufus stared down at his long fingers, and Spike wondered if he knew that Massetti's biological father had been hanged as a traitor. Probably – but if he did, he wasn't letting on. 'The Massettis were always very good to Christopher. Stuck by him through some tricky times. It was hard for them to manage, I think. And of course Josephine's health was never good. She died, oh, a long time ago. Her husband never really got over it.' Rufus looked up as Peter reappeared carrying a bottle of Rioja and three glasses. 'Nice people.'

Peter's face was flushed, and Spike wondered if he'd treated himself to a quick sharpener at the bar. His old friend's recovery from the hit-and-run accident that had almost killed him had been nothing short of miraculous, the doctors had said. Only two years ago, they hadn't thought he would regain consciousness, let alone walk again. But sometimes Spike wondered if the accident hadn't taken its toll in other ways. Especially when he saw the way and the quantity which Peter drank. As if on cue, he tipped a third of the bottle into each glass and held one out to Rufus. 'Not for me, Peter – I've had *quite* enough.' Rufus turned to Spike. 'Why not give Jessica a ring, son? It's getting rather late, isn't it?'

'Oh, give her ten more minutes,' Peter said. 'Live a little.'

Rufus's expression darkened. 'I was hoping to read the boy his story,' he said peevishly. 'We've just started *Fantastic Mr Fox*.'

'Charlie will be fine, Dad,' Spike replied. 'Ana's babysitting,' he added for Peter's benefit, but Peter just gave a distracted nod, suggesting that his business partner's childcare arrangements could not have been of less interest to him.

'I found Ms Lopes a little odd, *entre nous*,' Rufus said to Spike, then dropped his voice suggestively. '*Very* attractive though.'

Spike threw his father an uneasy look, wondering if the new medication that the specialist had prescribed might be having unwelcome side effects.

A mobile phone went off at the adjacent table. Then another. Suddenly the air was alive with the jarring sound of ringtones and vibrations, and Isola was on his feet, barking into a police radio. Spike caught his eye. 'What is it?'

'Fire in the Old Town,' Isola called back as he grabbed his jacket. Before he disappeared, Isola summoned the good grace to shout over his shoulder, 'Jessica's at the scene.'

Spike got to his feet and ran out into the street after him, hearing the slow lazy wail of sirens drifting down from the Old Town above.

26

Black smoke was already rising against the flank of the Rock as Spike pushed his way through the crowds on City Mill Lane. Somewhere in the distance, he heard the violent gush of water hoses. He could smell the fumes now, the woody scent of bonfire tainted by something acrid. A group of middle-school children jostled past him, whooping with excitement, and Spike felt a sudden stab of antagonism towards Jessica that even he recognised as unfair. But what the hell was she doing in the middle of all this chaos?

The people were five-deep on Governor's Street, a line of police officers struggling to keep them back behind the yellow-and-black-striped cordon. The blaze must have spread quickly: it seemed as though half the terraced street was alight.

'*Cagona*,' Spike swore to himself as he took in the scale of the conflagration. He'd never seen a house fire up-close before, and as he watched the dazzling showers of sparks crackle then fade, he had to admit there was something beautiful about it. Then he saw how the firefighters were struggling to get the flames under control, and realised that they didn't see any beauty in it at all.

The burnt-out shells of two houses rose above him, their blackening beams dripping with water, belching smoke. The adjoining building glowed orange and red through its upper windows, dark fumes billowing from what remained of the roof. With a jolt of panic, Spike realised that Chicardo's Passage was just fifty yards above, Charlie asleep in his cot bed. But he knew that Jessica was at the centre of the blaze, so he made himself press on through the crowd, puzzled to taste salt on his tongue until he remembered that the fire brigade pumped their water from the sea.

A taut face emerged through the smoke, and for the first time in years Spike found himself pleased to see DI Isola. 'Where is she?' Spike shouted. 'Where's Jessica?'

They both heard the sharp crack as something structural inside the burning house collapsed, then looked up to see a bright jet of embers erupt into the night sky. Spike watched the feverish eyes of the crowd widen as they took in the new constellation of golden stars above their heads.

'Over there,' Isola yelled back.

Spike could just make out a second cordon farther down the road, dividing the mob from another row of firefighters. He searched through the faces until he saw Jessica, then called out her name, but his voice was carried away by the spitting of the flames and the roar of the water, and he realised that there was no way that he could get to her through the throng.

So he pushed his way back through the onlookers, ignoring their cries of protest, trying to picture the layout of the Old Town in his mind, the warren of streets where he'd played as a child. He knew a back way.

Skirting above Governor's Street, his gaze was drawn upwards to the western face of the Rock, as mighty and indifferent to the fate of Gibraltar's insignificant hordes as it had always been. Then he felt something sear the flesh on the back of his neck, and slammed a hand against the skin to tamp out the burning ash. Pulling up the collar of his shirt, he ran down the passage that led to the other end of Governor's Street, then stopped for a moment to catch his breath, coughing out the stink of the fumes.

As he straightened up, he saw a figure standing twenty yards in front of him. He wiped the sweat from his eyes and looked again, knowing even before the smoke cleared that it was Christopher Massetti he would see.

Massetti was gazing up into the flames as though mesmerised. And suddenly Spike was transported back to Eloise Capurro's description of him standing beneath her bedroom window as he'd waited outside her house, night after night. The Capurro house was on Governor's Street. The street where the fire had started.

Spike called out his name and Massetti looked round, and for a moment their eyes locked, the older man's face unreadable. Then another shroud of smoke fell across the street, and by the time it had dissipated, Massetti was gone. And that was when Spike heard the high-pitched scream behind him, and turned to run back towards the heart of the fire.

27

Spike could hear his feet thudding on the cobbles, feel the rasp of his breath raw in his throat, but these sensations seemed to him vague and indistinct as he stared up at the top floor of the burning house. He drew closer, heart thumping as he caught sight of a figure behind the blackened glass of a sash window. Then came a tinkling crash, and the crowd covered their heads as a shower of broken glass hailed down on them.

Spike made out the figure more clearly now, and he knew it was a woman from the pitch of her screams. Twenty feet below her, a firefighter with a loudspeaker was appealing to her to stay calm as his colleagues scrambled back towards their truck. But his pleas went unheeded as the woman swung a leg out of the shattered window, and the crowd gasped. Her grey hair was dishevelled, the material of a white nightdress whipping around her thin body in the breeze.

Spike heard another collective inhalation from the watchers below as the woman stood up, bare feet on the sill, bloodied hands clasping the window frame. The orange glow behind her faded, then brightened again and the smoke began to blur her shape. On the pavement below, the side door of the fire truck rattled closed like a drum roll. The crash mat was readied and on the move.

'Jesus,' Spike whispered as he saw what happened next. At first, just the hem of the woman's nightdress was alight, but within moments, her whole body was engulfed by flames, hair flaring and crackling. Then her screams crescendoed to a level that Spike knew he would never forget, the writhing of her body like some kind of hideous dance. He closed his eyes, desperate to obliterate the memory, and when he opened them again, he saw her jump.

The speed with which she fell was extraordinary, as though a guy rope had yanked her down towards earth. The crowd fell silent, and somehow the noise of the flames seemed to quieten too, so that they all heard the hollow, sickening crump as she struck the pavement.

Then the panic began, people screaming and yelling, filled by some irrational urge to flee. Spike fought his way towards the safety cordon, where he saw the woman's body surrounded by an entourage of paramedics. One got to his feet, and Spike saw him wipe the sweat from his brow with the back of a gloved hand, the resignation clear on his face. To one side, watching in silence, stood Detective Inspector Isola.

Jessica still had her back to the cordon, reassuring an old man who was draped in a metallic silver sheet. The man was stroking his moustache with frightened, fast-moving fingers, and Jessica took his hand in hers and whispered something to him that made him raise his eyes and nod. Spike edged towards her, seeing her fluorescent-orange gilet unfastened around her baby bump. She looked up and saw him, and he pulled her into his arms. There was a smear of soot on her cheek, and he wiped it away with a thumb.

'We thought we'd evacuated the whole street,' Jessica said, eyes gleaming in the flicker of the flames.

Spike remembered the look on Christopher Massetti's face as he'd watched the house burn. 'You know who lives there, don't you?'

He must have whispered it as Jessica didn't seem to have heard. 'What?'

'Doesn't matter. Just stay here!'

'Spike!' He heard Jessica call after him, but he pushed on through, ducking beneath the cordon, dizzied by the foul aroma of drenched embers and something else. He reached the knot of emergency services personnel just as they were hoisting the woman up onto a stretcher. As they gently laid her down, the sheet covering her body slipped.

The woman's hair and eyebrows were gone, and all that remained of her nightdress was a blackened web entwined with her charred flesh. But beneath the blistered skin, Spike recognised the shape of her face, the small sharp chin that Dr Eloise Capurro had raised at him defiantly as he'd upbraided her on the stand.

Suddenly he felt a hand grab his forearm and twist. He glanced up and saw it was Isola, Jessica standing next to him, her face filled with bewilderment and irritation. Isola gave Spike a shove in her direction. 'Do your fucking job, Navarro,' he hissed. 'Get him out of here.'

Spike watched Isola stride away, then turned to Jessica. 'It's her.'

'What?' She wouldn't meet his eye.

'It's Eloise Capurro.'

28

The next morning Spike awoke, as he was prone to, exactly one minute before his alarm was due to go off. The sun was already streaming through the sides of the blue linen curtains, and just for a moment he felt happy, listening to Jessica snoring gently beside him. But then the image of Eloise Capurro's blistered face forced its way into his mind; the spectral figure of Christopher Massetti watching as the Old Town burned.

Jessica stirred; Spike was about to embark on the high-risk operation of coaxing her awake when he remembered she was now on maternity leave. So he rolled as gracefully as he could from the futon and crept into the shower, hoping that the warm, brackish water would do its work, soothe his body and mind. As he lowered his head beneath the spray, he tried to persuade himself again that there was still a possibility Massetti had had nothing to do with the fire. Perhaps Eloise Capurro had been a smoker; most doctors he knew were. And the fact that Massetti had been hanging around Governor's Street was hardly conclusive – it wouldn't be the first time. The police ought to be checking the Alameda Gardens: they'd probably find him slumped under a park bench, sleeping off another heavy night.

Stepping out of the shower, Spike picked up his razor and cleaned the mist from the mirror. Each swipe of the blade took a month off him. Five minutes later, he contemplated his tanned, angular reflection and decided he looked . . . well, forty. Finding the bedroom deserted, he slipped on a fresh cotton shirt and followed Jessica downstairs.

The scene that met him in the kitchen might have been the subject of a genre painting entitled 'Domestic Harmony'. Spike paused in the doorway to savour the tableau – Charlie kneeling on his chair over a bowl of Cheerios, tracing the letters on the back of the cereal box with one finger. Jessica, barefoot at his shoulder, edging him closer to literacy. And Rufus, comb grooves still clear in his silver hair, laying rashers of bacon into a frying pan that was only marginally carbonised.

'Morning all,' Spike said. Knowing that a peace offering was in order, he reached for Jessica's hand and pressed it to his lips. She gave him a small smile, which was probably more than he deserved, so he leant over and ruffled Charlie's hair. 'It's polite to say hello, Charlie.'

But the boy just pressed his lips together, as he seemed to more and more these days when Spike was about.

'Bacon sarnies all round?' Rufus called out, as he bullied the rashers about the pan with the corner of the plastic packet.

'Not for me, thanks.' Spike made a face: the smell of burning bacon was making him feel queasy. He turned to Jessica and lowered his voice. 'Any news?'

'Massetti's still missing.' Jessica glanced across at Charlie. 'The forensic team spent most of the night at the Capurro house. They found evidence of an accelerant. Some kind of flammable gel.'

'Right,' Spike said flatly, thinking of the portable stove in Massetti's apartment. 'Come on, Charlie. We'd better go.'

Rufus was holding an unbroken egg up to the light, contemplating it like Hamlet meditating upon Yorick's skull. Jessica rapped him on the arm with a look of affectionate exasperation. 'Come on, Delia. Hand it over.'

29

Midway down Line Wall Road, Charlie reached up and took Spike's hand. This small confidence touched him, and it must have shown on Spike's face as two tourists rewarded him with smiles of approval, flicking their glossy hair as they turned to go down the steps of the American War Memorial.

As usual, Spike let Charlie lead him beneath the high stone archway. At its top was a bronze plaque commemorating Gibraltar's role in Operation Torch, the Second World War invasion of North Africa by British and American forces. Normally Charlie liked to gaze up at it for a moment, then take Spike's hand and abseil down the steps three at a time, but this morning he didn't seem in the mood.

So when they reached the pavement below, Spike crouched down and placed his hands on the little boy's shoulders. 'I know I haven't been around much lately, Charlie. Work's been really busy.'

Charlie picked up a mimosa twig and ran it between the limestone blocks, watching as the pale dust passed into the close air.

'We're still looking for the new house. That sort of thing takes time. But we'll find somewhere nice, I promise. Jessica will make it nice after the baby comes.'

Charlie's chin suddenly crumpled, and Spike was horrified to see his large brown eyes brimming with tears. 'Don't want to go back to Nana and Pete,' he murmured.

'Nana and Pete?' The boy's grandparents, Spike thought. 'Of course not. You're staying with us. Wherever we go.'

Spike felt the little boy's arms clamp around his neck, his head slot into its place between his shoulder and chin. He found he was laughing, and realised once again that he had a lot to learn when it came to children.

Charlie's tread grew brisker as he retook Spike's hand, the little red LEDs on the heels of his dinosaur trainers dancing with each step. Spike decided to risk a question. 'Who do you like to play with at nursery?'

The boy's face fell again, but then he rallied. 'Max Macfarlane,' he replied, looking up at Spike with a shy smile. He crooked one finger and Spike leant down to hear him whisper, 'Max is a *ninja*.'

'I like the sound of Max,' Spike whispered back.

They'd reached the fence of the playground. Spike bent down and kissed the curls on the top of Charlie's head. 'Love you,' he said, trying to remember when he'd said it last. But then he saw Charlie's eyes flick towards the nursery gates, and ushered him forward. 'Come on, then, Sanguinetti. Playtime waits for no man.'

30

By the time Spike got back to Chicardo's Passage, his father had already left with his watercolour kit. When it came to choices of subject matter, Rufus Sanguinetti displayed mono-maniacal tendencies that would have put Monet to shame. So Spike knew where he would be – elegantly perched on his sketching stool above Catalan Bay, easel angled towards the Mamela Rock. The boulder had been christened by the Genoese migrants who'd first settled on Gibraltar's eastern shore, and its ribald meaning was clear at first sight of the smooth, rounded land mass lapped by the Mediterranean.

Spike was just studying his father's latest offering when Jessica walked in. Recognising the expression of alarm on his face, she laughed. 'You don't need to be Freud to inter-pret *that*.'

He pulled out a chair, and she eased herself into it, then opened up the polka-dotted file containing her maternity notes with a moue of distaste. 'Water birth, anyone?'

Spike threw up his arms in surrender. He was more than happy to put off thinking about the baby's arrival until he absolutely had to. He hovered by Jessica while she wrote; she put up with it for a minute, then dropped her pen and sat back. 'Shouldn't you be at the office?'

Spike remembered the sardonic tone of Peter's earlier voicemail – '*Started paternity leave already, have we?*'

'There's something I need to tell you,' he said, then sat down opposite her and explained about his summons to the hospital after Massetti's accident.

'But you told me you had to go back to work,' Jessica said.

Spike reached out and took her hand.

'When you actually went to the hospital.' She withdrew the hand. 'So you lied to me.' It wasn't a question.

'I thought it might be Dad.'

Jessica's chestnut eyes glinted. 'But it wasn't your father. It was Christopher Massetti.'

'The doctor said they needed someone to take him home.' Spike ran the side of one hand across his eyebrow; he was suddenly feeling rather hot. 'There wasn't anyone else.'

'So why not tell me about it?'

'I didn't want to worry you.' The excuse sounded lame even to his ears, and he knew she must think the same. But to his surprise, she reached forward and stroked the small scar above his eye. 'You were just trying to help, Spike. It's nothing to be ashamed of. But I still don't see why you didn't tell me. I deal with vulnerable people all the time. Maybe I could have done something.'

He had hurt her, he realised. Jessica didn't say anything for a moment, but then she lifted her eyes. 'I know things have happened in your life, Spike. Things that make you think it's better for everyone if you hold a little back. But what we're doing together . . .' She dropped her hand to her belly. 'All that has to end. We need to trust each other.'

'I'm sorry,' Spike said. And he was.

31

They lay side by side on the futon, the Massetti papers scattered around the bedclothes as though they were midway through the Sunday broadsheets. '*One country, one culture,*' Jessica read aloud, translating the Spanish with a facility that Spike couldn't help but admire. '*For only blood shall purify Iberia and give birth to a second Golden Age . . .* Christ. Is it all this bad?'

Spike shrugged. He'd only made it through the first few stanzas. Jessica picked up the photograph that Massetti had stolen from the Isthmus Museum and took another look at Raúl de Herrera. 'Hard to take a man seriously with that kind of facial hair.' She shot Spike a playful glance. 'But this Esteban Reyes is quite good looking.'

Spike rolled his eyes, then put an arm behind his head and lay back against the pillow.

'What about the other guy?' Jessica said, pointing at the overexposed figure next to Esteban.

'Massetti thought it might have been John Capúrro. But he couldn't be sure.' Spike sat up and rifled through the papers until he found the letter John Capurro had sent Massetti from his hospital bed. 'I could have used this before the trial,' he muttered.

Jessica read the note, then looked up at Spike, chewing her lower lip. 'I need to get this to Isola.'

They both heard the ping as an email landed in Jessica's in-box, and Spike automatically reached for her iPad, wondering exactly when this fabled maternity leave was going to begin. 'Speak of the devil,' he said. He watched as Jessica opened the email from Isola and registered its contents. Then she passed her iPad back to him and rolled off the futon.

Spike clicked on the attachment, and a sequence of black-and-white CCTV footage started to roll. The time code was dated 9.49 p.m. last night. The camera must have been mounted on the UK side of the Gibraltar–Spain frontier, as Spike recognised one of the Border Agency officials. A few moments later, a heavy man shuffled into shot and turned to the camera. Massetti had a sports holdall slung over one shoulder. He held out his passport. And then he was gone.

'It was recorded half an hour after you saw him on Governor's Street,' Jessica said, as she pulled on her elasticated jeans. 'They've issued a European Arrest Warrant. Can't be long now before the Guardia pick him up.'

'Unless he's already in the mortuary,' Spike said, wondering how long it would take Massetti to find a Spanish off-licence.

As he watched Jessica gather together the articles and memorabilia that Massetti had so painstakingly collated to persuade himself of his father's innocence, Spike couldn't help but wish that he'd done what his former client had asked of him – destroyed everything before it could be used as evidence against him in the murder of Eloise Capurro. But deep down, he knew that Jessica was right. 'There was a security camera at the Capurro house,' he called over. 'They installed it before the trial.'

Jessica nodded, then grabbed her things and left for work. Spike knew he should be doing the same, but there was something else he needed to do first.

32

Spike saw Marcela approach long before she realised he was there. The incline of Convent Ramp was steep enough to have quickened his own breathing, and the old woman certainly looked her age as she shuffled towards him, black caftan blowing behind her in the humid breeze. Her smile fell as she registered his expression. 'Well, if it's like that, I suppose you'd better come in.' She opened her handbag and took out her keys: 'You can help me open up.'

Spike followed her into the gloom of the restaurant. The shutters were closed, the air frowsty and warm. She reached for an old iron handle on the wall and started to rotate it, the sinews of her arms working beneath the papery skin, swollen knuckles trapping the unfashionably yellow-gold rings below. Those would have to be cut off one day, Spike found himself thinking. He pushed the morbid image aside. 'It's bad news, Marcela.'

She continued twisting the handle, one eye on the striped awning as it inched outwards.

'There was a fire last night in the Old Town.'

'I saw the smoke.' Marcela flicked a switch on the wall, then turned back to Spike, her wrinkled face impassive. 'Come on, then. Out with it.'

The displaced air from the ceiling fans did little to relieve Spike's discomfort. He tugged the side of his collar away from his damp neck with two fingers. 'Eloise Capurro was killed in the blaze. I'm so sorry, Marcela.'

Spike watched the notches around Marcela's mouth deepen. 'Was it him? Was it Massetti?'

'The police think so.'

She put out a hand to steady herself on the nearest table. Spike stepped forward to help but she waved him away. 'Have they arrested him?'

'I'm afraid not. They think he's fled to Spain.'

Marcela straightened up, then picked up a remote control from the waiter station. A moment later, the husky notes of Nina Simone's 'Don't Explain' drifted across the restaurant. 'Come on, then,' Marcela said, and Spike followed her out back.

The old woman opened the door to the kitchen garden and stepped outside, lowering her head against the glare. In the heat of the mid-morning sun, Spike could smell the fragrance of the herbs growing in neat beds by the far wall: oregano and rosemary, chives and thyme. Tomato vines and chilli plants were staked behind them, laden with dusty fruit.

Marcela knelt down before a row of beetroot and started snipping away at the green tops with a pair of orange-handled scissors, laying the stems in a wooden trug. 'I was evacuated to London during the war. Did you know that?' She cast Spike a penetrating glance over her shoulder, and he shook his head.

'No reason why you should. Young people are only interested in themselves. Or I was, at any rate.' She gave a wry smile and returned to her task, the blades of her scissors clipping back and forth. 'Your father was on the same boat as me. The *Gibel Dersa*. But I barely remember him. Toddlers, you know – not very interesting to a teenage girl.' She sat back on her heels. 'The whole evacuation was a fiasco, to tell the truth. They told us we'd be safer away from home, then they sent us into the middle of the London Blitz. But then, of course, I would never have found Andrew.' Marcela held a clawed hand over her eyes. 'We met during one of the air raids. At South Kensington Tube. He'd been invalided out of France.' She picked up another trug and thrust it into Spike's hands. 'Go on, make yourself useful. We need tomatoes and cucumber for the gazpacho.'

Spike heard Marcela's husky voice continue behind him as he set to work: 'After the wedding, Andrew and I opened a café on the Fulham Road. It did well at first, but after the war, things changed. Business was bad, and London was so bleak back then. So cold.' She shivered at the memory. 'We got back enough money from the Revenue to move to Gibraltar. I think Andrew hoped being close to my family might alleviate some of the disappointment of there not being any children of our own. But things never work out the way you expect.'

The stems of the cucumbers were sharp and spiny; Spike saw a bead of blood ooze from the pad of his thumb and put it to his mouth, hoping that Marcela hadn't noticed.

'My brother couldn't bear Andrew, you see.' Marcela inclined her head. 'I don't suppose you ever met Tito?'

'I'm afraid not.'

'Oh well. He died a long time ago. Killed himself, just like our father. They say these things run in families.' Marcela's green eyes darted round to meet Spike's as she suddenly remembered herself. 'But I'm sure that's just a lot of nonsense. We opened Marcela's together. And it was a disaster. And men, you know, there's something in them. They aren't built for failure. So in 1968, Andrew petitioned for divorce. Left me, and went back to live with his mother in Bethnal Green.' Marcela shook back her fringe of ice-white hair. 'But then Franco closed the border with Spain, and everyone was stuck in Gib with nothing to do but go to restaurants. Business boomed.' She gave a sudden cackle, sunlight glinting off the gold fillings on either side of her mouth, and Spike found himself feeling a little sorry for poor Andrew. 'I didn't really miss him, you know. But the divorce was hard, far harder than I'd imagined. It wasn't the done thing in those days. And going to court, well, it was really very distressing.' She laid down her scissors. 'So that was what I said to Eloise. Don't go to Law, not unless it's your only option.'

Marcela raised a bony arm and Spike helped her to her feet, seeing the swollen flesh cutting into the edges of her embroidered silk shoes as they walked back towards the restaurant. 'Maybe if I hadn't persuaded Eloise to drop the case, they'd have locked that bastard up and she would still be alive.'

As Spike held open the back door, Marcela grabbed his upper arm so firmly that it made him start. 'The police have to find him,' she hissed, green eyes searching his face. 'They must find Christopher Massetti, and lock him up.' Then she took the trug from Spike's hands, and disappeared inside the kitchen.

33

Within a week of the murder, the focus of the news coverage had shifted from Massetti's disappearance to the speed with which the fire had spread through the Old Town. Investigators had concluded that the accelerant was poured through Eloise Capurro's letter box; it had leaked beneath the floorboards, and the blaze had found force in the original wooden foundations that ran below the street – ancient timbers salvaged from scuttled Spanish warships. Rebuilding the Old Town had now become a priority, and Drew Stanford-Trench's calls to modernise the area suddenly seemed prescient. 'How many more people need to die?' Drew would ask solemnly in every interview, omitting to mention that Eloise Capurro's death had most likely been caused by a man he himself had failed to prosecute.

'Sanctimonious git!' Spike muttered to himself, as he finished reading Drew's latest panegyric in the *Gibraltar Chronicle*. Then he looked up to see Ana Lopes sauntering into his office, once again without knocking. If she discerned his irritation, she was untroubled by it, just handed him his morning post and turned on her kitten heels.

Spike's eye was caught by a thick cream envelope addressed to '*Mr Somerset Sanguinetti and Miss Jessica Navarro*'. Inside was an embossed card: '*Sir Anthony Stanford invites you to a Fund-raising Gala at Dragon Trees in honour of Liberal*

Party candidate Drew Stanford-Trench QC. Champagne Reception and Silent Auction. RSVP.'

Spike shook his head. Talk about striking while the iron was hot. Sir Anthony didn't miss a trick.

The next envelope was blank, but even before Spike tore it open, he knew that it would contain the form Peter had been pressuring him to sign for weeks. Spike had just picked up the phone to tell Peter exactly what he could do with it when his office door opened and the man himself appeared.

'Caught you!' Peter exclaimed with a diabolical smirk. He wore the houndstooth check suit that came out when business was good and summer on its uppers. His gold-topped walking cane was back in use; he claimed the autumn humidity made his legs ache. Once the grand production of lowering himself into the leather armchair was complete, Peter leant forward to examine the new photograph on Spike's desk – Charlie dressed in the Lost Boy costume Jessica had bought him, brandishing a wooden sword. Peter set down the frame without comment, but Spike didn't miss the smile playing at the edges of his lips.

Spike held out the sheet of paper. 'We've discussed this, Peter. I can't sign something confirming I've known some woman for more than a year when I haven't.' He pressed the document into Peter's hands. 'Even if she is the Chief Executive of our biggest client.'

'It's just a question of expediting . . .'

'It's a lie.'

Peter's voice hardened. 'Siri Baxter came to Gibraltar eighteen months ago. You could easily have met her then.'

'But I didn't.'

'Listen.' Peter took a moment to smooth down the brown goatee he still thought gave definition to a long-departed jawline. 'The whole Bonanza Gaming management team's on today's BA flight from Heathrow. Let's empty the Entertainment Account! Take Siri out to dinner at Marcela's. Get it signed over coffee.' Seeing the expression on Spike's face, Peter groaned. 'It's a formality, Spike. Be practical!'

'It's a fit and proper person test, Peter. That's why they need a lawyer to sign it.'

'There are plenty of lawyers in Gibraltar who've known Siri for a year.'

'Then there are plenty of lawyers in Gibraltar who'll *say* they have.'

The two men stared at each other, and Spike caught something in Peter's eye that he'd never seen before, that he didn't like. But then it was gone, and Peter was all smiles again. 'Why don't we discuss it later, Spike? When you're less, well . . .' He cupped a palm over the knob of his cane and pushed himself to his feet. 'She's here all week!' he wheedled over one shoulder as he opened the door.

34

On the night of Drew's party, there were no Rock Apes lurking on the approach to Dragon Trees, just a long line of executive cars preparing to avail themselves of the valet parking that Sir Anthony had provided for his guests. A stubby tongue of red carpet extended from the main entrance. 'Feels more like a victory parade,' Jessica observed, as they paused outside to let her catch her breath.

She'd found the walk harder tonight, Spike could tell. He took her hand, half-hoping she might go into labour there and then, if only to escape an evening of small talk. As usual, she seemed to read his mind. 'No such luck, Spike, I'm afraid.'

They were welcomed at the door by a tall blonde dressed in a black Nehru jacket that stopped midway down her skinny thighs. She ushered them over the threshold with a megawatt smile, then recalibrated her face for the next guest. The party was already in full swing, black-suited waiters and waitresses sweeping past them with silver trays – crystal flutes of champagne, smoked salmon blinis, miniature beef Wellingtons and Scotch quail's eggs. The uniform attractiveness of the staff was striking, and Spike found himself wondering if they were 'resting' actors and models who'd been flown in from London for the day. The irony was that the amount the party had cost would probably exceed that which it would generate, but Spike knew this was less about fund-raising than about establishing Drew as a serious candidate for Chief Minister.

The view through the glass cube was as breathtaking as Spike remembered, the shipping lights of the Straits flashing beneath a spangled dark-denim sky. Illumined against it was the man of the moment, flanked by two women, the younger and more attractive of whom Spike knew worked for the *Gibraltar Chronicle*. Hovering beside them was the owner of GibFuel, the Rock's largest ship-bunkering company, adjusting his yarmulke as he sourced kosher pickings from the passing trays.

At first glance, Drew looked every inch the promising candidate. This evening, he'd gone for a pale lightweight suit, which on a heavier man might have drawn unfortunate reminiscences of the Man from Del Monte, but which complemented Drew's clean-cut freckled complexion perfectly. By his standards, he'd acquired something of a tan since they'd last met, and Spike wondered if he'd been dragged to a salon by some newly employed stylist. But he knew Drew too well to miss the telltale shadows beneath the eyes – signs of sleepless nights and stressful meetings. He paused for breath to offer Spike and Jessica a wave, then returned to his attentive entourage.

'Jessie?' Spike looked round to see a petite brunette embracing Jessica. There was something oddly familiar about her delicate, elfin features.

'You remember Sofia Peralta, don't you, Spike?' Jessica prompted, and then it made sense. Marcela's great-niece.

Spike leant in to kiss her on both cheeks. The last time he'd seen Sofia she'd been an awkward teenager, sulkily waiting tables at Marcela's to pay for her gap year. People had always said she was bright, and the day she'd got her degree results from Cambridge, Marcela had done the unthinkable, clapped her hands together and said that drinks were on the house. Jessica had been surprised when Sofia had decided to move back to Gib after graduation, but perhaps, like so many of her overqualified peers, she just couldn't find work in England. So she'd taken an entry-level role in the online gaming industry three years ago. But her dress was so simple and well cut that Spike suspected it must be very expensive, and there were diamond solitaires sparkling in her ears, so maybe she'd inherited some of her great-aunt's famous work ethic after all. 'How are you feeling?' she asked Jessica.

Jessica sighed. 'Enormous.'

'You look radiant.' Sofia squeezed Jessica's hand, then turned her hazel eyes to Spike. 'And what about you, Spike? Ready for impending fatherhood?' The anxiety he felt must have been obvious, as both women looked at each other and laughed, the first unaffected sound Spike had heard all evening.

'Have you seen my great-aunt?' Sofia was scanning the room.

'Marcela's here?' Jessica said in surprise. 'I didn't think she would come.'

'Nor me.' Sofia hooked a hank of glossy dark hair behind one ear. 'Eloise's death has hit her pretty hard. She needs to slow down.'

'There she is,' Spike said. 'Talking to our estimable host.'

Marcela and Sir Anthony were standing in a huddle at the back of the kitchen, whispering intently. One of Sir

Anthony's arms was in a sling, Spike saw, and his face looked dark and angry. Marcela leant in to whisper something to him, but he shook her off and she turned away.

'Looks like a heated discussion,' Jessica said.

'I expect it's about the catering – Auntie M doesn't like to be overlooked.' Sofia pulled a face. 'I'd better go and rescue her.'

Spike suspected that the argument might have more to do with a fund-raising event that capitalised on the recent death of a mutual friend, but he put that out of his mind as they watched Sofia move through the crowd.

'Be a while before I'm back in a dress like that,' Jessica murmured.

Spike handed her a tumbler of elderflower pressé and kissed her cheek. 'No contest,' he said, and was rewarded with a smile.

35

Minesweeping canapés, Spike led Jessica over yards of polished cedar flooring to the west wing of the house. As a teenager, he'd always been awed by the vastness of Dragon Trees, and from the look on Jessica's face, he could tell she felt the same. On numerous occasions, he'd heard Sir Anthony relate the tale of how the then Governor had built it in the eighteenth century as a summer-house for one of his many mistresses, and he knew that the only way to get a sense of its true size was to view it from the Straits – storey after storey huddled against the Rock.

When they finally reached the drawing room, Spike recognised the Bloomsbury-era oils that had once hung in the kitchen, now framed in antique gilt and over-lit on the panelled walls like in some gentlemen's club. The sofas had been shunted to one side to make room for a trestle table displaying items for the silent auction.

Spike examined the list of lots, finding mostly vouchers for the dolphin safaris, spa breaks and personal-training sessions that were the staple entertainment of bored tax exiles counting down their days in Gib. But there were also a few antiquities, and his eye was caught by a rather lovely pair of Victorian watercolours of the lighthouse at Europa Point, which he imagined would fetch enough to fund a couple of advertising billboards for the Liberal Party and its thrusting new leader.

Recognising Peter's well-liquored boom of a laugh, Spike turned and saw a triumvirate he would have preferred to avoid. Peter had donned his midnight-blue dinner jacket for the occasion, belly straining his silk cummerbund to its limits. Alan Cassar QC looked hot and thirsty, and between them stood a tall, androgynous figure in a black satin cigarette suit that Spike suspected was – but hoped was not – the infamous Siri Baxter. They were clustered around a replica of Alexander Calder's 1936 sculpture, *Gibraltar* – the Rock hewn from hardwood, encircled like a witch's hat by a smooth brim of walnut.

Spike tried to steer Jessica away, but it was too late. 'Spike!' Cane clicking in one hand, glass of champagne in the other, Peter drew Jessica into his moist embrace, leaving Spike to nod at Cassar, then turn warily to face Siri Baxter. 'We haven't met in person, Ms Baxter. How do you do?'

Siri stood there and appraised him for a moment, one lean arm wrapped across her waist, clasping her elbow, her free hand toying with the stem of her champagne flute. With her magenta lips and short blonde hair waxed like that of a schoolboy from the 1930s, she looked like an elegantly malevolent character from an Evelyn Waugh novel. She held out a long, cool hand. 'Your work for Bonanza has been outstanding, Mr Sanguinetti.'

Spike heard Alan Cassar let out a scoff. 'He's half-decent when he bothers to prepare.'

'Alan's known Siri for years,' Peter confided. 'They're both patrons of the Royal Opera House.'

'Do you care for the opera, Mr Sanguinetti?' Siri asked.

'Not especially.'

Siri's watery blue eyes slid over to Jessica, fell moment-arily on her belly, then returned to Spike's face. 'Maybe on your next trip to London we might change your mind?'

In the corner of his vision, Spike could see Jessica biting her lower lip, struggling to hold her temper. He picked up her hand and squeezed it. 'That's very generous, Ms Baxter. But I don't have any trips to the UK planned in the short term. As you can see, Jessica and I have a busy time ahead of us.'

Siri gave a confident, empty smile, as she searched the room for more amenable prey. Then she turned for the door and Peter hurried to catch her up, glowering back at Spike over his shoulder.

'Unusual approach to client management, Spike.' The amusement was clear in Cassar's face. 'But I can't fault your judgment. If there's one woman you don't want to be trapped in a box with for a performance of the *Ring Cycle*, it's Siri *bloody* Baxter.' Catching sight of another QC, Cassar gave Spike an avuncular pat on the arm, then took his leave.

'That was awkward,' Jessica said.

'Sorry,' Spike replied, pushing open the door he hoped led to the library. 'Peter's been driving me mad.'

Spike was relieved to find the library largely unchanged. Running a fingertip along the mahogany writing desk that he'd always envied, he turned to the bookshelves, as packed with leather-bound classics as the Garrison Library in town. Trollope, Galsworthy and Dickens; Shelley, Coleridge and Tennyson. Authors and poets whose intimidating canons he had barely penetrated, something he knew that Rufus, a passionate reader, considered a baffling shortcoming. Spike had always hoped to remedy this, perhaps when he had more time, but now he had Charlie to think of, the baby coming – and a hefty mortgage to take on. He couldn't see himself settling down after a long day in court with a copy of *Crime and Punishment* in the immediate future.

Jessica was looking at a framed picture on the wall. Spike crossed the frayed Moroccan rug to join her, and she pointed to a black-and-white photograph of a group of uniformed men lined up along the docks of Gibraltar Harbour. They were beaming with pride, medals pinned to their chests.

Spike recognised the bearded man in the admiral's uniform from the trademark vacant look in his eyes. 'King George V,' he said.

'Not *him*,' Jessica chided, pointing at the stocky young man at the end of the row. The hawkish nose and thick swept-back hair were just the same. 'Sir Anthony Stanford,' Spike murmured, leaning closer. 'Bloody hell. Is that a George Cross?' Then Spike saw the card beneath the picture: 'King's Medal, 1945'. A war hero – he should have guessed.

But Jessica was tapping an impatient finger on the glass. Spike took a closer look: hanging around the young man's neck, just visible above his collar, was a pendant. Spike tried to remember where he'd seen the teardrop shape before, then it came to him. The third man in Christopher Massetti's photograph hadn't been John Capurro at all. It had been Anthony Stanford sitting in that smoky bar with Esteban Reyes and Raúl de Herrera.

Hearing voices outside, Spike and Jessica stepped back, fidgeting like a couple of guilty teenagers as they waited for the door to open.

36

It was Drew who reacted first. 'There you are,' he called out, as though he'd been searching for the pair of them for hours. Sir Anthony said nothing, but the notches between his eyebrows evidenced his displeasure, and Spike wondered if they'd trespassed into some private domain. 'I hope we aren't intruding, Anthony,' he said.

'My fault, I'm afraid,' Jessica cut in, offering her most demure smile. 'I felt a little faint.' She looked up at their host through her eyelashes and fanned her face: 'All those people!'

Sir Anthony's expression softened, and he waved away their apologies with his good hand.

'It's a hell of a party, Drew,' Spike said.

'Full of the great and the good,' Drew shot back. 'The perfect place for a hungry lawyer to hustle up some new clients. Or so your business partner seems to think.'

The sourness in Drew's tone gave rise to an uncomfortable silence. 'Looks like you've been in the wars, Sir Anthony,' Jessica said.

The old man cupped an ear in irritation. He'd lost ground since they'd last met, the skin on his cheeks hanging more loosely, the shape of his skull more visible around the nose and jaw. It was his left arm that was injured, Spike noted.

'What happened?' Jessica asked.

'Slipped in the shower – the silliest thing,' Sir Anthony replied in a terse voice that made clear he was disinclined to discuss the matter further. He turned to leave, but Jessica called him back. 'We've just been admiring your pictures.' She pointed up at the photograph: 'I thought I recognised *this* handsome young war hero.'

Sir Anthony reached up to unhook the frame from the wall, and smiled for the first time that evening. Then he handed it to Jessica with a wink. 'I can neither confirm nor deny.'

'Typical.' Drew rolled his eyes. 'Ask Dad about his war and he starts spouting the Official Secrets Act.'

Spike turned to the bookcase and pulled out what he suspected was a Siegfried Sassoon first edition.

'Do you like war poetry, Spike?' Sir Anthony asked, the scepticism clear in his voice.

'I'm no expert,' Spike replied. 'But the other day a friend mentioned a Spanish poet he's discovered.' Spike ignored Jessica's attempts to catch his eye and looked instead at Sir Anthony. 'Raúl de Herrera?'

Sir Anthony's left knee buckled, and he knocked his injured arm against the bookcase. Drew stepped forward to help his father, but Sir Anthony pushed him away, face creased with pain. 'Oh stop fussing, would you?' His sling had rucked up, and he pulled it down over his wrist, trying to recompose himself. 'We should get back. The auction will be starting soon.' He raised his head. 'You might find yourself in one of these photographs, Spike. Somewhere near the ox-eye window.'

The door closed, and Spike looked round to find Jessica glaring at him. 'What?' he said, automatically crossing his arms.

Jessica turned away with a sigh of resignation. 'You never can leave well enough alone, can you?'

Spike just bit his tongue and followed her meekly across the room. The walls around the oval window were studded with pictures, and it took them a while to find the one Sir Anthony had mentioned. But there it was: a sun-faded Polaroid of the Sanguinetti family on Eastern Beach in . . . 1977? 1978? Spike plucked the frame from the wall and recognised himself, a tiny boy kneeling in the sand with his bucket and spade, blue eyes grave and watchful, skin the colour of melted chocolate. Rufus stood beside him in a pair of yellow Speedos that Spike had forgotten and hoped some day he would again, mouth open in the sort of toothy grin Spike hadn't seen in years. Then his mother, sleek in a black swimsuit, staring at something off camera, far out to sea. Catherine Sanguinetti. Present but not present.

Spike passed the photograph to Jessica and she stared at it. 'Your mother was very beautiful.' She sounded surprised, and Spike realised with a pang of guilt that she probably hadn't seen a picture of his mother before. Rufus didn't like them around the house these days – said they made him feel maudlin.

Feeling Jessica's hand on his sleeve, he glanced round, hoping she wasn't going to interrogate him further. But she wasn't thinking about his mother at all. 'This thing with Esteban Reyes. It intrigues you, doesn't it?' She looked into his eyes. 'But there's something you need to realise about cold cases, Spike. No one ever quite knows where they are going to lead.' She reached forward and hung the picture back in place, and Spike was reminded of what Josephine Massetti had said to her son before she died: *'There's no point raking up the past.*' Christopher had ignored her warning and now Eloise Capurro was dead. It was a sobering thought, but Jessica hadn't finished yet. 'You know another thing?' she asked. 'If Christopher Massetti had really wanted to clear his father's name, he would have done better not to have followed in his footsteps.'

37

The next morning, Spike blew on his coffee as he watched Peter Galliano stride around his office, wondering how long it would take before they could get started on the weekly work-in-progress update. Quite a while, he suspected, as Peter tucked his thumbs into his purple braces and puffed out his cheeks. 'Siri Baxter! What a woman!'

Spike gave a diffident nod of the head.

'The Russian market is opening up, and if you can handle yourself in that kind of environment, well . . .'

The stuffed Spanish wildcat on Peter's overmantel peered down from its dusty case. For the first time, Spike sensed a note of exasperation in its glass eyes.

'And your pal Drew seems to have made *quite* the impression,' Peter continued. 'Siri's even considering making a donation to the Liberal Party.' He slapped one palm on the desk. 'She knows how to recognise talent, Spike. And that's a real skill.' He seemed to be waiting for Spike to agree.

'It's tax efficient, I suppose,' Spike conceded.

Peter clenched a fist and shook it in his face. 'Exactly!'

Judging by the bloodshot quality of Peter's eyes, and the syrupy smell on his breath, he'd kept drinking long after the party had wound up. Spike wondered idly with whom.

'And about that document we discussed,' Peter resumed. 'Alan Cassar says he's more than happy to sign it, though

I must say I'm a touch disappointed that you'd put such a petty point of principle before . . .'

Mercifully, this morning's 'Peter Galliano Ethics Lecture' was cut short by a rap at the door. Peter swung round in irritation, but as ever, Ana Lopes was entirely unmoved by her employer's histrionics. 'Apologies for interrupting *such* an important meeting, gentlemen,' she said with that sly, innocent smile she did so well. 'But Sir Anthony Stanford is here.'

Peter's face lit up.

'Bad luck, Peter. He didn't ask for you.' Ana turned to Spike. 'I put him in your office.'

'Whatever he wants,' Peter called out, rubbing his hands together like a housefly, 'sign him up.'

The whistling had started before Spike even reached the door. Spike recognised the tune: the Ginger Rogers standard, 'We're in the Money'.

38

Sir Anthony had already made himself at home in the armchair opposite Spike's desk, legs crossed, one foot jogging with impatience. 'Glass of water?' Spike asked, and the old man gave a brisk nod without meeting his eye.

Spike turned towards the crystal decanter set on the sideboard, another of the expensive affectations Peter had demanded when they'd started up the firm. Spike was unsure when its contents had last been refreshed, but if Sir Anthony noticed the motes of dust swirling in the water, he didn't say.

As soon as Spike sat down, he could see that Sir Anthony was not himself. He'd missed a coin of silver stubble on the side of his jaw and the front of his monogrammed shirt was creased. He was hunching over his sling, so it was only when he sat back that Spike realised he was almost shaking with anger.

'Now you listen to me,' Sir Anthony said, raising an index finger, the nail split and ridged. 'I don't care for scurrilous insinuation, particularly in my own home.'

'I'm afraid you've lost me, Anthony,' Spike replied, clasping his hands on the desk in front of him.

'You know exactly what I mean. Taunting me with talk of that fascist charlatan.'

Spike opened his desk drawer and took out Massetti's photograph of the three young men at the bar in La Línea.

He slid it over the desk and waited, intrigued to see how the old man would react. Sir Anthony used his good hand to remove a pair of spectacles from his breast pocket and nudge them on. The furrows on his brow deepened. 'Where did you get this?'

'Does it matter?'

Sir Anthony took a sip of water as he considered his next move. 'What you need to understand is that at the time, these were issues of national security. We can talk off the record, I suppose?'

'I'm not a journalist, Anthony.'

The old man raised his damaged wrist so he could rest it on the arm of the chair. 'At the start of the war, Gibraltar was in a precarious position.' He lowered his head to peer at Spike over his spectacles, perhaps trying to ascertain how much the younger man was likely to know about 1940s Gibraltar. Not much, thought Spike, and it didn't take Sir Anthony long to reach the same conclusion as he sighed and prepared himself to begin with the basics. 'General Franco was in hock to Hitler for his assistance in the Spanish Civil War, and by the end of 1939, Spain was full of Nazis. There were howitzers in the hills above Algeciras, their barrels trained on the Rock.' Sir Anthony shook his head at the sheer audacity of it. 'Then Mussolini entered the war, and it looked as though the Italian fleet would take control of the Mediterranean. Vichy France had captured Morocco, so the threat to the Rock was threefold – from Spain, North Africa and the sea.' Sir Anthony looked up from under puffy pink eyelids at the flaking paint on the ceiling. 'I was sixteen at the time. My father was a retired British corporal, but he was also an alcoholic. He could be . . . unpredictable. In retrospect, I suppose it must have been very hard for my mother.' He dropped his gaze to meet Spike's. 'But you'd know all about that, of course.'

Spike looked away, remembering his own mother's volatile moods. The litany of painful incidents she'd begged him to conceal from Rufus. The shaming relief he'd felt when she'd finally given up on herself – and them.

'Money was tight' – Sir Anthony was still talking – 'so in the holidays I took whatever casual work I could find. Water carrier. Pot washer. But as the hostilities increased, more and more servicemen began streaming into Gib, and servicemen, as I expect you remember, have certain appetites. U-boat activity made the beer ships unreliable, so those with a bit of entrepreneurial flair could make good money importing essentials from Spain. There was a market for Red Biddy, the soldiers called it – a mixture of red wine and methanol that would strip the flesh from the back of your throat. They needed a team of boys to run it over the border – that, and a few other contraband items as well.'

'So you were a black marketeer, Anthony?' Spike couldn't help but smile.

'I was a young man trying to help keep his family afloat,' Sir Anthony retorted. 'The immorality of the thing never occurred to me. At least, not until the night I was stopped at the frontier.' Sir Anthony pulled off his glasses and sat back. 'The guards took me in for questioning, and I assumed they would transfer me to the Moorish Castle. Lock me up. But then a man came into the hut. I didn't learn his real name until much later, but he called himself Bowers. Claimed he'd fought with my father at Cambrai. Well, Bowers told me I had a choice. That there was a way I could pay off my debt – and help the war effort at the same time.' Sir Anthony snorted derisively. 'Some choice! The penalties for marketeering were harsh – a fine I could never have paid and two years in gaol. But then Bowers said I'd be working for the SIS, and that was it, I was sold. Hook, line and sinker.' Sir Anthony raised his tufted eyebrows. 'He'd massaged the truth, of course, as they all do, but I wasn't to know that then.' He paused, eyes clouding a little as he remembered that conversation from so long ago. 'La Línea was swarming with German spies, Bowers told me. They needed people they could trust to keep an ear to the ground. It wasn't much at first. My reports, such as they were, were anecdotal – a sense of the German presence in La Línea, that kind of thing. But Bowers seemed pleased, and after a few weeks, he made contact again and said he had a mission for me.' Even now, the memory brought a boyish glow to Sir Anthony's face. 'The Security Service had a particular interest in a Spanish nationalist living in La Línea. A man who was working with the Germans to plan an assault on military targets in Gibraltar. His name, of course, was Raúl de Herrera.' Sir Anthony enunciated the Spanish slowly, with relish and precision. 'De Herrera was building a network of spies and potential saboteurs, seeking out the disenfranchised, the disillusioned – young men he could influence and mould. Like many of us in Gib, I had relatives in Spain, and an uncle on my mother's side had been killed by the Reds in the Civil War. Bowers was aware of that, of course, and knew it was just the kind of thing that would make me an appealing target for de Herrera.' Sir Anthony's smile was thin now, bitter. 'The first meeting wasn't hard to engineer. I made sure to frequent de Herrera's usual haunts, then one evening he asked me to join him at his table. Plied me with brandy, tried to impress me with his poetry.' Sir Anthony gave a sniff. 'Dismal stuff, but then I've never had much of a taste for it. Before long, we were meeting regularly, and each time I gained a little more of his trust. Made him think he'd found a willing acolyte he could manipulate.' He rolled the shoulder of his bad arm with a grimace, and Spike found himself wondering to what lengths a teenaged boy might have been persuaded to go for King and Country. 'It wasn't long before de Herrera began talking openly about the need for direct action against the British. An act of sabotage so daring it would send a message to the Allies – and devastate morale amongst Gibraltar's civilian population. And then, one night, he revealed his target. The Royal Navy Dockyard.' Sir Anthony allowed himself a small smile of satisfaction in recognition of a job well done.

'So why did the bomb go off, Anthony?' Spike asked, making no effort to temper the scepticism in his voice.

Sir Anthony frowned.

'De Herrera had told you of his plans. But this man' – Spike tapped a finger on Esteban Reyes's handsome brow – 'still succeeded in blowing up the Dockyard.'

Sir Anthony gazed back at Spike for a moment with his bright crow's eyes, but then he looked away, and it was as though a door had slammed shut. When he spoke again, it was in that patronising tone his son favoured when questioning a witness he wished the jury to conclude was well meaning, but a tad slow-witted. 'Intelligence is an imperfect art, Spike. Especially in times of war. Not every act of sabotage can be prevented.' He placed one hand on the desk and started to prise himself out of the low chair. 'Our overriding objective was to prevent Spain from entering the war. And in that regard, we succeeded admirably.' The look on Sir Anthony's face left Spike in no doubt that the discussion was closed, so there was nothing left to do but take the old man's elbow and escort him through reception.

'How's the arm?' Spike asked, feeling the weight of Ana Lopes's inquisitive gaze upon them.

'At my age, these things take a little longer to heal.' Sir Anthony turned and, almost as an afterthought, added, 'So where *did* you get that photograph? The National Archives at Kew?'

Two can play at that game, Spike thought. So he just smiled. 'Do give my best to Drew.'

Perhaps it was the intensity of the expression on Sir Anthony's face when he'd enquired about the photograph, or maybe it was just that he was the second person to have mentioned Kew to Spike in the space of a month. But when he got back to his desk, something made him flip open his laptop and log onto the website of the National Archives. There was a box marked 'Explore our Records' at the top of the screen; Spike clicked on it, then dragged the cursor down towards 'Second World War'.

39

As usual at this time of year, the humidity had caused the lock at Chicardo's to tighten like an oyster, and it caught on the first twist of Spike's key. Nerves frayed by an afternoon spent needlessly redrafting an opinion on the instructions of an overpaid London associate many years his junior, Spike felt a sudden burst of rage, and had to stop himself from doing further damage to the woodworm-raddled door-frame with his foot. At last the lock yielded, and the blare of the telly struck him like a cosh – 'You can fly, you can fly, you can fly, you can fly . . .' *Peter Pan* – again. Spike checked the time. 7.40 p.m. Rufus must still be in charge.

In the sitting room, he found both man and boy topless. But seeing the wide-eyed exhilaration on Charlie's face, Spike felt his frustration ebb away. Charlie raised a hand for a distracted high-five, eyes trained on the screen as Michael and John Darling defied gravity.

Spike sank down into the sofa and leant his head back. A new canvas was drying by the wall, a study of the chapel in Catalan Bay. 'What happened to the Mamela Rock?'

'Old Davey wouldn't let me sketch from his terrace today,' Rufus replied, the perceived slight obvious from the set of his lips. 'Had to find something different.'

'*Old* Davey? He's younger than you, Dad.'

Rufus ignored him. 'He told me he's selling up. Downsizing, he called it.'

That got Spike's interest. Properties in Catalan Bay rarely came up for sale. 'Is the house on the market?'

'No clue. Look, Charlie, there's Skull Rock,' Rufus said, and the little boy shrieked in anticipation, shuffling into a kneeling position in his red underpants.

'Is Jessica in bed?' Spike asked.

'Eh?' His father was as engrossed as the four-year-old. 'No, no. Gone to the station.'

'She's on maternity leave, Dad.'

'Well, that's what she told me.' Rufus jabbed a finger at the screen. 'That rascal is Smee, Charlie. He's the evil genius of the operation, that's my theory. It's always the ones you least suspect . . .'

Jessica's number went straight to voicemail. Spike lay back for just a moment, then forced himself to his feet. 'Bye, son,' he heard called behind him as he wrestled with the lock once again.

40

As he reached the police station, Spike looked up to see the blue glass lamps on the facade of New Mole House fizzing with suicidal moths. Shaking off the inexplicable sympathy he felt for the doomed, euphoric insects, he pushed open the doors and presented himself to the desk sergeant. 'I'm looking for DS Navarro. Tell her it's her fiancé.'

The sergeant pivoted a heavy forearm on the edge of his desk and nudged his mouse. His placid, bulging eyes scanned the screen. 'She's on maternity leave.'

Spike resisted the urge to bludgeon the man over the head with his keyboard. 'I know that. Why don't you try the sign-in book?'

The desk sergeant inched across for the ledger. The pace at which he moved suggested he was on a mission to burn as few calories as possible. 'She's in Interview Room Three. With DI Isola.'

'Could you please let her know that Mr Sanguinetti is here?'

Spike watched as the receiver was slowly hoisted, then took himself off to wait in one of the chairs at the back of the room. The battery of his BlackBerry was dead, so there was nothing to do but stare up at the walls, at the cracked paint covered in sun-bleached bulletins and alerts. 'Operation Gib Watch', one poster said. The logo showed a magnifying glass enlarging the Rock above the tagline: 'Working Together to Put Crime Between a Rock and a Hard Place'. Christ: who paid these people? Spike looked away, then found himself staring into the eyes of a mugshot he recognised.

'WANTED: CHRISTOPHER ALEJANDRO MASSETTI', the text beneath it read.

> *Massetti is sought in connection with the murder of Dr Eloise Capurro. He was last seen crossing the Spanish border at 9.50 p.m. on 4 September. He is white, around 6'2" tall with long grey-brown hair and grey eyes. At the time of his disappearance, he was wearing dark tracksuit trousers, a blue T-shirt and carrying an Adidas holdall. He should not be approached, but anyone who sees him should call police on 199. Note: If calling from Spain, please ring 900-111-555. A reward of up to £3,000 is on offer.*

Who had put up the money, Spike just had time to wonder before his eyes closed.

41

'Spike?'

He opened one eyelid, trying to work out where he was – if he'd been asleep for five seconds or five hours. Then he blinked, and Jessica came into focus, wearing the same clothes as he'd left her in that morning. She pushed a styrofoam cup of coffee into his hands and eased herself down next to him.

'You're meant to be at home,' Spike growled. 'On maternity leave.' He took a gulp of coffee, wincing at the temperature and taste. At the periphery of his vision, he saw DI Isola emerge from an internal door with a petite young woman. Spike pinched the bridge of his nose between finger and thumb. 'Was that Sofia Peralta?'

'That's why I'm here,' Jessica said in a strange, flat voice. 'Marcela didn't turn up at the restaurant this morning. First time in forty years.'

Spike sat up, feeling the fogginess that always assailed his mind after an unplanned nap give way to a creeping sense of unease. 'Have you tried her apartment?'

'Sofia has a key. The place had been turned over.'

Spike got to his feet and started to pace. 'What about her mobile?'

'Straight to voicemail. I've been trying to persuade Isola to pay for a trace, but he wants to wait another day.'

The tightest man in the Royal Gibraltar Police, Spike thought. 'Did Sofia file a missing persons report?'

Jessica nodded. 'She also said the staff at the restaurant thought Marcela had been acting strangely. Jumping every time a customer came in.'

'As though she was scared? Of what? Massetti?'

'Maybe.' Jessica looked unconvinced. 'But if Massetti had crossed the border back to Gib, we'd know about it.' She shifted about in her chair, trying to find a more comfortable position, and Spike glanced across to see a tiny muscle twitching under her eye, like it always did when she was exhausted. 'We should go home.' He drained his coffee. 'Get some sleep. There's nothing more we can do tonight. I'll order a cab.'

This time Jessica didn't protest, so Spike gestured for her phone and waited for the line to connect. 'Have you eaten anything?'

She made no reply, and when he turned back, he saw her resting her head against the wall. So he leant down and kissed her cheek, aware of the sergeant watching them from behind his desk, blinking his melancholy, bovine eyes.

42

The next morning, Spike sat at his desk with a headache, staring at the latest set of directives proposed by the European Gaming and Betting Association. EGBA missives never made for the most scintillating reading, and Spike's task was not helped by the fact that it had been past 2 a.m. when he'd finally persuaded Jessica to come to bed. Neither of them had slept much after that, lying awake side by side, waiting for news of Marcela.

Spike's phone rang and he snatched it up.

'Peter here.'

'Peter *who*?' Spike said, hearing the murmur of his business partner's voice reverberate from the next door office.

'Very droll. Listen, I need a favour. Details of the private client account.'

'Filing cabinet too far for you?'

'Oh, for the love of God, Spike! I've just had Siri Baxter on the phone.' Peter let out a heaving sigh. 'Help out an old cripple, would you?'

Spike flipped open his desk diary and read out the log-in information for the firm's account. 'That it, then?' Spike caught the words 'Siri' and 'donation' in Peter's reply, and laid the receiver down on his desk. Thirty seconds later, he picked it back up and heard '. . .via the Client Account.'

'Sorry?' But Peter had already rung off.

Whatever, Spike thought, returning to the broader implications of Case C-98-14. The print danced before his eyes. Maybe he should ring Jessica again, see if she'd heard anything. But just as he picked up his phone, he heard a knock at the door and saw Ana Lopes holding a large brown envelope. 'It's from the National Archives,' she said as she laid it down on his desk.

Spike nodded. 'I should get my head down for an hour. No disturbances, please, Ana.'

'Busy, busy, Mr Sanguinetti,' Ana muttered. The door closed, and Spike sat back for a moment, trying to work out if she was being ironic. Then he tore open the envelope, took out the declassified MI5 file and started to read.

PART THREE

PART THREE

P.F. No. 66072 RA

SUPPLEMENTARY VOLUME HELD BY S.L.B.1.

REYES, ESTEBAN ALEJANDRO

Section: DG

Date: 24.03.41

33/15982/2/53

<u>IMMEDIATE SECRET</u>

Dear Major Shawfield

I refer to our conversation of 2nd October inst. regarding the draft obituary notice. As you will recall, it was my suggestion at that time that a copy of such notice should be sent to the Foreign Office for their comments and amendments, so as to be ready for timely distribution to the press in the United Kingdom and Gibraltar in the event of the sentence of death being carried out upon Esteban Alejandro Reyes.

We have now received confirmation from the Governor of Gibraltar that he has considered the case of Esteban Alejandro Reyes and, in accordance with Rule XXIII of the Royal Instructions, has concluded that the sentence of death should be carried out.

Having contacted the Foreign Office, I was disappointed to learn that they have received no such communication from you. It is therefore as a matter of urgency that I ask you to provide the Foreign Office not only with the draft notice, but also with the full statements and reports of the case. As soon as their concurrence is obtained, they will telegraph the official obituary notice to the Colonial

Office, Privy Council Office and Security
Service.

Your sincerely,

E.B.H. Hayward, Esq.

From: D.S.O., Gibraltar
Office File No.: PF. 55051
Date of Origin: 22.10.40
Date of Receipt: 23.10.40
Deciphered by: MN

1. Draft obituary notice sent to you
   to-day by aeroplane
2. Copy of complete statements and reports
   in same transit
3. Apologies for delay; somewhat busy this
   end

COMPLETE STATEMENTS AND REPORTS OF THE CASE
REX ... v ... ESTEBAN ALEJANDRO REYES

DEFENCE SECURITY OFFICE
GIBRALTAR
SEPTEMBER 1940

STATEMENT OF KENNETH MICHAEL SHAWFIELD, DEFENCE
SECURITY OFFICER, GIBRALTAR, made at DEFENCE
SECURITY OFFICE, GIBRALTAR on 17th June, 1940.

1. I have held the position of Defence
   Security Officer, Gibraltar, since March
   1937. Prior to that, I worked for the
   Imperial Security Service in London
   and abroad. Given the unique strategic
   position in which the Rock of Gibraltar
   finds herself during this conflict, my
   role, by its very nature, is broad and
   somewhat imprecise in its remit.
2. In view of the increasing Abwehr presence
   across the border in Spain, a signifi-
   cant amount of my time is devoted to
   investigating the activities of enemy-
   inspired sabotage organisations operating
   in Gibraltar and beyond. To assist me in
   these investigations, I have constructed
   a secret network of agents and sources.
3. At approximately 9.45 p.m. on 10th April
   this year, I heard an explosion from
   my house on Ragged Staff Road, and saw

161

smoke rising from what appeared to be
the Admiralty Fuel Depot. As soon as I
reached H.M. Dockyard, however, it became
clear that the smoke was in fact coming
from inside the Dry Dock enclosure.

4. I made my rank known to the Dockyard
Policeman on duty, P.C. SIMON RAMIREZ,
who informed me that the Dry Docks
were clear of personnel. As a result,
the emergency services focused their
efforts on controlling the blaze from the
outside. However, when the firefighters
came to enter the enclosure, they discovered in Dry Dock 3 the bodies of two
Royal Naval Engineers, ENGINEER COMMANDER
ARTHUR URQUHART BAINES and ENGINEER
LIEUTENANT HAROLD JOHN BECK. They also
found a third man, alive but gravely
injured, later identified as ESTEBAN
ALEJANDRO REYES.

5. As a consequence of these developments,
I summoned P.C. RAMIREZ back to the
scene in order to take a second
statement.

FIRST STATEMENT MADE BY POLICE CONSTABLE SIMON PEDRO RAMIREZ, P.C. NO. 8, H.M. DOCKYARD, AT THE DETECTIVE OFFICE, H.M. DOCKYARD, GIBRALTAR, AT 10.30 P.M. ON 10TH APRIL, 1940.

Question: Were you the Police Constable on duty at the Dry Docks this evening?

Answer: Yes, I relieved P.C. THOMPSON at 7 p.m.

Question: What are the functions of your role?

Answer: Seeing to it that no one goes into the Dry Docks what's not supposed to be there.

Question: Did you see anyone enter or leave the Dry Docks during your shift?

Answer: No, I didn't see no one.

Question: Was there any evidence of a fire before you heard the explosion? Smoke, perhaps, or flames?

Answer: Just a bang. That was when the fire started.

Question: Can you describe the sound of the explosion?

Answer: It come from nowhere. I felt it in my chest. My ears still ain't right.

Question: And you were at your post all night?

Answer: That's right, Sir. Until the explosion. Then I got myself off to get help.

Signed: SIMON RAMIREZ,

Police Constable,

GIBRALTAR

SECOND STATEMENT MADE BY P.C. SIMON PEDRO RAMIREZ AT 1.30 A.M. ON 11TH APRIL, 1940.

Question: In light of the new information that has come to our attention, I would ask you to give careful consideration before answering the following question, P.C. RAMIREZ. Where were you between 8.30 p.m. and the time of the explosion?

Answer: In the Mess Hut with P.C. DAVID MCDOWELL and P.C. JEREMY TORRES. We get together sometimes for a poker game. Just a few cards, it's good for morale.

Question: Would it have been possible for someone to enter the Dry Docks during the time that you were away from your sentry box?

Answer: No, Sir. We always look out for each other's stations, so there ain't no risk.

Question: But you were in the Mess Hut at the time of the explosion, weren't you?

Answer: We stick our heads out every now and again. Keep an eye on things.

Question: And you consider that to be a sufficient discharge of your duties, P.C. RAMIREZ?

Answer: Look, I've never seen no one trying to get into the Dry Docks after hours, and I've been sat in that box every night for six months.

Question: How often do you play poker?

Answer: Once a week on Wednesdays, when the others are on shift.

Question: So it's a regular arrangement?

Answer: I suppose you could say that.

Question: So if someone were familiar with your routine, they would know there was likely to be a period on a Wednesday night when you were not at your post? When it might be possible to access the Dry Docks unseen?

Answer: Like I said, Sir, I do what's asked of me and I never let no one come in or out without the proper papers. All the other P.C.s have got reprimands for sleeping on the job. But not me, I never close my eyes.

Signed: SIMON RAMIREZ,

Police Constable,

GIBRALTAR

STATEMENT MADE BY ENGINEER CAPTAIN CLIVE LEWIS CHIVERS, CAPTAIN OF NAVAL ENGINEER CORPS, AT BRITISH MILITARY HOSPITAL, GIBRALTAR, ON 11TH APRIL, 1940, AT 10 A.M.

I am Engineer Captain Clive Chivers, Captain of the Corps of the Royal Naval Engineers currently stationed in Gibraltar.

I identify the bodies in this mortuary as belonging to ENGINEER COMMANDER ARTHUR URQUHART BAINES and ENGINEER LIEUTENANT HAROLD JOHN BECK, two men of my command.

ENGINEER COMMANDER BAINES led the unit tasked with fitting out fishing vessels requisitioned from Gibraltar and Malta by H.M. Navy. His command was exemplary and his technical knowledge and skills irreproachable. I cannot conceive that the source of the explosion within the Dry Docks could have been related to the valuable work in which his unit was engaged, although it is my understanding that explosive devices are occasionally required in connection with that work.

ENGINEER LIEUTENANT BECK was a subordinate but highly valued member of the team. A recent officer fitness report praised not only his diligence and level-headedness, but also his meticulous approach to his work. Although he, like many young servicemen stationed far from home, on occasion drank to excess, he was not an habitual drinker, and I strenuously refute the contention that he would jeopardise his career by mishandling dangerous materiel whilst under the influence of alcohol in the workplace.

I cannot say why ENGINEER COMMANDER BAINES and ENGINEER LIEUTENANT BECK chose to return to Dry Dock 3 after hours, nor if they were acquainted with a man named ESTEBAN ALEJANDRO REYES.

Signed: ENGINEER CAPTAIN CLIVE CHIVERS,

Royal Navy, Gibraltar

STATEMENT MADE BY GREGORY CAMILLERI, BRITISH SUBJECT, CHARGEMAN OF MOULDERS, H.M. DOCKYARD, GIBRALTAR, AT BRITISH MILITARY HOSPITAL, GIBRALTAR, ON 11TH APRIL, 1940, AT 11 A.M.

I am the Chargeman of Moulders, C.E. Department, H.M. Dockyard, Gibraltar.

ESTEBAN ALEJANDRO REYES, No. 3561, works as a labourer under my supervision.

REYES entered my employment on 12th July, 1939. I set him to work transporting brass and iron casings from the moulds. He is a good strong worker, but can sometimes be uncivil in his manner.

I confirm that the Dockyard Identification Card you have shown me is the one issued to REYES. But I cannot identify for certain the man lying here because of the bandages on his face.

I declare this to be true.

Signed: G. CAMILLERI

STATEMENT OF KENNETH MICHAEL SHAWFIELD, DEFENCE
SECURITY OFFICER, GIBRALTAR, made at DEFENCE
SECURITY OFFICE, GIBRALTAR on 17th June, 1940 —
CONTD.

1. The witness known as 'LAUREL' first
   came to my attention in December 1939,
   when he was stopped by Border Police
   crossing the frontier from La Línea
   to Gibraltar in possession of contraband. Through his illegal activities,
   LAUREL had built up a number of useful
   contacts in La Línea, and with a degree
   of coercion, was persuaded to work for
   the Security Service as an informant.
2. Over the past year, a man of especial
   interest to the Security Service has
   been RAÚL DE HERRERA, a Falangist poet
   and pamphleteer who moved back from
   Madrid to his native La Línea in the
   summer of 1937. DE HERRERA is believed
   to have been working as an agent of the
   German Abwehr, specifically tasked with
   the recruitment of potential Spanish
   saboteurs.
3. Over the course of one of my regular
   briefings with LAUREL, it emerged that he
   had already forged a loose acquaintance
   with DE HERRERA, although he professed
   to know nothing of DE HERRERA's political inclinations. I therefore encouraged
   LAUREL to cultivate this connection,
   and he and DE HERRERA began to meet

often in the cafes and bars of La Línea.
Consequently, LAUREL's value as an opera-
tive increased.

4. On the day after the explosion, I
   instructed LAUREL to meet me at the
   Defence Security Office for a private
   debrief.

5. I wish to emphasise that LAUREL has
   never received payment for his information, and that it is my considered
   opinion that any and all assistance he
   has given is evidence of his good character and loyalty to the British cause.

FIRST STATEMENT GIVEN BY 'LAUREL' AT DEFENCE
SECURITY OFFICE, GIBRALTAR, ON 12TH APRIL, 1940.

*THE ORIGINAL DOCUMENT RETAINED IN DEPARTMENT
UNDER SECTION 3(4) OF THE PUBLIC RECORDS ACT
1958.*

<u>MEMORANDUM</u>

To the Governor and Commander in Chief, Gibraltar

1. Given the sensitive nature of certain testimonies, particularly those pertaining to Security Service investigations which stray into foreign territory, I would counsel that when the Reyes case is tried, all such evidence be given <u>in camera</u>.
2. In the interests of national security, this is particularly apposite as regards the evidence of LAUREL, a key witness in this case.
3. I therefore propose that for the entire duration of the trial, LAUREL be referred to only by his pseudonym, and that the Judge be appraised that this measure is necessary to secure the protection of the witness.

<u>S.L.B.1.</u>

15.04.40

Signed: K.M. Shawfield

TECHNICAL REPORT ON SABOTAGE MATERIAL

The 'galapago' bomb comprises a small quantity of high explosive, typically not more than 2 lbs. 'Galapago' means 'tortoise' in Spanish, and the curved, shell-like shape of the metallic device makes clear the reason for the name. At one end of its upper side lies a hole into which a time fuse mechanism can be inserted. Fixed to its flat underside are magnets, which are used to secure the device to a metal surface — as, for example, the shaft of a torpedo.

The time fuse mechanism used is colloquially known as a 'pencil'. It is composed of three compartments. The first is made of copper and contains a glass ampoule of acid. A strand of copper wire attaches this to the second, which encloses a suppressed spring and a striker. The third compartment contains the detonator. A thin strip of metal prevents the striker from detonating the firing cap, and also operates as a rudimentary safety mechanism and timer. The strip is painted a particular colour to indicate the length of delay for which that 'pencil' is designed.

In order to operate the time fuse, the glass ampoule of acid is broken by squeezing or biting the copper casing. The safety strip is then removed, and the 'pencil' can be inserted into the explosive. Once released, the acid eats through the copper wire. As soon as the wire breaks, the spring is released, the striker hits the detonator, and the device explodes.

CONCLUSION

Having studied the aftermath of the Dockyard explosion, I can confirm that its characteristics conform in every essential to those I have seen created by other 'galapago' bombs.

The extent of the damage was such that it was unlikely to have been caused by a 'galapago' in isolation. Accordingly, it is my contention that the perpetrator or perpetrators sought to intensify the blast by triggering the torpedoes of the trawler berthed in Dry Dock 3. The 'galapago', therefore, was most likely clamped to the shaft or cap of one of the torpedoes.

These findings have been corroborated by Naval Bomb Safety Officer, D.R.T. ANGSTRUTHER, LT., R.N.V.R., who examined the scene with me at the personal behest of ENGINEER CAPTAIN CLIVE CHIVERS.

> Signed: KENNETH SHAWFIELD,
>
> DEFENCE SECURITY OFFICER,
>
> 16.04.40

Dear Major Shawfield

I must begin by offering you an apology for my behaviour towards you last night at the Bristol Hotel. Whilst the reasons underlying my vexation must be apparent to you, I sincerely regret my conduct, and hope that you will accept my unreserved apology, and also pass on these sentiments to Mrs Shawfield.

But the fact remains that this intolerable stalemate cannot be permitted to continue. I feel this so keenly that I was tempted to petition His Excellency, the Governor, himself. I only refrained from doing so because the tone in which I write would likely be deemed unbecoming of the gap between our ranks.

So I must ask you once again what you mean to do to bring to justice the perpetrators of the Dockyard bomb. An atrocity has been committed on our soil, two of my Naval Officers have lost their lives, and the dismissal of one member of the Dockyard Police, and the suspension of two others, seems to me a woefully inadequate response. What is more, the perceived hesitancy of your investigation is having an adverse effect on morale amongst all Forces personnel here in Gibraltar.

I am not given to sentiment, as you well know, but allow me to tell you this. The widow of Engineer Commander Baines lost her eldest son six months ago in the submarine attack on Scapa Flow. She has another son departed for France with the B.E.F. The widow of Engineer Lieutenant Beck, moreover, is but twenty, and on learning of the death of her husband, entered into such a collapse that she is reported to have lost the child that she was carrying.

It seems to me that the very <u>least</u> you can do is order the immediate repatriation of both bodies.

Yours sincerely,

CLIVE LEWIS CHIVERS, E.C.

MEMORANDUM

To the Governor and Commander in Chief, Gibraltar

Perhaps I should let you draw the sting from this one, Your Excellency. Time for the Governess to unleash the cocktail trolley? Pink gins in the Convent garden? I fear my shiner may preclude my attendance, alas. *Buena suerte*, one and all.

S.L.B.1.

18.04.40

Dictated by: K.M. Shawfield

STATEMENT BY PETER MATTHEW ZAMMIT, BRITISH SUBJECT, OF 9 CRUTCHETT'S RAMP, GIBRALTAR, TAKEN AT THE DEFENCE SECURITY OFFICE, GIBRALTAR, ON 18TH APRIL, 1940.

I am the Acting General Manager of the Piccadilly Café, 14 Main Street, Gibraltar.

The Piccadilly is often patronised by British servicemen. On a good night, we can have as many as 80 customers between 7 p.m. and 10 p.m.. Under my orders are 2 barmen, 3 waiting staff and 1 'chucker-outer'.

I have been shown photographs of ENGINEER COMMANDER BAINES and ENGINEER LIEUTENANT BECK, and I remember seeing them come into the café at about 7.30 p.m. on the evening of 10th April. Many of the servicemen are 'rowdies', but these two sat quietly at the bar and drank a few bottles of ale. The younger man did most of the talking, whilst the older listened. When they stood up to leave, both appeared steady on their feet.

That was at exactly 9.15 p.m. I remember the time because it was when the Flamenco dancers arrived. They are nice enough girls, but I understand they are not to everyone's taste.

I make it my business to recall particular details about customers. That is why so many of them come back to the Piccadilly.

I have had this read to me and it is true.

Signed: Peter Zammit

First statement made at British Military Hospital at 10 a.m. on 20th April, 1940 by ESTEBAN ALEJANDRO REYES, Spaniard, born in La Línea on 18th August, 1919. Working at H.M. Dockyard, Gibraltar, as a labourer at the Foundry. Living with Gibraltarian wife, MAGDALENA PAULA REYES, née MONTEGRIFFO, at 17b Sefarty's Passage, Gibraltar. No dependents or children.

—

I have been warned that I do not have to answer any questions but that anything I do say will be taken down in writing and may be used as evidence.

(Signed) Esteban Alejandro Reyes

Question: Please confirm that you can fully understand the questions being put to you.

Answer: I understand what you say. My English is good.

Question: And are you well enough to proceed?

Answer: I want to see my wife. The other man said I could see my wife.

Question: Please answer the question.

Answer: Yes. Yes, I feel stronger today.

Question: Please give your name, address, occupation and nationality.

Answer: My name is ESTEBAN ALEJANDRO REYES. I live at 17b Sefarty's Passage, Gibraltar, with my wife, MAGDALENA. I work at the Dockyard as a labourer. I was born in Spain but my wife is Gibraltarian.

Question: When did you arrive in Gibraltar?

Answer: On 6 April, 1939. The day we got married.

Question: And when did you first obtain employment at the Dockyard?

Answer: In July last year. I don't remember the day.

Question: Do you remember what happened on 10th April this year?

Answer: What day is today?

Question: 20th April. Do you remember what happened ten days ago on 10th April?

Answer: I'm not sure. My head is still confused.

Question: Do you know why you're in hospital?

Answer: The doctor said there was an explosion.

Question: Why were you at the Dockyard on the evening of 10th April?

Answer: I work there.

Question: You work at the Foundry, not at the Dry Docks. Is that correct?

Answer: Yes.

Question: But you were at the Dry Docks on 10th April, weren't you? What were you doing in a different sector of the yard after dark?

Answer: My wife is pregnant. Sometimes she needs time alone. I told this to the other man.

Question: Go on, Señor REYES.

Answer: I needed to breathe. So I went for a walk by the Dockyard — I don't know why. Then I saw a light in the Dry Docks.

Question: Why didn't you alert the Police Constable on duty?

Answer: The sentry box was empty. Maybe the guard was playing cards. But I could still see the light. And my boss, CAMILLERI, always tells us to be watchful. That we must be on our guard. So I ran through the gate. I remember seeing two men in British uniform. Then, everything is black.

Question: What were the two British servicemen doing when you saw them?

Answer: Just standing. On the dock floor.

Question: Why do you think they were there?

Answer: I don't know. Why don't you ask them?

Question: Because both ENGINEER COMMANDER BAINES and ENGINEER LIEUTENANT BECK are dead.

(Prisoner attended to by medical staff — pause for fifteen minutes.)

Answer: Now I remember better. I think maybe the two servicemen were setting a bomb. Yes, I remember the cap of one torpedo was unscrewed. One man was keeping watch while the other put something inside.

Question: Did you see the bomb?

Answer: I think so, yes.

Question: Was it a 'galapago' or a 'puro'?

Answer: A 'galapago'. It looked like a 'galapago'. You call it 'tortoise' in English, I think.

Question: How do you know what a 'galapago' bomb looks like?

Answer: Everyone from La Línea knows this.

Question: Do you know a man called RAÚL DE HERRERA?

Answer: No.

Question: RAÚL DE HERRERA. Perhaps you know him from La Línea?

Answer: No, I am a resident of Gibraltar now. When my papers come through, maybe I'll sign up and join the war.

Question: Please look at this photograph.
  (Shown a photograph.)

Question: Is that you?

Answer: Yes.

Question: Who is the man in the moustaches sitting next to you?

Answer: I don't know.

Question: The man in this photograph is RAÚL DE HERRERA. If you don't know him, then why do we have a photograph of you drinking with him at a bar in La Línea?

Answer: I don't know. I can't understand.

<u>Question</u>: RAÚL DE HERRERA gave you the 'galapago' bomb, didn't he?

<u>Answer</u>: No, I have never seen this man before.

—

I have had this read to me in Spanish and English and it is all true and made of my own free will.

                (Signed) Esteban Alejandro Reyes

(Above statement completed at 11.40 a.m. — prisoner given lunch.)

SECOND STATEMENT: Made at 3 p.m. 20.04.40 at
B.M. Hospital.

Yes, I have again been cautioned that I need
not say anything or answer any questions unless
I wish to and anything I do say will be written
down and may be given in evidence.

(Signed) Esteban Alejandro Reyes

(Shown a strip of metal retrieved from the site
of the explosion.)

Question: Do you know what this is?

Answer: No. I want to see MAGDALENA now. Please
let me see my wife.

Question: This is a metal safety strip. It has to
be removed from the time fuse mechanism before
a 'galapago' bomb can be primed. Can you see the
traces of yellow paint at the end?

Answer: Yes.

Question: The yellow paint tells us that the
bomb was set to explode between ninety minutes
and two hours after it was planted.

Answer: I'm just a labourer, Mister. I don't
know anything about bombs. I don't believe in
violence. Ask my friends. Violence is the lowest
part of a man.

Question: ENGINEER COMMANDER BAINES and ENGINEER
LIEUTENANT BECK spent the evening together in
a bar until just thirty minutes before the bomb
exploded. Do you understand what that means?

That it would have been impossible for them to have planted the bomb.

Answer: One of them could have left the bar, no? Run to the Dry Docks, set the bomb, then come back without anyone seeing.

Question: But you told me that when you entered Dry Dock 3, you saw two British servicemen interfering with the torpedoes on the trawler.

Answer: My memory is confused. I have been very ill.

Question: Let me tell you what I think, Señor REYES. I think that RAÚL DE HERRERA gave you the bomb. And that is how you know what a 'galapago' looks like.

Answer: No. No.

Question: Then DE HERRERA paid you a sum of money to carry it over the border and plant it. You work at the Dockyard; you know how to slip in and out undetected — and where to plant a device to cause maximum damage. But you were interrupted by two Royal Naval Engineers as they passed the Dry Docks on their way back to their sleeping quarters.

Answer: If the bomb had a timer, why would I wait at the Dry Docks for it to explode? You didn't think of that, did you?

Question: Perhaps you mis-set the timer.

Answer: Or the other men did.

Question: Maybe you were keeping watch nearby after you planted the bomb. Making sure that everything went to plan. You saw the two Naval Engineers enter the Dry Docks, and you tried to distract them, worried that they would find the bomb.

<u>Answer</u>: Can you not hear how you sound? How ridiculous you English are with your 'maybes' and 'perhaps'? You have nothing on me.

This has been read to me in Spanish and English and I have said all this of my own free will because I want to tell the truth.

(Signed) Esteban Alejandro Reyes

STATEMENT OF KENNETH MICHAEL SHAWFIELD, DEFENCE
SECURITY OFFICER, GIBRALTAR, made at DEFENCE
SECURITY OFFICE, GIBRALTAR on 17th June, 1940 —
CONTD.

1. The discovery by D.R.T. ANGSTRUTHER,
   LT., R.N.V.R. of the yellow safety
   strip, taken with the eyewitness
   account of PETER ZAMMIT, General
   Manager of the Piccadilly, means
   that there was no conceivable way in
   which ENGINEER COMMANDER BAINES and
   ENGINEER LIEUTENANT BECK could have
   been involved in the explosion, regardless of ESTEBAN ALEJANDRO REYES's best
   efforts to deflect the blame onto his
   innocent victims.
2. Despite such compelling evidence of
   REYES's guilt, no confession was forthcoming. Given the likelihood that his
   case would pertain to a capital offence,
   after further discussion with the
   Commissioner of the Gibraltar Police, it
   was decided that stronger evidence was
   needed against REYES before any charge
   could be brought. To that end, I made
   contact once again with LAUREL, and told
   him to broaden his enquiries with regard
   to REYES's precise movements in the days
   leading up to the explosion.

SECOND STATEMENT GIVEN BY 'LAUREL' AT DEFENCE
SECURITY OFFICE, GIBRALTAR, ON 21ST APRIL, 1940.

*THE ORIGINAL DOCUMENT RETAINED IN DEPARTMENT
UNDER SECTION 3(4) OF THE PUBLIC RECORDS
ACT 1958.*

STATEMENT GIVEN BY NICHOLAS CONSUELO ISOLA, POLICE SERGEANT NO. 13, GIBRALTAR SECURITY POLICE, AT THE DEFENCE SECURITY OFFICE ON 22ND APRIL, 1940.

For the last ten months I have been stationed at the Four Corners, where it is my job to examine the passes of all civilians entering the Garrison from Spain. I am permitted to search the clothing and luggage of any person crossing the frontier, but this is not an absolute requirement. As anyone on border duty will tell you, sometimes it is too busy to take everyone into the searching sheds, and individuals known by face get let through quickest.

I confirm that MAGDALENA PAULA MONTEGRIFFO is my second cousin, and that she is married to ESTEBAN ALEJANDRO REYES.

I also confirm that REYES makes regular trips across the border to La Línea to visit his family.

On one or two occasions, REYES has brought me cigarettes purchased in La Línea as he knows I am partial to Spanish tobacco. The fact that REYES makes me these small gifts has no bearing on my decisions to search him.

On the afternoon of 9th April this year, REYES crossed to and from Spain. I remember this because on his return he gave me a packet of cigarettes and that was the last time I received a Spanish packet.

I have been shown a diagram of a 'galapago' bomb and can confirm that a device of that size

would be easy to conceal in the deep pockets
of the Dockyard dungarees that REYES tends to
wear.

This is true.

Signed: NICHOLAS ISOLA, P.S. 13,

Gibraltar Security Police

THIRD STATEMENT BY ESTEBAN ALEJANDRO REYES: Made at D.S.O.'s Office at 11 a.m. on 4th May, 1940.

I have again been cautioned that I need not say anything or answer any questions unless I wish to and anything I do say will be written down and may be given in evidence.

(Signed) Esteban Alejandro Reyes

Question: Do you know a man called RAÚL DE HERRERA?

Answer: No. You must believe me. The guard told me they turned my wife away. I need to see her. It's a long way to come to Detention Barracks to be turned away.

Question: You are being detained under the Gibraltar Defence Regulations, 1939, Señor REYES, and your rights, such as they are, are in the gift of the Governor.
  (Prisoner shown a photograph.)

Question: I ask you once again. Do you know the man sitting next to you in this photograph?

Answer: No!

Question: Can you read Spanish?

Answer: Of course I can. Spanish and English. You think I'm stupid?
  (Prisoner handed a book.)

Question: Look at the dedication in this book. Can you read what it says?

Answer: No. My head hurts.

Question: Let me read it for you. It says, 'For Esteban Reyes, a true Son of the Revolution'. Signed, 'Your friend and fellow linense, Raúl de Herrera'.

Answer: You bastard. You've been in my house.

Question: We had a warrant, Señor REYES. You must try to control yourself.

(Prisoner shown two 500 'peseta' notes.)

Question: Where did you obtain this money?

Answer: From my mother. What, I can't have Spanish money in my house?

Question: I think that these banknotes were given to you by RAÚL DE HERRERA.

Answer: Now I see it. You come after me because you need a scapegoat. That's how you English say it, isn't it? Un chivo expiatorio. I am a Spaniard in Gibraltar, so I am an easy target. You hid the book and the money in my house for them to find so you can hang me.

Question: The book was found beneath the floorboards in your bedroom. The money was in your kitchen dresser. There were witnesses present when both discoveries were made. We now have all the evidence that we need to charge you. The metal safety strip; an eyewitness account proving that the two Naval Engineers could not have planted the bomb; evidence confirming your personal connection to RAÚL DE HERRERA; two high-denomination Spanish banknotes in your house. And then, of course, there is the

192

simple question to which no satisfactory answer presents itself. If it wasn't you who planted the bomb, then who was it?

Answer: That is your job, Sir, not mine.

Question: Why not make it easy on yourself, Señor REYES? Confess now. Perhaps the Governor will let you see you wife. She is not well, I understand.

Answer: I want to speak to a Spanish lawyer.

Question: I'm afraid that will not be possible, Señor REYES.

(Signed) Esteban Alejandro Reyes

FOREIGN OFFICE

S.W.1.

25th October, 1940

(C 437/301/G)

<u>Secret</u>

Dear Shawfield

I know that Hayward wrote to you on 18th October regarding the draft obituary notice for Reyes.

I can now confirm that the draft notice has been agreed subject to the omission of the line 'and his conviction was secured thanks to the courage of certain members of the local community' in the final paragraph.

Many thanks for your timely assistance in this matter.

Do send my fond regards to Margery.

Yours sincerely,

S.W. Andrews

K.M. Shawfield, Esq.,

M.I.5.

[This document must be paraphrased if communi-
cated to any person outside Government service.]

[CIPHER]   DEPARTMENTAL NO. 1

FROM GOVERNOR AND COMMANDER IN CHIEF GIBRALTAR
                TO FOREIGN OFFICE

D. 25th October, 1940
R. 3.10 p.m. 26th October, 1940

Repeated to War Office (M.O.5)
Madrid

IMPORTANT
MOST SECRET

Received unofficial visit today from Spanish
Consul-General. Purpose of meeting was to plead
for life of saboteur Reyes. I responded that
regrettable etc. but evidence was firm and my
hands were tied. No clemency could be extended
to a man responsible for murder of two British
servicemen.

Consul-General suggested it was in interest of Allied forces not to aggravate Spanish
government. I responded that to all intents and
purposes the Axis has free run in Spain already
and he grew agitated and terminated interview.

As you know, execution of Reyes now fixed for
30th inst. Perhaps some sort of official dinner
for Consul-General and his wife once dust has
settled? Governess not in favour as pair of
them known to have fearsome appetites. But such
are demands of diplomacy.

TELEPHONE MESSAGE

Major Shawfield

Major Andrews, D.3.b., telephoned to report that the two men travelling to Gibraltar in connection with the REYES case have now been granted passports and exit permits by M.I.5. and that everything has been arranged to his satisfaction.

1300 hours 26.10.40

AR

From: D.S.O., Gibraltar
Office File No.: PF. 55053
Date of Origin: 27.10.40
Date of Receipt: 28.10.40
Deciphered by: MN

IMMEDIATE

Reference your DS/113/40/12a of 26.10.40

Execution to take place on morning of 30 October provided hangman and his assistant are not delayed by weather. Information to be released immediately thereafter.

MINISTRY OF INFORMATION — For Official Use of Censors Only

QUALIFIED RELEASE No. K.153   **Serial No.** 21

<u>Subject</u>: EXECUTION OF REYES

The following P. & C. Memo has been issued today:

'The obituary notice released today concerning the execution of Esteban Alejandro Reyes includes every item of information about this case that may safely be published.

Editors are requested in the interest of security to publish <u>no other details whatever</u> either of the case itself or of the man, his history and relatives, apart from the photograph of Reyes leaving his trial which has already appeared in the Gibraltar press.'

The obituary notice hitherto mentioned reads as follows:

'A Spanish national was executed today at Gibraltar, having been sentenced to death for offences against Regulation 23 of the Gibraltar Defence Regulations 1940:-

Esteban Alejandro REYES was executed today at the Moorish Castle in Gibraltar in accordance with the sentence of death passed upon him by the Supreme Court of Gibraltar Special Court on 12 October, 1940.

REYES pleaded "Not Guilty" to charges of treachery by acting with intent to help the enemy contrary to Regulation 23 of the Defence Regulations, 1939, as amended by paragraph 2 of the Defence (Amendment) (No. 17) Regulations, 1940 (Gibraltar). His trial took place on 9 October, 1940, before the Chief Justice of Gibraltar (His Honour Henry Percival Fawcett). REYES was represented by Mr Samuel T. Alonso.

REYES was recruited by a Spanish agent working for the German Secret Service and tasked with committing an act of sabotage in Gibraltar. As an employee of H.M. Dockyard living in Gibraltar, he succeeded in smuggling a bomb into Gibraltar on 9 April this year and secreting it the following day aboard a vessel berthed at the Dry Docks. The explosion caused the deaths of two Royal Naval Engineers, ENGINEER COMMANDER ARTHUR URQUHART BAINES and ENGINEER LIEUTENANT HAROLD JOHN BECK. REYES himself was injured in the blast, but recovered sufficiently to attend trial. He is survived by a wife.'

Censors, please act accordingly.

AUTHORITY: COLONIAL OFFICE TIME: 15.25 DATE 30.10.40

PART FOUR

43

Spike turned over the last document of the file, registering the twist of disgust in his gut as he stared down at the thick sheaf of A3 pages. So that was how it was done, he thought. That was how you orchestrated an execution. At Bar School in London, worthier contemporaries had spent their summer holidays working for Amnesty International or the Death Penalty Project, offering their untested services pro bono to death-row convicts incarcerated in the less evolved states of the US, or the Caribbean. But Spike had lacked both the funds and moral energy to indulge in such adventures, so it was a new experience for him now to see the relentlessness with which the apparatus of the State could collude to condemn a man to death.

Spike was against the death penalty on principle, having encountered enough unjust verdicts in the course of his career to confirm that the justice system was far from infallible. And on the basis of this evidence, the case against Esteban Reyes was weaker than most. He would have liked to have seen the court transcripts, but even without them, the glaring anomaly was one which Reyes himself had identified – namely, why a man who had just planted a bomb would hang around waiting for it to explode. It felt as though Reyes's conviction had been hurried through without much consideration of his actual innocence or guilt.

A more hawkish lawyer might have felt that the end justified the means: that Gibraltar was at war, and under such circumstances, the Governor had needed to set an example to deter other potential saboteurs. But Spike was no hawk, and the fact that the inconsistencies in Reyes's case had been subordinated to serve a political end troubled him deeply.

Then there was Sir Anthony's role in the affair. For there could be little doubt that Sir Anthony Stanford was the witness referred to in the file as 'Laurel'. Every one of his statements had been redacted from the record to protect his identity, and Spike wondered how many favours the old man must have called in from his pals in Whitehall to achieve such anonymity. Spike could understand that urge; what was odd was how the account that Sir Anthony had given to Spike in his office had differed from that in the file. Sir Anthony had implied that the Security Service had exhorted him to befriend Raúl de Herrera, yet the official version made clear that their acquaintance had been forged long before Sir Anthony had even been recruited.

Spike gazed through the French windows at the weed-strewn patio, thinking, as he seemed to more and more these days, of his mother. Rufus rarely spoke of her death now, but when he did, Spike would notice that certain details of his story changed over time – nuances, sometimes even facts. It was human nature, he supposed. He couldn't blame his father for constructing a narrative which gave him comfort, and which – even if it couldn't make sense of his wife's suicide – at least absolved him of some responsibility. A subtle reworking of a painful story: who could claim never to have done the same? Certainly not Sir Anthony, Spike thought, pulling himself back to the matter at hand.

In the end, what did it all matter? The events described in the file had taken place so long ago that the UK Government had allowed the documents to be declassified. Esteban Reyes had been dead for over seven decades, just a footnote in history. And the chances were he *had* been guilty – as the DSO had pointed out, if it wasn't Reyes who'd planted the bomb, then who?

Hearing a knock at the door, Spike looked up and saw Ana Lopes lurking in the doorway, looking uncharacteristically flustered. 'I know you asked not to be disturbed, Spike. But your, ah, well, Jessica is here. She said it was important.'

Jessica appeared in the doorway. From the set of her mouth, Spike could tell that something was wrong. He got to his feet. 'What is it?'

Jessica waited for Ana to retreat. 'They found the body of an elderly woman. In Rosia Bay.'

It took a few seconds for the implication of Jessica's words to sink in. Then Spike cleared his throat, trying to repress the lump in it. 'Have you told Sofia?'

'She's in Cadiz; I didn't want to worry her until we knew for sure.' Jessica dug her fist into the small of her back and grimaced. 'Do you think I could have a glass of water?'

Spike helped her into the leather armchair and reached for the decanter. At least he'd refreshed it since Sir Anthony's visit.

'I told Isola I'd identify the body.' Jessica drained her glass. 'It seemed the least I could do.' She stared down at her fingers as they plucked at a loose thread in the taut white cotton of her top.

Spike refilled her glass, then kissed the top of her head. 'I'll go.' As he pulled closed the door, he realised that neither of them had mentioned Marcela's name.

44

There were three of them inside the tent – four if you counted the person in the black body bag at their feet. The heat was dizzying, but it was the smell that made Spike's stomach keel, the sweet, rotten reek of decay. It seemed the young police photographer felt the same, his face ashen as he scrolled through images on his iPad.

'Who found the body?' Spike asked.

'There were two kids out crabbing,' Isola began. It sounded like the first line of a joke. In the confined space of the tent, Spike smelt the lunch on the detective's breath, and automatically reared back. 'One of them spotted a foot sticking out beneath the jetty,' Isola continued. 'The body must have drifted in. The bay was calm overnight, so the crabs had a field day.'

The photographer staggered just a little, and for a moment Spike thought he might be about to faint. He took hold of the young man's forearm and steered him towards the front of the tent. 'Why don't you get some air?'

Isola looked with contempt as his more artistic colleague lurched outside onto the crumbling jetty of Rosia Bay. Then he turned back to Spike. 'You ready?' he asked, his dark brown eyes sliding over Spike's face, as though weighing up whether Jessica Navarro's chosen mate was up to the task. Probably not, Spike concluded, aware of the sweat sheeting down his back. But he nodded anyway, and Isola fixed a white elasticated mask over his nose and mouth and dropped to one knee.

As the black plastic began to part, Spike made out the pale crown of a head covered in ice-white hair. Then that heavily lined forehead, and a pair of startled, carefully plucked eyebrows. *It's her*, he wanted to say, but it was too soon, he knew it was too soon. The zip continued on its journey, and Spike closed his eyes rather than have to stare into Marcela's empty pink sockets.

'The crabs go for the softest parts first, I'm afraid,' Isola said. '*Heri hof.*'

Spike frowned – how could things get any worse? – but then he opened his eyes to see Marcela's protruding yellow teeth, the damage done to her lips and gums, and turned away. 'It's her.'

Isola looked up, and Spike formed his hand into a C-shape and pinched his cheeks. 'The gold fillings. Marcela had one on each side of her mouth.'

Isola zipped the body bag closed and got to his feet. '*Tenkiù, compa.*' He stood for a moment next to Spike in the sweat box of the tent. Through the rear flap, Spike could see a massive liner cruising towards Ocean Village, three thousand new souls venturing in for their first and most likely only experience of Gib. Fish 'n' chips at Casemates, quick trip to see the monkeys, a few jars on Main Street. In and out in a couple of hours.

'Did you know her well?' Isola asked abruptly.

'Not really,' Spike replied, wondering if that was a lie. 'My family used to eat at her restaurant when I was a boy.'

'No husband, at least. No kids. That's something.'

'Marcela had family. Friends. She'll be missed.'

Isola shrugged, then held out a hand. Spike shook it. 'That's it, then?' he asked.

'That's it.'

45

Spike found Jessica talking on her phone outside New Mole House, biting the little fingernail of her left hand. When she saw Spike approach, she gave a small smile and wound up her conversation, 'OK. Well, let's just wait and see. We'll know more after the post-mortem.' She hung up, then turned away from Spike to pick up her bag from the steps. As she straightened up, he put his hands on her shoulders and she leant back against him.

'Was that Sofia?' Spike asked.

Jessica nodded.

'How did she take it?'

'She didn't say much. I expect it'll be a while before it sinks in.' She twisted her head round to look at him. 'She asked about the body. Was it very bad?'

Spike thought of Marcela's mutilated lips, of the foetid smell in the tent. Something of what he felt must have shown on his face as Jessica reached up and squeezed his hand. 'Come on. I'll shout you a coffee. Compliments of the RGP.' Then she pulled away and he followed her into reception.

The same slow-moving desk sergeant was on duty, immersed in a book of Sudoku. 'Any rooms free, Winston?' Jessica called over. The man raised three plump fingers and buzzed them through.

Spike waited in the interview room while Jessica got the drinks. He was pleasantly surprised when she handed him a cappuccino in a porcelain cup, complete with dusting of chocolate. 'Isola keeps a Gaggia in his office' – she managed a wink – 'but I know where he hides the key.' Then she sat down and pulled her iPad out of her bag. 'I want to show you something.'

Her face was serious again, so he drew up a chair while she busied herself with the screen, eyes narrowed in concentration. 'Need some help?' he teased, but she didn't smile back.

'Just give me a minute, would you?' She swiped one finger across the screen and a file opened to reveal a dark still of camera footage. Spike sat forward. 'Is that Governor's Street?'

Jessica nodded. 'On the night of the fire.'

He pulled the screen towards him. 'You found the camera?'

'Installed above Eloise's porch.' Her fingertip hovered over the 'play' button, then she looked up, directly into Spike's eyes. 'This is just between us, right?'

'Of course.'

She held his gaze, then hit play. The footage was grainy, but in the glow of a street lamp, Spike saw the first floor of a row of terraced houses. As they watched, the top of a man's head came into view. The face was impossible to make out clearly.

'The camera was installed too high,' Jessica said.

So that was why Drew hadn't submitted any CCTV footage as evidence at trial, Spike thought. He watched as the front door opened, and the man stepped inside the house. 'Eloise *let* Massetti in?'

Jessica held out a hand, demanding patience, so Spike tipped back on the legs of his chair, trying to make sense of it all. Eloise had been terrified of Massetti: anyone could see that from the way she'd looked at him in the courtroom. What possible reason could she have had for allowing him into her house?

Jessica touched a button on the screen, and Spike righted his chair, watching the time code fast-forward, one minute, two . . . Then she hit play and they saw the front door open and the man re-emerge. The doorstep added an extra six inches to the man's height, so his head was now in shot, face angled away from the lens. Then suddenly he turned to the camera, and Spike prepared himself to see Christopher Massetti captured on screen, fleeing the scene of his crime. But then Jessica pressed pause, and Spike saw that it wasn't Massetti at all. 'Jesus,' he said.

A lock of Sir Anthony Stanford's grey hair had fallen over his forehead, but there was no doubting it was him.

'Now watch this,' Jessica said. She hit fast-forward again, and Sir Anthony vanished from shot. Moments later, the houses opposite began to blur as the smoke overwhelmed the lens. Then the footage shook, and went blank.

Jessica closed the iPad, and Spike rubbed his eyes. Surely Sir Anthony couldn't have done this thing. There must be some alternative explanation, some other reason for him to have been at the Capurro house. But if so, why hadn't he come forward of his own volition? Spike twisted his fingers through his hair. Eloise had been locked into her bedroom, Jessica had said. Spike imagined the panic, the fear she must have felt as the fire took hold, and thought that he couldn't conceive of a worse way to die. But then he remembered Marcela's body, and wondered if she would agree. 'So Massetti didn't start the fire.'

Jessica shook her head. 'He must have panicked when you saw him. Assumed he'd get the blame.'

'He was right,' Spike said, realising how little it had taken for him to have been persuaded of his client's guilt. He looked back at the screen, seeing the panic in Sir Anthony's eyes, the smear of soot on his face. 'Have you questioned Anthony yet?'

'Isola's petitioning Judge Bossano right now for a warrant to search Dragon Trees.' Jessica's phone rang, and she rolled away her chair to answer it. '*Vale* . . . OK, I'll let them know. Yes, I'll be around for a while. See you later.' As she hung up and turned to Spike, he saw that her cheeks were flushed, her chestnut eyes glistening, and though he knew she had a right to be pleased with her work, he couldn't help but find her exhilaration a little distasteful. 'They got the warrant, then?'

'Six a.m. tomorrow.'

Spike pictured Sir Anthony jolted from sleep as the heavy fists banged on the door. 'Do you really think it's necessary, Jess?' They both heard the censure in his voice. 'Anthony's a bit frail for a dawn raid, isn't he?'

'He didn't look too frail in that video,' Jessica retorted. Her phone rang again. She looked at the caller ID, then back up at Spike. 'I've still got a few things to sort out. Maybe I should just see you at home.'

Spike got to his feet. 'Don't stay too long.'

Jessica didn't reply. She'd already picked up her phone. 'Detective Sergeant Navarro . . .'

Spike closed the door quietly behind him and walked away.

46

The Cathedral clock was tolling eight as Spike rounded the corner into Gunner's Lane. There seemed little point in hurrying home: Jessica would probably be at the station for hours, Charlie would be in bed, and Spike was in no mood to deal with his father. The Old Town was emptying out, as it always did at this hour, its citizens dissipating into the steep-rising labyrinth of streets that had formed itself piecemeal over the centuries. Camp followers, the Spanish still called them – tailors, fishermen, vintners, pimps; men and women who'd moved here to provide what the Garrison had needed. Genoese, in the main, though the town they'd built resembled something from North Africa – crumbling stucco facades, narrow twisting gulleys, shutters that couldn't open without striking the buildings on the other side.

Passing what was left of Governor's Street, Spike saw a Liberal Party poster wire-tied to the scaffolding. 'DST – The ONLY Candidate'. DST . . . Christ: Drew even had his own acronym now. Today's *Chronicle* had identified Drew as an early front-runner for the premiership. Spike wondered how the pollsters would react when news broke that his father had been arrested on suspicion of murder. He knew what Jessica would say – that Drew had hitched his wagon to his father's star, and must live with the consequences if that star happened to implode. But Jessica had always had strong views about people like the Stanfords. He couldn't blame her, he supposed. She'd grown up sharing a bedroom with her brother, Nuno, on the wrong side of the Varyl Begg Estate. She and Spike had never discussed why she hadn't gone to university, but he knew that money had always been tight, and that she still sent a part of her salary home to her mother. Her father had now made himself a new family to disappoint in Marbella, and Jessica had had no one to smooth her passage through life. Maybe that was why she had scant respect for those who did – though she'd always professed to like Drew.

Spike knew he ought to be pleased for her. Most officers in her position would be starting maternity leave unsure of their future prospects. But Jessica would head off knowing that she'd just made a breakthrough in one of the biggest investigations the RGP had faced in years. It would give her confidence a much needed boost, and for that he was grateful.

But he still couldn't shake from his conscience the thought of Sir Anthony clad in his pyjamas, watching his beloved Dragon Trees being torn apart. Spike had always had faith in Jessica's judgment, but in this case, what if she were wrong? He'd seen her eyes light up when she'd shown him the CCTV footage, knowing that she'd just found the crucial piece of evidence that would lead the police to Sir Anthony – a man so revered in Gib that only incontrovertible proof of guilt would suffice. So maybe, in this instance, Jessica's judgment wasn't infallible. Maybe it was clouded by a little ambition of her own.

On the corner of Cornwall's Parade, Spike pulled out his phone and stared at it, mind suddenly flooding with memories of all those occasions over the years when the Stanford family had come to his aid. How a few weeks after Spike's mother's funeral, Sir Anthony had persuaded Rufus to let him accompany them on a trip to Provence, where he'd offered Spike his first taste of champagne, and had looked away when he'd found him smoking on the balcony with Drew. How he'd given Spike a brisk talking-to just before his A levels – told him to buck up his ideas, not to let his mother dictate his future as she'd done his past. How he'd introduced Spike to the senior partner at Ruggles & Mistry when he'd been forced to return to Gib to look after Rufus – put in a good word, as he always did. So before he could change his mind, Spike scrolled through his contacts and hit dial.

Drew answered almost instantaneously. 'I can't talk for long. They'll want me back in the conference room any minute.'

'Where are you, Drew?' The connection was poor.

'In London. For the GibFuel arbitration. Why? Is something wrong?'

Spike sensed that he was about to step off a cliff, and this was his last chance to back away. But he forced Jessica's disapproving face from his mind, and jumped. 'It's about your father . . .'

Drew remained quiet for a long while after Spike had finished talking. When he did speak, his voice was thick with emotion. 'There must be some misunderstanding.'

Spike wished he could agree.

'I can't make it back by six a.m. tomorrow.'

Spike could tell what was coming . . .

'Dad needs someone with him when the police arrive.'

'I can't, Drew.'

'Why? Because of Jessica?'

'Jessica, my connection to Eloise Capurro, the Massetti case. Take your pick.'

'I'd do it for you.'

'I've already gone out on a limb.' In the background, Spike could hear Drew's name being called. 'Just hold the fort until I arrive, OK?' Drew said. 'You don't have to be there in an official capacity, just make sure the police do everything by the book.' He lowered his voice, 'I won't forget this, Spike.'

Spike hung up. He had no doubt that Drew meant it. The problem was he knew that Jessica wouldn't forget it either.

47

When he finally got home, Spike had hoped to find every-one in bed. No such luck: Charlie was sitting at the kitchen table with a plate of cucumber batons and a jar of Nutella. He stared up at Spike with a hint of defiance, then dipped a piece of cucumber into the chocolate spread and licked his lips.

Rufus was beside the kitchen sink, observing the scene with evident pride. 'Jessica insisted he start with vegetables. Seemed the easiest way.'

'He's meant to be in bed by seven, Dad.' Spike glared at his father. But then he remembered that Rufus had no idea that Marcela was dead, and that Sir Anthony was a murder suspect, and tried to hold his temper. '*Please* don't play with your food, Charlie.' He stooped down to pick up the cucum-ber stick just in time to see another baton hit the floor.

Charlie slowly raised his head. His dark eyes were hooded; he was practically asleep at the table.

'I spoke to Old Davey today,' Rufus said. 'Davey Lavagna?' he enunciated, reading the blank expression on Spike's face. 'Owns the house in Catalan Bay?'

'Right,' Spike said, only half following what his father was saying. He felt a sudden, irritating buzz against his thigh and checked his phone. The number was withheld – out of habit, he ignored it.

'He said you could go down there tomorrow and take a look.'

'I'm working tomorrow, Dad,' Spike snapped, hearing Drew's stricken voice echo in his head. 'There's no way I'll have time to get to Catalan Bay.'

'Oh well,' Rufus said. 'Entirely up to you. Forget I mentioned it.'

Spike forced himself to focus. 'I'll give Davey a call, OK?' His eye fell on another piece of cucumber wilting on the floor. 'Can you pick that up please, Charlie?'

The boy ignored him, just dipped a fresh baton into the pot.

'Charlie?' Spike raised his voice. 'Get down and pick that up.'

'*I'll* do it,' Rufus said. Delivered curtly, it was a rebuke. But Spike was already hoisting the boy out of his chair. He set him down on the cork-tile floor and crouched beside him. 'I said *PICK IT UP*!'

Charlie stared up at Spike in shock. His mouth started to quiver, then Spike felt a hand grip his shoulder, surprisingly strong. He swung round to face his father.

'Leave it, son. We're all just a bit tired.'

Charlie clamped himself to Rufus's legs, and as Spike watched the old man scoop him up, he felt his anger fade until all that remained was a healthy measure of self-disgust. He turned away, found an open bottle of red wine and went upstairs.

Twenty minutes later, he heard a knock at his bedroom door and saw Rufus's frail frame silhouetted in the light of the landing.

'Is he asleep?' Spike asked.

Rufus nodded. 'I shouldn't have let him stay up so late, son. That sponsored scoot really took it out of him.'

Spike lowered his head into his hands. 'That thing was today?'

Rufus placed himself gingerly on the futon beside him. 'I don't know how you can bear this contraption,' he grumbled.

Spike let slip a smile. 'Sorry about earlier.'

'You need to spend more time with the boy. Both of you.'

There was a long pause. Spike knew what he wanted to say. That Rufus was a hypocrite who'd preferred to stay late at the school he ran rather than come home to face the fact that his wife was drinking herself to death. But seeing the tender, sheepish look on his face, Spike could tell that his father had anticipated his thoughts, and that, in some way, every kindness he showed Charlie was an attempt to atone for his own failings. So all he said was, 'I know, Dad.'

Rufus creaked to his feet. 'Jessica's working late again.'

Spike knew he couldn't put it off for ever – and he didn't want to leave it up to Jessica to break the news. 'She's still at the station. They found Marcela Peralta's body this morning in Rosia Bay.' He reached over and squeezed his father's bony shoulder. 'I'm so sorry, Dad. I know you two were close.'

Rufus swayed on his feet, pale blue eyes glassy in the lamplight. 'Was it an accident?'

'That's what Jessica's trying to work out.'

Spike stood up to embrace his father, but Rufus was already at the door. He reached for the handle. 'You think some people are going to last for ever. Stupid, really.'

Then he stepped into the corridor and pushed the door to behind him.

For a moment Spike considered following him. But he knew his father had always preferred to grieve alone, so he reached for his jacket and took out his BlackBerry. The unknown caller had rebounded with a text. '*I wondered if you might join me tomorrow for an early breakfast. 6 a.m. at Dragon Trees? All best, Anthony S*'.

Spike sighed. He'd come this far; it was too late to turn back. '*See you tomorrow*' he texted back. '*Try to get some sleep.*'

48

Four pairs of amber eyes tracked Spike's progress as he climbed the dusty road towards Dragon Trees, an alcohol sweat drying cold on his back. The apes were meant to be a reassuring presence on the Rock, but it didn't feel that way this morning. Maybe it was just Spike's hangover, but he was sure that he could sense disapproval in their gaze as they watched him from their rocky crags, scratching at their genitals. As though they knew that he'd pretended to be asleep when Jessica had finally crawled into bed after midnight. Or that he'd done all he could not to wake her as he'd sneaked out of the house at 5 a.m., reluctant to face uncomfortable questions about where he was going and why. So he turned his back on them as well, and pressed the buzzer by the main entrance.

A minute later, a wooden door set into the stone wall ten yards down the road creaked open, and Sir Anthony Stanford stepped outside. He'd jettisoned his sling, Spike saw as he walked towards him. This morning, he wore a freshly pressed powder-blue suit and, nestling in the silver hairs of his chest, Spike recognised the teardrop pendant he'd seen in Christopher Massetti's stolen photograph.

Sir Anthony must have seen the dip of Spike's eyes, as he tucked the necklace into his collar with a half-smile.

'I came across it the other day. Quite by chance. It was a gift from my mother.'

Spike cleared his throat. 'I'm here because Drew asked me to come. As a family friend, not as your lawyer. I would ask you not to share anything substantive with me.'

Sir Anthony clasped Spike's hand in both of his, black eyes wet with emotion. 'I can't tell you how grateful we are.' Then he turned, and Spike followed him down a set of steps hewn from the Rock, feeling the green-painted hand-rail already warm in the sun.

The garden was as impressive as Spike remembered, still the largest of any private house he'd seen in Gibraltar. It had been Drew's mother's great passion and, until the last months of her illness, she'd delighted in show-ing it off, pointing out to every visitor each of the plants she'd coaxed to thrive in Gibraltar's thin, alkaline soil – narcissi, asphodels, candytuft. In the middle rose an antique stone sundial, as accurate as the clock on Spike's phone, he noted as he saw the shadow line nudging 6 a.m. Beneath the garden's back wall ran a broad herbaceous border, and in each corner rose the eponymous dragon trees, their trunks bulked out by serpentine roots that had somehow absorbed themselves into the wood, their can-opies formed by individual bunches of fleshy, cactus-like leaves. Beneath the largest, a weathered teak table had been laid for breakfast; Sir Anthony sat down at the head and smoothed out a linen napkin on his lap. 'Does Jessica know you're here?'

Spike shook his head. 'She's been caught up at the station. They found a body yesterday in Rosia Bay.' He watched Sir Anthony's face for his reaction, but the old man barely seemed to register the words. 'Ships in the night,' he murmured with a faint smile.

Spike didn't smile back, just poured two tumblers of freshly squeezed orange juice from the white china jug and set one down in front of his host.

'It's all lies, Spike. You must know that. Eloise was a friend. An innocent.' Sir Anthony fidgeted with the silver cufflinks in his sleeve. One oval was engraved with his initials, the other with the MCC monogram.

'There's a tape,' Spike said. 'A video recording of you entering Eloise Capurro's house a few minutes before the fire was reported.'

It was as though Sir Anthony hadn't heard. He reached out and placed a fond hand on the bark of the dragon tree next to him. '*Dracaena draco*,' he said, then looked over at Spike. 'I read Greats at Oxford, you know. Came down from Teddy Hall in 1948. The first member of my family to have had the benefit of a university education. It would never have been possible, of course, were it not for my war service.' Sir Anthony picked up a stainless steel knife from the table and ran the blade across the bark, and they both watched as a bead of blood-red sap oozed out. 'Dragon's Blood,' he said. 'Valued as a medicine throughout the ages.' He stretched the tacky red gum between his thumb and forefinger. 'Dab it on a human wound and it hardens like a new skin.'

In the still of the early morning, Spike could hear the cicadas thrumming, a lone blackcap singing merrily in a pine tree. The idyll was broken by the sound of car tyres on the road above, but Sir Anthony continued regardless. 'It's not like a rubber tree, you understand. You can't just keep on tapping it indefinitely. The wounds don't heal. So the harvesters had to go all out. Make a thousand cuts and bleed the tree dry.'

The doorbell rang from inside the house. Spike looked over to check Sir Anthony had heard, and saw him clench his lips, then nod to let Spike know that he should answer it. So he stood up and walked across the garden, inhaling the lemony vanilla scent of the last magnolia blooms as he climbed the steps back up to the road. He unlatched the wooden door and called across to a man standing outside the main entrance to the house. 'Detective Inspector Isola?'

Isola looked round, holding up a hand to shield his eyes from the glare. '*Bartoleo*,' he swore in *yanito*. 'You're remarkably well-informed, Sanguinetti.' He signalled to the men sitting in the police van behind him, then walked up the road towards Spike.

'I'll need to see a warrant,' Spike said.

Isola handed over the document marked with the Royal Crest and waited, arms crossed, as Spike checked all was in order. It was, of course, so Spike held open the gate, hearing the van doors slam behind him. On the crags above, the family of apes slunk quietly back up the Rock.

'Your men can come and go through the basement,' Spike called over one shoulder as they started to descend. 'I'll be in the garden with Sir Anthony. Anything you want to remove, you'll need to run it past me first.'

They reached the garden, and Isola peered up at the glass structure protruding from the back of the house, shaking his head in disgust at the extravagance. Then he turned to Spike with such naked hostility that Spike could see why he'd always been the most unpopular senior officer on the Force. 'The old man better be paying you well' – Isola screwed the tip of his forefinger into Spike's lapel – 'because your fiancée won't even be able to draw her pension once the disciplinary board is done with her.' Then he pushed past and called out to his team, 'Well, get on with it!', before disappearing inside.

Spike found Sir Anthony hunched beneath his dragon tree. He'd taken a white handkerchief from his pocket and was rubbing his fingers clean with an intensity Spike found unsettling. 'Sanguinetti . . .' he murmured. 'I've always liked that name.' He must have felt the weight of Spike's gaze as he looked round with a strange smile. 'All the perfumes of Arabia, eh?'

Spike took him by the elbow and guided him back to his chair. 'Why don't we sit for a while, Anthony? I expect the police will take their time.'

They sat opposite one another in what in other circumstances might have been a companionable silence, Spike admiring the espalier fig tree on the wall opposite, its branches drooping with overripe fruit. Then suddenly Sir Anthony spoke. 'It was Marcela, wasn't it? In Rosia Bay.'

And though Spike knew that his indiscretion had already landed Jessica in enough trouble, he reasoned that it was only a matter of time before news of Marcela's death was leaked to the press. So he told the truth, 'I'm afraid so.'

The old man said nothing, but then Spike heard a sharp intake of breath, and when he looked across at Sir Anthony – invincible, incorruptible Sir Anthony – he saw a tear catch in the deep seams of his face. He knelt down by the old man's chair.

'It's my fault, son,' Sir Anthony said. 'You'll see.'

A volley of raised voices came from inside the house. Spike scrambled to his feet to see Drew Stanford-Trench emerge from the basement, dragging a smart black suitcase behind him.

Sir Anthony beckoned Spike back. 'Look after Drew,' he whispered. 'He needs you.' Then he found his most congenial smile and stood up to watch his son crossing the paving stones towards him.

Spike stuck out a hand, but Drew ignored it and threw an arm around him. 'Bloody hell, Spike. You look even rougher than me.'

'Mr Stanford-Trench?' came a curt voice.

They both turned and saw Isola standing in the basement doorway, hands on his lean hips. 'A moment of your time?'

Drew leant in, and Spike could hear the tremor in his voice. 'Thank you.'

As Drew walked away, Spike turned to see Sir Anthony staring up at his dragon tree with vacant eyes. Spike raised an arm in farewell as he walked past him towards the steps, but if the old man saw him, he made no sign. As he passed the sundial, Spike checked its face, wondering if he would ever see it again. It was only 6.40 a.m. All that for forty minutes.

49

Jessica must have oiled the lock at Chicardo's, as the front door flew open to Spike's shoulder and clattered against the wall. He put down his briefcase in the hallway, feeling weariness enshroud him like a cloak. The house was silent, which could mean only one thing – Rufus and Charlie were out. The Gibraltar Museum were running Saturday morning activities for under-fives, and Rufus had been threatening for some time to expose Charlie to the joys of simulated cannon fire and papier-mâché Neanderthals.

Spike was just on his way upstairs for a shower when he heard a noise in the kitchen. He pushed through the bead curtain and found Jessica sitting at the kitchen table, an overnight bag at her feet. Her back was to him, but he could tell everything he needed to know from the way she held her head. When she spoke, it was in a cold voice that frightened him. 'It's not my hospital bag, Spike, if that's what you were wondering.'

He wasn't sure how to respond, so he just turned to the kettle and flicked it on.

'Isola called,' Jessica said.

Spike unhooked two china mugs from the rack.

'At least you can fucking look at me!'

He'd rarely heard her swear. He put down the mugs.

'How could you *do* it?'

It wasn't that he hadn't considered the ramifications of what he'd done, but now that he was standing there, seeing the betrayal in Jessica's eyes, the reasons seemed so small. 'Drew's my friend' was all he could manage.

'I've been suspended, Spike. Pending a conduct review. I think they would have fired me if I wasn't pregnant.'

The kettle reached boiling point and began to rattle. As Spike poured out the water, he saw his hands were trembling, so he focused on the ritual – remove bag, add milk, stir . . . He took a sip and it burnt his tongue. Serves you right, he thought.

'I can't stay here,' Jessica said. 'I'll be at my brother's place.' As she picked up her overnight bag, he saw her wince a little. Her hips and wrists had been aching for weeks, he knew. He made as if to help her, but she stilled him with a look. 'Here.' She slid a package across the table. 'This came.' And then she was gone.

Spike was about to go after her, but for some reason his feet wouldn't move. So he stood where he was, knuckles white as he gripped his mug of tea, waiting for the front door to slam.

Then he looked down at the parcel, stuck a thumb through the envelope and tore it open. What else was there to do? *Run after her*, a small, insistent voice urged in his head. But it was a very small voice, and easy to suppress, so he just held open the envelope and shook out a faded blue notebook with a cracked spine.

Inside, he saw pages of handwritten script with dates at the top: December 14th 1939, January 9th 1940. He turned to the first page. Written in a looping, girlish hand was a name he recognised: *Marcela Elena Peralta, 16 Lower Castle Road, Gibraltar*.

'Jessica?' Spike called out. Then he remembered she was gone, and sat down at the kitchen table and started to read.

PART FIVE

October 18th 1939

Jack was waiting on his mother's porch again. He got to his feet as soon as he saw me and started wiping his hands on the sides of his greasy dungarees. I didn't notice at first there was someone with him, but then Jack hunched down to light a cigarette, and I saw Esteban Reyes standing behind him, looking at me. I'd never seen him up-close before, so when he gave me that smile of his, my cheeks started to burn and I walked away as quickly as I could.

I don't see how I can sleep. I've never seen anything so beautiful in my life.

October 21st

I could tell something had happened as soon as I walked through the gates. All around the schoolyard, everyone was standing in little huddles, and Veronica Felleti had already burst into tears like she always does whenever there's any sort of excitement. I don't see why they were all so shocked! Everyone knew we were to be evacuated, and now they say only men with 'essential jobs' will be allowed to stay. All the girls were in <u>agonies</u>, but Sister Margaret gave them short shrift. Said we'd be better off worrying about how we could contribute to the war effort rather than wasting our time on idle gossip. That's as may be, but I can't see how we're going to defeat the Germans by knitting socks and collecting scrap metal.

October 23rd

Antonia told me I might find Tony at the Four Corners, and as usual, she was right. I only had to wait a few minutes before I saw him, wearing his favourite black suit, as though at any moment he might be summoned to a funeral. The way he's been carrying on, it will probably be his! There are more soldiers than ever at the frontier now, sitting in their jeeps. And when I saw Tony stroll between the border posts, lugging that suitcase of his, I thought they would take him into the searching sheds for sure. But no one did. They just laughed as he clicked his heels and gave them a mock salute. And seeing Tony dole out his handshakes and cheeky winks, I remembered how Mama used to tell me that she'd always known Tony Stanford would go far, no matter what his father said. I daresay she was right, but if Mama had heard the way he spoke to me this afternoon, I don't think she would have liked it. Not one little bit.

He was at it as soon as he clapped eyes on me. 'Well, look at you, Marcie! All grown up.' I didn't reply, just gave him my haughtiest glare, but that just made him laugh, and before I knew it, I was smiling too.

I waited until we reached Main Street before I asked him – <u>very</u> casually – if he thought he might be able to get me a couple of bottles of wine. He looked at me side-ways, and I could tell he was trying to work out what it was worth to him. A bit of sport, it seems, as when he made me tell him what it was for, he howled with laughter and said that a girl like me should aim a little higher than a pelota like 'Little Jack'. That was when I told him to mind his own business thank you very much and wasn't my money as good as anyone else's. That shut him up.

November 5th

God must have been smiling on me tonight, as for the first time ever he answered my prayers. Esteban was already there when I got to Jack's house, but his wife Magdalena was ill, so she'd decided to stay in bed!!! I tried to look sympathetic, I really did, but inside I was just <u>bursting</u> with joy.

And it really was quite lovely rushing around making the place pretty for our evening together. Even Tony Stanford turning up uninvited couldn't spoil it, at least not for me, though I could tell that Jack was <u>seething</u> as he led him into the parlour. But Tony couldn't have been more pleased with himself, grinning wickedly at everyone.

I didn't talk much over dinner, and when Jack leant over and asked me in the most <u>gauche</u> way how Tito had been since Mama died, I just wanted to shrivel up in my chair. And I know people have begun to talk – especially since Father Ignacio came to call on Papa to ask him why Tito hadn't been to school. But it's nobody's business but ours! And that's exactly what I would have said to Jack, if Esteban hadn't turned to me then and told me how sorry he was to hear about my Mama. Then he spoke to me about his brother, who'd died at Jarama – murdered by the Reds. And across the table, I could see his grey eyes glistening with pain, and I wanted to run to him. But I didn't move, I just watched as he set his mouth into a brave smile and recited a few lines of the most beautiful poem I have ever heard. But then Tony ruined it all with a guffaw. So everything was spoilt, and Esteban didn't even stay to finish his calentita.

I stood up as well, trying to ignore the hurt look on Jack's face as I kissed him goodnight. But it was worth it to feel Esteban's hands brush against my shoulders as he helped me on with my coat. We crossed the road together to my front door, then, on the step, I looked up into his eyes and told him how much I'd loved the poem. He leant in to kiss me on the cheek, and I felt him press something into my hand. I looked down and saw it was a little book, and when I looked back up, he gave me the most devastating smile. 'It will make you laugh and cry. Till next time.'

Next time! Esteban said there's going to be a <u>next time</u>.

November 7th

It's only been two days since Esteban kissed me, but already I must have read the book he gave me a hundred times. I keep it under my pillow, so it's near me while I sleep. I realised what a special gift it was the moment I opened it. 'For Esteban Reyes', it says inside. 'A true Son of the Revolution, from your friend and fellow linense, Raúl de Herrera'.

When I saw that, I cried, because I knew that surely I must mean <u>something</u> to Esteban for him to part with such a treasured possession.

November 9th

A terrible night. I woke to the sound of breaking glass. At first I thought it was Tito sleepwalking, but when I went to check on him, he was safe in his bed. Then I saw a lamp burning downstairs. So I crept down to the kitchen and found Papa on his hands and knees on the floor. He was sweeping up a broken tumbler with one hand, while the other was tucked into his armpit. He wouldn't meet my eye, not even when I helped him into his chair and set down a bottle of oloroso beside him. I poured him a glass and took his hand in mine and turned it to the light. And I could see that his middle finger was fat and black and sticking up in a way that made me feel quite sick. So I fetched an old sheet and tore off some strips. Then I bound up his hand like Mama did the afternoon I fell out of Dr Stagnetto's dragon tree and sprained my wrist.

Papa didn't say anything until half the bottle was gone. Then he leant his head back and stretched out his legs for me to undo his shoelaces. And his voice when he spoke wasn't like my Papa's at all.

The Piccadilly had been full of Naval Engineers, he told me. They were drunk when they got there, and Papa heard one of them say that they'd been thrown out of the Imperial. But he agreed to serve them one last drink, and at first they were all smiles. But then Papa rang the bell. One of the officers offered him more money, and when Papa refused, the man pushed past him behind the bar and started tipping rum into his mouth while his friends held Papa back. Then the man started smashing every bottle he could find while the others all jeered and clapped. When there was nothing left to break, Papa said that they must leave right away – threatened to report them to the Security Police. So the officer grabbed Papa by the collar and pushed him against the wall. And when Papa told him he was mad, the man took his hand and pulled off his glove and bent back his middle finger, saying he was a filthy Spic bastard liar. Papa thinks he must have fainted then, for the next thing he remembered was seeing Jack standing over him. And all the men had gone.

November 12th

Papa didn't go to work the next day. Nor the next. He just stayed in bed. And when I finally plucked up the courage to ask him if he'd thought about the Piccadilly – about the state those men had left it in – he just rolled over onto his side and closed his eyes. So last night, I went down to the Piccadilly myself, and my heart was beating like a drum when I saw lights burning inside and heard the sound of voices. But I made myself go in, and when I did, I found Esteban Reyes in his shirtsleeves – mopping the floor!! Jack was there too. They'd been there every night after work, clearing up after those British bastards. Well, it took us a good few hours, but we finally got everything shipshape, and as we walked back to Lower Castle Road together, Jack told me that the squaddies deserved a whipping for what they'd done to Papa. How, if he hadn't heard the screams and come in when he did, God knows what they would have done to him.

When I told all this to Papa, he said he felt better. This morning, he got up and had a wash, then he went to the Piccadilly himself to see what needed doing. When he came back, I suggested that wouldn't it be nice if I cooked supper for Jack and Esteban to thank them for what they'd done. Papa agreed, and he said I should ask Tony too, as he's been so helpful about the stock.

238

November 24th

At least the chicken stew was a success. Papa left us a bottle of sherry, and we ought to have made a very jolly band, except that all evening Jack had a face like a wet Wednesday. When I asked him what was the matter, he just grumbled on about how much he hated his job at the Dockyard. Said that the Brits treated them all like scum, ordering them about and making sly comments about why the 'lazy Gibbos' hadn't joined up yet.

Even Tony seemed low. Little wonder given the state of his face. He just sat there brooding and topping up his own glass and no one dared ask him how he'd got that black eye, but I'll bet that the cut on his cheekbone came from his father's signet ring.

Things didn't get really heated until after dinner. I'd fetched Esteban's little book, and when I asked him if he might choose a poem to read aloud, I could see that Tony was about to make some spiteful comment, so I told him to hold his tongue – that it was my evening and he wasn't to spoil it. So he just sat back and crossed his arms while Esteban recited 'El Peñón', which is my favourite one as it happens, and not just because it means 'The Rock'.

Tony was silent after Esteban had finished reading, but then he picked up the book. And when he saw the inscription, he wagged a finger at Esteban and said that he didn't think good Gibraltarians like us should be seen consorting with a Spanish Nationalist. And though I know he probably thought he was being <u>terribly</u> droll, nobody else found it amusing. It was only after Esteban had left that I realised he'd taken his book with him. I expect he just forgot it had been his gift to me, but I have to admit I shed a few tears.

December 2nd

The strangest thing happened today. I was getting ready for evensong, when there was a knock at the door and there was Tony Stanford blushing on my doorstep, holding out a package tied with string and saying that he was sorry for spoiling my night. Then he made me open it and inside was a copy of Raúl de Herrera's collection of poetry, bound in crimson calfskin! He's made his peace with Esteban too. They went together to La Línea last night and found Raúl de Herrera drinking at Los Caminos – he even asked them to join his table!

It <u>was</u> a thoughtful gesture on Tony's part – and naturally I'm pleased to own such a handsome book – but it's not quite the same as the one I lost, because Esteban didn't give it to me. And afterwards, I wondered if what I was thinking might have shown on my face, as just as Tony was about to go, he put his hands on my shoulders and whispered in my ear that he thought I ought to know that Esteban's wife was going to have a baby. Then he stuffed his hands in his pockets and walked away.

December 14th

Today I went down to HMS Cormorant to make an official complaint. Papa says he just wants to forget about what happened at the Piccadilly, but I can't – and he didn't try to stop me. Jack came too, and seeing the British officer stifle his yawns Jack stammered his way through the whole sorry tale, I found myself wishing that it had been Tony I'd asked to come – Sharp Tony, who's so good at dealing with these self-satisfied Brits.

I didn't want to talk about it over supper, but Jack drank too much as usual, and started ranting again about 'British tyranny'. If Tony had bothered to turn up, he could have calmed him down, but nobody's seen Tony all week, so we had no choice but to sit and wait until Jack had burnt himself out. Then he slumped back in his chair, and said there was nothing we could do about it anyway.

But then Esteban refilled our glasses. 'We have a phrase in Spanish. "Mil Cortes".' A thousand cuts, I said, and Esteban nodded. 'Small acts of resistance. We may be few, but together we can change the world. To the "Mil Cortes". Salud.'

As we all chinked glasses, Esteban gave me that wicked smile of his again, and just for a moment, anything seemed possible.

January 9th 1940

There are planes in the sky every day now. They give me the willies, but Tito likes them. He spends hours sitting on the steps of Lime Kiln Gulley, watching them weave and duck like murderous swallows.

At least the Christmas celebrations are over. I tried my best – Tito and I made paper chains, and decorated the mantelpiece, and I even scraped together the ingredients for a plum pudding. But it wasn't the same without Mama. Papa just sat in his chair smoking cigarette after cigarette, and on New Year's Eve, he got so drunk that we had to carry him up to bed.

And business at the Piccadilly is very bad. The service-men have all but deserted the place and yesterday, when Papa went to open up, he found that someone had thrown a can of red paint through the window. It took us all day to clean the floor, and it'll take a good few more to get rid of the stink of turps, not that there will be any customers to notice.

March 16th

I passed Jack on Main Street today. He didn't see me, so I kept my head down and walked on by. Poor Jack. Esteban says he's not really strong enough for the work at the Dry Docks, and now he's been told that he is to be evacuated with the women and children – probably within the month. Everywhere we go there are rumours of where we might be sent. Some say French Morocco, others Madeira or Jamaica. What worries me is if there will be enough boats, and how we'll get across waters swarming with German submarines. But it seems that the Governor is too busy renovating his summer residence to concern himself with such trifles. His wife can't bear the humidity, we hear.

March 23rd

Papa died today.

He must have waited until Tito and I left for the market. For when we got back, there was a note pinned to the front door. It didn't say much, just that we shouldn't go in, and that we must fetch Dr Stagnetto as he would know what to do. Then Papa wrote that he was sorry, but that he didn't feel that he could go on without Mama. So I sent Tito for the doctor, and when I pushed open the front door, I saw my father's feet in his best shoes, lying at a strange angle on the kitchen floor. The smell of gas made me choke, so I turned off the oven and opened the windows, all the time trying not to look at Papa's face and think about what a coward he was to leave us here all alone.

Dr Stagnetto was very kind. I couldn't find the right words, so he just patted my hand and tucked Papa's letter into his breast pocket. Then, after we'd heaved Papa into his chair, he turned away and started polishing his spectacles, while he said in a very quiet voice that grief can kill a man just as surely as any tumour, and that he thought it had probably been Papa's heart.

March 28th

We buried Papa this afternoon. Not nearly as many people came as had done to Mama's funeral. I expect it's because of the rumours. Dr Stagnetto promised he would make it right with Father Ignacio, but his homily was very short, and he said he could only spare a plot on the north side of the cemetery.

Peter Zammit laid on some bread and butter and a bit of cake at the Piccadilly, and a few people came on afterwards. Tito didn't say a word to anyone, but Sister Margaret was good enough to sit with him, working away with her crochet needle while he sat in the corner, letting his tea go cold. By 4 o'clock, almost everyone had left, and when Jack's mother offered to take Tito home and give him a proper meal, I was grateful for a moment to myself.

So in the end it was just me and Tony. He was wearing his black suit again, and I realised that he'd finally found that funeral he'd been dressing up for all this time. The thought made me giggle, and soon I was bent over double, tears of laughter running down my cheeks. But then the tears wouldn't stop, and before I knew it, Tony was holding me tight as these great sobs came out of me. He was whispering in my ear all the time, telling me about that bully of a father of his, how nothing he could do would ever be good enough and that I was lucky not to have anyone left to disappoint.

That made my blood boil, and I pushed him off me and said that he didn't know what he was talking about. That my Papa had been a fine man but he'd been brought low by those British bastards who'd attacked him and then closed ranks against us when I'd dared to complain. That they'd practically bankrupted us, and that we might lose the bar – and the house, and how would I support my brother then?

Then I told him to leave.

April 2nd

When I got home from the notary, there was a brown paper package sitting on the kitchen table. The front door was locked, and Mrs Stanford keeps the spare key, so I knew it must have been Tony. Inside it was a wad of notes – enough to pay off the rent we owe on the Piccadilly.

Tito was over at Jack's house again. His mother doesn't seem to mind, and Jack is very patient with him. He's got this clapped-out Royal Enfield motorcycle engine from somewhere, and they spend hours tinkering with it. Jack says Tito's got a good mind for mechanical things – he even took him to the Dockyard the other day to meet some of the boy labourers. I suppose I should be pleased that he's got something to keep himself busy. All I have is my journal.

April 7th

Yesterday the evacuation roster was published. We are to leave on the 'Gibel Dersa' on May 21st. Tito was horribly upset, so when Jack and Tony called round to ask if they could take him over the border to get some part for the Enfield, I didn't have the heart to say no.

I should have known better. For they decided that the best way to cheer my little brother up was to take him drinking in La Línea. Then they knocked on my door at 10 p.m. and slunk away, leaving me to deal with a vomiting 14-year-old who's too heavy for me to get up the stairs on my own. And the fact that they left a case of oloroso on my doorstep 'For the "Mil Cortes"' didn't make me feel any better at all.

April 9th

I still can't believe it. Just when things seemed to be getting a little better, it has all gone wrong. And as always, it is Tony's fault.

It was Tito who found it, hidden in that box of sherry. When I saw what it was, I sent him to fetch the others. And when they all got back, I packed him off to bed.

As soon as Jack saw the small metal weight, curved like a tortoiseshell, he put his head in his hands, while Esteban just paced around the kitchen. Only Tony seemed to be master of himself, checking the blackout curtains and helping himself to a spoonful of my soup. I wanted to knock it out of his hand! How could they have done it? Taken my little brother out drinking with <u>Raúl de Herrera</u>? Because that's what they'd done. And I wanted to know everything. Whether they'd known what was in the box? Let <u>Tito</u> carry it over the border?

Tony did all the talking. Denied everything, said Raúl had been going on for months about 'direct action', but that he'd never taken him seriously – not until now. Then he opened a bottle of Papa's best brandy and said he'd sort it all out and that I wasn't to worry about a thing.

The brandy certainly did its work for Jack. Why <u>shouldn't</u> we? he kept saying. Why the hell <u>shouldn't</u> we do it? Not to hurt anybody, just to teach those British bastards a lesson. They told us they were coming here to protect us – but what had they done? Attacked my father; lorded it over loyal men like him who broke their backs on behalf of the Empire at the <u>Royal</u> Naval Dockyard. And I have to admit, something of what he said made me consider, just for a moment, if he might be right. But then Esteban told Jack that he didn't know what he was talking about. That there was no such thing as violence without bloodshed, and that anyone who'd lived through a war like him would know that.

But what about the "Mil Cortes", I was thinking? Esteban must have seen my face, as he turned to me with this sad smile and said that poetry was just pretty words. And though I knew he was right, for the first time I noticed that his grey eyes were just that little bit too close together.

Then Tony stood up and said he'd find a way to get rid of the thing, but that we must lock it up till he worked out what to do. So though I wanted it out of the house there and then, somehow it ended up in Mama's rosewood bureau, next to her book of pressed flowers. As I closed the door behind them, I thought I heard the tread of footsteps on the stairs. Just for a moment I thought it was Papa, but when I looked round there was no one there.

April 10th

As I sit here in my bedroom, with Tito's head in my lap, I still don't understand how it could have happened. It's my fault, I suppose. I should never have let Tony persuade me to keep that <u>thing</u> in our house.

I knew something was wrong as soon as I came through the door. The grate was cold and even before I'd turned round, something told me that Mama's bureau would be open and <u>it</u> would be gone. I ran up the stairs, calling Tito's name, but his room was dark and empty. So I started pulling open all the drawers. I don't know what I thought I was looking for, but what I found when I turned over Tito's mattress chilled my blood. There were two words written on the square of paper – 'Dique Seco' – and even a child would have recognised the tortoise from the drawing on the other side.

I felt horribly light-headed then, but there was no way of knowing how long Tito had been gone, so I staggered downstairs and hurried over the road to Jack's house. When he saw my face, he told me to go home, and that he would be over with the others right away.

I remember Jack made me sit down as they all stood around the kitchen table watching Tony examine that bit of paper. All I could hear was the tick of the clock – and all I could think of was whether they would have caught Tito yet.

Then Tony started firing questions at Jack. Asking him what a boy like Tito could know about the Dry Docks. About how he imagined he could get in at night without anyone seeing. Then Jack started stammering, saying, yes, he'd shown Tito round the Dockyard, but he couldn't be sure what he'd said to him – or who else he'd spoken to – but in any case, everyone knew that Tito wasn't all there, so no one could blame him if he'd... Well, I don't know what Jack would have said next, because I flew at him and I would have scratched out his eyes if Esteban hadn't come up behind me and pulled me away. Then Tony put on one of Papa's old coats, and Esteban did the same, and they were gone.

They'd told Jack to stay with me, I suppose. But I couldn't <u>bear</u> to look at his pasty stricken face, so I turned Papa's chair towards the fireplace and waited. Then finally we heard it – the sound I'd been dreading.

The explosion was like nothing I've ever known. The whole house shook, and when I ripped away the blackout curtains, I saw a funnel of smoke rising into the sky. Then the sirens sounded, and I started to shake, because I knew then that Tito must be dead.

So when Jack came over and took me in his arms, I didn't have the strength to push him away. I let him cover my face with kisses, and I probably would have let him make love to me if Tony hadn't burst through the door, his face all covered in soot, holding Tito in his arms.

As Tony laid Tito down on the kitchen floor, he told me that Esteban had been lost, and there was nothing to be done. And even though that should have made me sad, when I looked down and saw Tito open his eyes, I felt nothing but joy.

April 14th

The whispers are everywhere. This morning, the 'Chronicle' said that two men were killed in the blast. The authorities have confirmed there was one survivor, but that he is badly injured – and no one knows who he is.

Tito still won't speak. He just stares up at me from his pillow with those pleading eyes that remind me so much of Papa, then turns away.

April 15th

Tony came to see me tonight. When he saw Tito he barked at him – said he should make himself scarce – and my little brother jumped to it like a beaten child.

Tony told me to sit down, and then he said that Esteban was still alive. He didn't look especially pleased, just said that we must all get our stories straight. And then he told me what I was to say when they came.

I was relieved when he got up to leave, but at the door he turned and asked me if I was sure I could make Tito understand what must be done. Because otherwise, he said, he would deal with it himself. And when I saw that icy glint in his eye, I made myself smile and say thank you, but that I was sure I could manage things quite well by myself.

Later, when I was washing my hair, for the first time I thought about what Esteban has done for us. And though I felt grateful, all I could think of was of the police dragging

Tito away in the middle of the night because of something that Esteban might tell them. And the darker part of my heart wished that he was dead.

April 21st

The knock came last night. An Englishman with a black eye and a fake smile. He showed me a photograph of Esteban and Tony at a bar with a man in waxed black moustaches. And then he pointed at Esteban and asked if I knew him, and I swallowed and said, 'Yes. Why yes. That's Esteban Reyes. Doesn't he look handsome!' Then I opened my eyes up wide like Antonia used to do when her father smelt cigarette smoke in the parlour, and I heard myself say, 'He works at the Dockyard, doesn't he?' Once the man had left, I was sick in the sink.

May 15th

Tito is a little better. We spent today shutting up the Piccadilly. I suppose we could have kept it open longer, but I can't muster the energy to smile at the customers – and there's still so much to do before we leave. I've seen other families packing up heirlooms and turning up on the quayside in their Sunday best, only to have their treasures discarded as they're led wailing onto the boats. And looking around the house where Papa and Mama died, I can't think of much that doesn't fill me with sadness anyway.

May 21st

As we waited for the ship to be ready, there was the most distressing scene. It's been very humid, and as no one is sure where we will end up, all the evacuees were wearing over-clothes and swooning in the heat. Then there was this horrible sound of wailing, and I turned to see three British officers dripping with sweat as they dragged Magdalena Reyes along the gangplank, kicking and scratching like a cat. Then she fainted, and they picked her up like a sack of flour and laid her on deck. They kept their heads low as they marched back down the gangplank so as not to meet anyone's eye.

She is lying on a blanket now ten yards in front of me. I can see the swell of the child inside her as the ship rolls up and down. Everyone knows who she is. Who her husband is.

May 22nd

The soldiers have pitched tents for us in the scrubland behind Tangiers Harbour. The stink is almost as bad as on the boat. But I try not to think of my own troubles.

May 25th

Our 'official representative' has just come into the tent to break the news. We are to be moved to a derelict phosphate mine in the desert.

Today is my sixteenth birthday.

July 4th

Paris has fallen and France has surrendered. Everyone at the camp says we will be made to leave French Morocco. The uncertainty is terrific, and every time I pass Jack I can tell from his eyes that he feels as I do. That however bad this may be, all three of us deserve it.

July 6th

Magdalena was well enough to get up today. Her legs are so thin that I can't imagine them bearing that swollen belly of hers much longer. She smiled at me as she passed, but I was too ashamed to hold her gaze, so I looked away.

July 15th

The Vichy soldiers are expelling us, and we are to return to Gibraltar.

July 19th

When the Captain weighed anchor, everybody cheered. But then he sent us a message to say that the Governor will not give us leave to come ashore. Most of the children are ill with dysentery, and Magdalena is very weak. She just gazes out at the Rock, thinking of her husband, I imagine – wondering what they have done to him. And seeing Esteban's beloved so reduced, I find myself thinking that if there is a God, He must be a vengeful one to have dreamt up such a torment for me.

July 20th

Today we were given permission to disembark. But only for one night – so they can clean the boats. Then tomorrow we set sail again. This time for England.

And walking through Irish Town past my school, everything boarded up and silent, I realised that the Gibraltar I knew is gone. That there is nothing left here for us. Just tanks and aeroplanes and soldiers and sailors.

When I passed the Piccadilly, I saw workmen inside. The notice on the door said it is being converted into an Officers' Clubhouse – under the management of Peter Zammit, Esq.

July 21st

Thinking back, I suppose they could have done it on purpose. For as we were funnelled down Line Wall Road towards the Nissen hut, the officer blew on his whistle and ordered us to stop to let an armed guard pass by.

We all turned to stare at the prisoner, at his manacled arms and that horribly twisted foot dragging behind him as he walked. Then Magdalena gave this terrible shriek and tried to run to him, but the stevedores held her back.

But I think that Esteban saw me, standing there holding my brother's hand before they led us back onto the boats. It was only for a moment, but our eyes met and I saw no anger in his. Then they took him away.

PART SIX

50

That was the last mention of Esteban Reyes in the diary. Spike skim-read the few entries that remained and found no trace of the voluble, naive young girl who'd fallen in love with somebody else's husband. It was a more cynical Marcela who'd written in London, and she described her life as an evacuee as though it were being lived by someone else – someone she didn't care for especially. There were perfunctory descriptions of the dilapidated boarding house on the Fulham Road where she and Tito had been billeted; the temporary Catholic school that they'd attended at the Victoria and Albert Museum. Then, some months later, a report of the death of the first Gibraltarian evacuee during a London air raid, notable only for its phlegm. The last entry, dated March 7th 1941, amounted to little more than a complaint about the bitterness of the English winter and the unrelenting blandness of the food.

Pushing his hands through his hair, Spike sat back from the kitchen table, trying to take in the enormity of what he'd read. He never would have claimed to have known Marcela well, but the events that she described seemed impossible to reconcile with the forthright, high-minded woman he remembered. But there was no way to get around it. Every one of them – Marcela, Anthony and their friend Jack – had colluded to let Esteban Reyes take the blame for Tito's crime. Hard as it was to believe, Christopher Massetti had been right all along. There *had* been a conspiracy against his father. What Massetti couldn't have known was that Esteban had been complicit in the deception.

Spike picked up the Jiffy bag and turned it in his hands. The postmark was local, the address label computer-generated. Who could have sent it? And why to him and not the police?

He was just trying to work out which of Jessica's colleagues she might persuade to run the diary for prints, when he remembered that she had left him, and was finally able to place the nagging dread that had been lurking at the back of his mind. Now that his anger had faded, he couldn't believe he'd been so stupid as to let her go. He dialled her number, feeling his chest tighten as he waited for the call to connect. But it rang straight through to voicemail, as he'd known it would, so he slipped the diary into his briefcase and headed for the front door.

Outside, the Church of the Sacred Heart was chiming eleven. Jessica had an antenatal appointment at noon; he might catch her if he hurried. As he moved through the Old Town, he replayed their argument in his head, rehearsing better excuses, more persuasive justifications for what he'd done. But the lawyer in him knew there was no defence for putting his future wife's career in jeopardy, and that the only way he could have salvaged the situation was to have offered her some kind of explanation, rather than retreat into a detached silence, as he always did when he knew he was in the wrong.

Somewhere in the distance, he caught the beat of march-ing drums, a sound he'd always found faintly sinister. The

Gibraltar Regiment, rehearsing for the Ceremony of the Keys, the tedious annual re-enactment of life during the Great Siege. How had a year passed since the last one?

Slipping into a side street to avoid the crowds, Spike pressed on towards Nuno Navarro's apartment. He couldn't recall the exact address, but he'd picked Jessica up from the flat often enough in the early days of their flirtation, checking the time in irritation as he'd waited for her to run down the stairs to him. On more than one occasion, he remembered looking up to see her younger brother laughing down at him from the balcony, cigarette dangling from one corner of his mouth.

The medium-rise tower block was as unloved as Spike remembered. But today, the third-floor balcony was deserted, a small drift of dead leaves heaped against the closed shutters. Spike rolled his shoulders, then held down the buzzer.

A throaty voice responded, '*Sí?*' No surprise to find Nuno at home at this hour. The travel agency where he worked used him only in high season, and only when no one else was available, which suited Nuno and his surprisingly lucrative online-poker habit just fine. The brief coughing fit that followed suggested his most recent attendance at smoking cessation classes had lapsed. Jessica would not be pleased.

'It's Spike.'

There was a long pause, then a sigh. 'I don't know what you've done, man,' Nuno said. 'But this time she's really *craka*, know what I mean?'

Spike almost smiled. 'Yeah, Nuno, I know what you mean.' He and his future brother-in-law usually restricted their conversation to the vagaries of Spanish football, so this territory was as unfamiliar as it was uncomfortable. 'Can I come up?'

Spike heard the buzzer click off, and guessed that Nuno was consulting with Jessica. He could imagine her leaning against the door-frame, chewing her lower lip as she ran through a mental profit-and-loss account of their relationship. His most recent indiscretion would put him deeply in the red, that much he knew. He heard another click: 'She doesn't want to see you.' Nuno lowered his voice: 'You know what Jessie's like when she's pissed off. Just give her some space, *compa*. A couple of days.'

The intercom fell silent, and Spike stared up at the shutters, willing them to creak open. But a minute went by and nothing happened, so he turned away, catching the desolate wail of a military bugle in the distance.

On the roundabout of Harbour Views Road, Spike paused to look at the bronze statues of the Evacuation Monument, a tearful father running with arms thrown wide to greet his returning wife and children. Usually the mawkishness of the thing brought out the cynic in him, but this time he leant in to read the plaque: 'The Evacuation of the Gibraltarians, 1940–1951'. A list of the outposts where the evacuees had been sent was engraved around the plinth: Madeira, French Morocco, Jamaica, England, Northern Ireland . . . Marcela had married Andrew and stayed in London after the war. After reading in her diary what she and the others had done, Spike couldn't say he blamed her.

He wished he'd never seen that bloody journal, he thought as he walked on, wondering what the hell to do with it. Under normal circumstances, he would have shown it to Jessica, asked for her advice. But now he was just going to have to wait until she was ready to talk to him.

His phone buzzed: another chasing email from Harriet Baldwin at Van der Bijl & Zimmermann. He checked the time. He'd never had that shower, he realised, but at least he was wearing a suit. And for once he felt grateful to have some urgent corporate work pressed upon him. Something which, for a few hours at least, might take his mind off the unnavigable mess in which he found himself.

51

Spike spent a long afternoon working on the legal opinion for Van der Bijl & Zimmermann. Harriet Baldwin, he had quickly surmised, was an idiot. Those of her amendments which were not entirely asinine demonstrated such a lack of market knowledge that he wondered, not for the first time, if she had ever handled this kind of matter before. He forced himself to be more charitable. Maybe she was just a trainee solicitor, thrown in at the deep end by a neglectful partner. Then again, noting Ms Baldwin's fondness for the imperative mood, perhaps even a trainee solicitor thought herself above a lawyer with a funny name sending her emails from a tinpot firm in Gibraltar. Either way, the challenge of dealing with each of her objections in a manner which did not disclose his contempt for her legal abilities stretched his diplomatic skills to their limits.

So it was past 7 p.m. when Spike finally finished the email and hit send. Peter and Ana were long gone, so he switched on Radio Gibraltar and settled down at his desk with a glass of one of Peter's better Riojas. And sitting there by the light of his old anglepoise lamp, listening to Bruce Springsteen coaxing Mary to go down to the river, just for a moment he felt relaxed. But then the song ended, and he remembered Sir Anthony and Drew and Jessica and Marcela's diary and all the things he wanted to forget, so he killed the music and reached for the Brusati file, a convey-ance he'd been working on for another of Peter's Italians of dubious means.

Last month, Spike had fixed Signor Brusati up with Juan Felipe, and apparently the Italian had opted for the first apartment the estate agent had shown him. Evidently time – or the sustainability of his country's latest coalition government – were pressing hard on the man's finances, and the sooner he could avail himself of Gibraltar's tax breaks the better.

Logging onto the private client account to check if Brusati's deposit had arrived, Spike saw the screen and blinked. The balance was nearly four million euros higher than it ought to have been. Either Brusati had settled on a very different property than they'd discussed, or he'd wired through the asking price rather than the deposit. For a brief, dizzying moment, Spike considered absconding to Buenos Aires with the company debit card, but contented himself with ordering a detailed statement of the account instead.

His neck was aching; as he flexed his shoulders, he caught sight of his reflection in the blackness of the French windows. Christ: he was starting to look old. It might have been him farming out work to the sticks from an office in Canary Wharf, he thought with a sudden surge of bitter-ness. The scholarship he'd won at Bar School in London had caught the attention of a number of Magic Circle firms, all hoping to persuade him to cross-qualify. But then the call had come in from his father, followed by a surreal meeting with the specialist. 'Connective tissue is the cement of the body,' the doctor had explained. 'It joins the lens to the eyeball, the valves to the chambers of the heart.' Spike remembered Rufus sitting in the corner of the examination room, one leg crossed elegantly over the other, looking strangely – infuriatingly – amused. 'Your father's connective tissue is deteriorating,' the specialist had concluded. So Spike had moved home, and here he still was, some twenty years later.

As he swivelled around to replace the Brusati file in the bookcase behind him, his elbow caught the bottle of Rioja on his desk. '*Manascada*!' he spat, and ran outside to retrieve the hand towel from the office's tiny lavatory, a once yellow thing which, to his knowledge, had never been washed.

Mopping up the spillage on his knees, Spike was relieved to see that it was only the Esteban Reyes file that had taken the brunt. He set about peeling apart the saturated pages, laying them out to dry one by one on the conference table they so rarely used. As he turned back to his desk, he saw a sheet he'd missed busily welding itself into the carpet. Only when he'd picked it up and placed it on that day's *Chronicle* to dry did he see that it was an index of the contents of the file.

'Memorandum to the Governor and Commander in Chief, Gibraltar (p. 17)', he read. 'Technical Report on Sabotage Material (p. 18)'. He worked his finger down the list of statements: 'Statement of Chief Witness . . . "LAUREL" (p. 35)'; 'Statement of Accused . . . ESTEBAN ALEJANDRO REYES (p. 38)'. Then he inhaled sharply. 'Statement of witness . . . MARCELA ELENA PERALTA (p. 41)'; 'Statement of witness . . . JOHN FERNANDO CAPURRO (p. 43)'.

'John Capurro?' he said aloud. What had John Capurro to do with the events of the Dockyard bomb? Heart quickening, Spike stood up and started leafing through the sodden pages on the conference table. Both Marcela's and John Capurro's witness statements had been completely redacted from the file.

Spike sat down at his desk, swivelling in his chair as he rubbed his neck. If John Capurro had given a statement, then he must have known something about what had gone on that night at the Dockyard. An eyewitness perhaps, or another informant. But Marcela had never mentioned John in her diary. Just Tito, Anthony, Esteban and . . . Spike closed his eyes and tipped back his head. 'Jack' and John Capurro were the same person. Of course they were.

He leant forward in his chair. John Capurro and Marcela Peralta. Both had been involved in the conspiracy against Esteban Reyes. And both were dead. As was Eloise Capurro, John's wife and confidante. And the one man who inter-linked them all? 'Laurel'. Tony. Sir Anthony Stanford.

Spike folded the index page into his briefcase, turned off the lights and locked the front door. There was no choice now: he had to turn the diary over to the police. But as he set off for New Mole House, he couldn't help but wonder what these revelations would do to Sir Anthony's case. Whether or not the prosecution could use Marcela's diary as admissible evidence was a moot point, but the RGP would now have everything they needed to charge Sir Anthony.

Drew would have destroyed the diary, that much he knew. Spike had always suspected that Drew was not the type of lawyer to be overly troubled by the niceties of the Law – not when they threatened his own comfort, or career. And one night, not long after Drew's mother had finally surrendered to cancer, he had confirmed Spike's intuition. They'd sat out in the garden at Dragon Trees until the early hours, drinking a bottle of tequila down to the worm, and Drew had told him about the night that he'd learnt he hadn't got tenancy. Sir Anthony had managed to swing Drew a pupillage at a small criminal set in Lincoln's Inn, but not even his influence could secure the permanent gig for his son – not when he was 'up against a Hardwicke Scholar with a Double First and a cracking pair of breasts', as Drew had so delicately put it. Drew's response had suggested that his pupil master's judgment had been sound – because he'd gone off on a bender and somehow ended up in Cornwall. And in the early hours of that frosty, nasty night, Drew had driven his car into a wall on the outskirts of Penzance. He was drunk, and he was a lawyer, albeit one without a job, so instead of calling the police, he'd doused the car in petrol and torched it, then reported it stolen the next day. So Spike knew he wouldn't hesitate to bend the Law, especially if it was his father who was in trouble.

But though Drew was Spike's oldest friend, Jessica was going be his wife, and sometime in the next week or so, the mother of his child. So he pushed open the doors to New Mole House and asked the desk sergeant if DI Isola was available, hoping that he could persuade the detective to keep his mouth shut about where he'd obtained such compelling new evidence against Sir Anthony Stanford.

Because the one thing he was sure of was that if Drew ever found out that Spike had betrayed his father, he would never forgive him.

52

Two days went by, and Spike lost count of the number of voicemails he'd left for Jessica, begging forgiveness, swearing to do better. But nothing worked, and it was becoming harder and harder to explain away her absence. Meanwhile, the house had regained its former level of disorder with a speed that both would have alarmed Jessica and vindicated her complaints that she was the only adult in residence at Chicardo's Passage.

At work, Spike did his best to keep out of Peter's way and to avoid tormenting himself by constantly checking the online papers. So far, the press didn't seem to have picked up on Sir Anthony's arrest. Spike was just starting to believe there was a possibility it might stay that way when his phone rang.

'It's Drew. Can we meet?'

A moment's hesitation: 'Now?'

'It'll only take a minute. I'm in the Alameda.'

Spike hung up and headed for the exit. On Main Street, he had to flatten himself against a wall to give passage to a baton-twirling Band Major. The Ceremony of the Keys wasn't even on until next week – he couldn't wait for the damn thing to be over.

It was only as he neared the Alameda Gardens that he felt his palms start to sweat. He must have been mad to have trusted DI Isola. The man wasn't known for his integrity – even when dealing with people he didn't actively dislike.

But it was reassuring somehow to find Drew standing beneath the bust of General Eliott, hero of the Great Siege. As ever, Drew had dressed with care, but as Spike sat down on the bench beside him, he could see the shadows beneath his eyes were now so dark they looked like bruise marks. He felt a sudden stir of guilt as he realised for the first time how much his friend was starting to resemble his father.

'The injunction failed.' Drew was studying some unidentified spot in the distance. 'It'll be in all the papers tomorrow.' He slid a pack of Marlboro Reds across the bench to Spike; for old times' sake, Spike accepted. 'They've charged Dad with three counts of murder.'

'*Three?*'

Drew took a deep pull on his cigarette, then curled his lips into a facsimile of a smile. 'It came as something of a shock. The CCTV evidence was undeniably damaging, so we knew they'd probably charge Dad with Eloise Capurro's murder. But the other counts blindsided us.' Above Drew's head, Spike saw wisps of cloud rising over the peak of the Rock, like a volcano waking from sleep. 'The charge relating to the death of Marcela Peralta was particularly unexpected.'

'The police are treating it as murder?' It was just as Spike had feared. He dropped his cigarette and crushed it out with his foot. The nicotine was making him nauseous.

'According to the Coroner, she was dead before she hit the water. Broken neck.'

Spike closed his eyes, trying not to think about how Marcela might have sustained that sort of injury. But Drew was still talking: 'The RGP found traces of her blood at

Dragon Trees. They're working on the assumption that she was killed there, then the body was dumped at sea.' Drew pinched out his fag end between thumb and forefinger and flicked it away.

'They can't seriously think your father was responsible?' Spike said. 'At his age?'

For the first time, Drew looked encouraged. 'Perhaps not. But there's also the third charge. The police found a phial of morphine at the house. And last week, the Attorney General ordered John Capurro's body to be exhumed.'

Spike had trouble keeping the incredulity from his voice. 'But John Capurro's death was never in dispute. He had pancreatic cancer.'

'And as we all know, "There's no recovering from that."' Drew's impression of Eloise Capurro's flat Essex accent was poor in both execution and taste. His lip curled again, and for a terrible moment Spike thought he was going to laugh. 'It seems that John's death was premature. The post-mortem concluded that he died of a morphine overdose.'

Spike took a careful moment to formulate his next question. 'How did the police make the connection with John Capurro?'

Drew rubbed his neat cleft chin and shook his head in resignation. 'They must have some evidence they haven't shared with us yet. And whatever it is, I think Dad knows more than he's prepared to admit.' Drew turned and looked Spike in the eye. 'I wondered if he'd said anything to you. That morning in the garden before they arrested him.'

'No,' Spike replied, letting his eyes slip away from Drew's penetrating gaze to the ornamental tree draped over the wall ahead, forcing himself to focus on the clusters of purple seeds hanging from its branches. As Drew shook another white tip from his pack of Marlboros, the name of the plant hovered at the fringes of Spike's mind, then slipped away.

'All Dad cares about is the impact on my career,' Drew went on. 'Ironic, really.' Another sour curve of the lips: 'I withdrew my candidacy this morning to concentrate on his defence. I'd assumed the party might have the good grace to try and talk me out of it. But the Secretary General couldn't snatch the letter out of my hand fast enough. '

Spike reached over and touched his old friend's shoulder. 'If there's anything I can do, Drew. Anything at all.'

As they walked back towards the gates of the Alameda, Spike looked back at the wrinkled, finger-like pods hanging over the wall and suddenly remembered what the shrub was called. Judas tree.

53

The next day, as Drew had predicted, the scandal hit the press. The legal profession on the Rock – like every other – was not immune to the baser attributes of humanity, and Spike could easily imagine the scores of 'close friends' and colleagues sniggering into their cappuccinos as they read of Drew Stanford-Trench's withdrawal from the political fray after his father's spectacular fall from grace. Peter Galliano was never one to deny himself a little *Schadenfreude*, and Spike felt a mild sensation of disgust as he watched his partner flip through the *Gibraltar Chronicle*, emitting little tuts and gasps as he lapped it all up. Finally replete, he closed the paper and heaved his feet up onto Spike's desk with a sigh of satisfaction. 'Rejoice not when thine enemy stumbleth, and all that, but I mean, really, Spike! The old goat must have lost his marbles. A knighthood? That magnificent villa? And then he goes and kills three people.' A rope of smoke unfurled from each nostril. 'It must be dementia. I'd put money on it. Make sure you ship me off to "Dignitas" before that ever happens.'

Spike suppressed the temptation to suggest they put the idea in writing there and then, and just said, 'They'll have a job pinning three murders on a man his age.'

'Then they must have some pretty compelling evidence in reserve.'

Spike looked away. So far Isola had kept his word. The article made no mention of Marcela's diary.

'Well' – Peter reached for his gold-topped cane – 'I must get on.'

But Spike hadn't finished. As Peter turned towards the door, Spike held out the statement from the firm's client account. 'This BACS payment, Peter,' he called over. 'I assumed it was related to the Brusati conveyance. But it isn't, is it?'

Peter dismissed the question with an airy wave of the hand. 'Oh, the donation. Don't you remember? From Siri Baxter's people.'

'Siri Baxter donated 3.5 *million* euros to the Liberal Party?'

Peter scratched one eyebrow. 'Like I said, she was very taken with your friend's political prospects.' He picked up the *Chronicle* and tucked it under his arm with a smirk. 'I expect she'll be wanting her money back now.'

Peter closed the door, and Spike looked back at the statement, wondering if he should just stuff it back into the filing cabinet and forget all about it. Probably, he thought. But then he heard Peter's phone laugh resonate from the next door office and realised that his mind was already made up.

So he walked into the hallway, finding Ana at her desk, sipping some foul-smelling herbal concoction from a mug marked 'I'd Rather Be Reading *Ulysses*.' He reached into her pen pot for a biro and circled the transaction code that was troubling him. 'I'd like some more detail on this deposit.'

Ana cocked her head. 'What sort of detail?'

'The provenance of the money.' Spike didn't lift his eyes from the sheet of paper, but he could sense Ana narrowing hers as she tried to work out what he was up to, and if she wanted any part of it. 'Housekeeping,' he improvised.

'Housekeeping,' she repeated. There was a long pause, then she leant forward and plucked a stray hair from his shoulder. 'I'll see what I can do.'

54

It was the waiting Spike hated the most. He always had. As a child, his impatience had infuriated his mother – she'd never understood how deeply he loathed that sense of powerlessness, as though he were some passive creature that could only stand by until others acted. And here he was once again. Waiting for Jessica to decide if she was prepared to forgive him. Waiting for Isola to divulge to Drew where he'd acquired the new evidence that had strengthened the police's belief that Sir Anthony might be capable of murder.

Three days had now passed since Jessica had left. At first, the work had helped, but now Spike found that his in-box was clear. Even the invoices Peter had been nagging him to get off his desk for months had been drafted and sent. Charlie was otherwise engaged with Rufus, so that afternoon, Spike found himself sitting on a bus to Catalan Bay, staring out at a lone fishing boat tacking in towards the harbour's golden sickle of sand.

The bus reached his stop, and Spike got off, pausing on the step to savour the gentle salty breeze on his face. Then the driver pulled away, and Spike made out the Rock's disused water catchments on the other side of the road, the steep flattened bank sheering down into empty underground reservoirs – no doubt about to be snapped up by some hi-tech company for its new R&D centre.

Clusters of pastel-painted fishermen's cottages framed the path down to the sea. In the distance, Spike saw the early evening sun dapple the white frontage of the Caleta Hotel, a vast and invariably empty art deco palace favoured by couples in town for a quickie Gibraltar wedding. At its foot rose the Mamela Rock. No kids paddling around it today: the October sea was too chilly for local tastes.

A white-stubbled, Italian-looking fisherman sat outside the Catalan Bay Social Club, eking out a tumbler of grappa. He wiped his mouth on the sleeve of his jersey. 'Who you after?'

'Davey Lavagna.'

The man jabbed his roll-up southwards, and Spike continued along the cobbled road that ran above the harbour. Then, just past Our Lady of Dolours church, he saw the house, and an involuntary smile spread across his face. Faded pink stucco, salt-streaked turquoise shutters, roof undulating with ancient terracotta tiles. He had to ring the bell three times before a short leather-skinned man opened the door. The shutters behind him were closed, and in the darkness, Spike could just make out a pair of shrewd blue eyes. 'Mr Lavagna?'

The man squinted in the sunlight. 'You Spike?'

Spike nodded, and Old Davey held open the door with a grunt. Spike followed him into the sitting room, nose wrinkling at the pervasive stench of stock cubes. Davey lowered himself into his chair with a grimace that suggested both knees and hips were in need of medical attention, then rammed a forkful of instant noodles into his mouth. He looked Spike up and down. 'When Rufus comes, he brings me pastries.'

'Sorry.'

Davey's mouth twisted like a petulant old woman's as he swept his fork back through the bowl. 'The place is too big for me now. Since Vera passed.'

Spike made his usual gesture of sympathy, somewhere between a shrug and a double-nod. 'May I?' he said, waving a hand towards the ceiling.

'*Vai, vai,*' Davey urged in impatient Italian as he grappled with the remote control. As Spike turned for the door, he heard Davey call after him, 'The estate agent's coming tomorrow.'

The urgent tattoo of the GBC-TV evening bulletin followed Spike up the steep oak staircase. He pushed open the first door on the landing. Though it was crammed with packing cases, and the wallpaper looked like it dated from the First War, even Spike could appreciate that beneath the chaos might lie a room that befitted the title of 'master bedroom'. The ceiling was high and the floorboards, though uneven, looked original. A rusting iron bedstead stood in one corner, and just for a moment Spike imagined himself on the beach below, warming his hands over a bonfire as the hated futon burned. He forced open the shutters and stepped out onto the balcony. The view of the sun-burnished bay was bewitching; in his mind's eye, he pictured himself and Jessica sitting there with a glass of oloroso, watching the terns dive into the wavelets as the sun went down. The room next door was smaller, but filled with nooks and alcoves he knew Charlie would love to fill with his treasures. There was even a palm tree outside the window for him to shinny down once he'd reached his teens and wanted to sneak out to Casemates to join his friends.

Hearing a creak behind, Spike turned from the window to see Davey Lavagna standing in the doorway, bald head shiny from the effort of the stairs. Davey pointed at the easel in the corner. 'That's where your father does his pictures.' He crooked one arm, and Spike followed him as he began his slow progress back downstairs, emitting a wheeze with each step. 'Rufus tried to flog me one the other day,' he called over his shoulder. 'I told him my knees might be shot, but there's nothing wrong with my eyesight.' He gave a throaty chuckle at his own wit, and Spike met him with a half-smile.

'My daughter's found me an apartment in Both Worlds,' Davey confided at the front door. 'Sheltered housing. Says it'll be easier for me.'

Watching how the old man moved, Spike suspected the daughter might be onto something. 'My fiancée will have to see the place before we make a decision.'

Davey's grin revealed more gum than tooth. 'Isn't that always the way? In the end, it's the women who hold the reins.'

Spike shook Davey's hand. 'I'm starting to think you may be right, Mr Lavagna.'

55

The sun was setting as Spike walked back through Catalan Bay. The grizzled fisherman was gone, the only evidence of his presence an empty tumbler and an ashtray brimming with the twisted stubs of his roll-ups. Spike sat for a while at his table with a bottle of beer, watching the sun bleed down into the horizon, staring out at the unbroken Mediterranean. The view from this side of the Rock was infinitely superior, he'd decided – no rusting oil tankers or Commercial Dockyard to mar the composition, the only sounds the unhurried roll of the waves and the scream of the gulls as they waited for the fishing boats to return with their spoils.

Thinking of that house, picturing the balcony where Rufus might settle into his dotage trying and failing to capture the Mamela Rock, where they could finally give Charlie a real home, Spike knew he had to have it. This might be the grand gesture, he thought, the thing that brought them all back together. Maybe it was just the Peroni, or the sunset, but he decided to let the last bus rumble by and walk home.

When Spike finally got back to Chicardo's Passage, the house was sleeping, and he wasn't sorry. He opened a bottle of Rioja, trying to make up his mind whether to try Jessica again. Maybe if he told her about the house in Catalan Bay, it might make a difference. He took out his phone, draining his glass to give him courage, then heard a knock at the door and felt his heart lift. The lightness of touch suggested that whoever it was knew a child would be in bed at this hour.

But as he threw open the door, his smile fell. The man standing on his porch was bearded, his face so lean and tanned it took Spike a few moments to recognise him. Then Christopher Massetti gave one of his shy, lopsided smiles. 'I know it's late . . .'

It was late. And a wiser and more sober lawyer would probably have told his fugitive client to get the hell off his doorstep and turn himself into the police. But Spike wasn't that lawyer. And he wasn't that sober. So he just held open the door and beckoned Massetti in.

The two men stood together in the kitchen, looking at each other in awkward silence. Beneath the unforgiving glare of the naked ceiling bulb, Spike realised that what he'd taken for a winter tan was actually a jaundice so severe that even the whites of Massetti's eyes had taken on a yellowish tinge. Aware that he was staring, he turned to the sink and waited for the lukewarm water to run cold. Then he passed Massetti a glass and sat down.

'I shouldn't have run,' Massetti said. 'I know that now.'

Spike raised one eyebrow: he'd never known the man to be so forthcoming. 'Where have you been, Christopher? The police still have a warrant out for your arrest.'

'At a campsite in Ronda. They know me a bit. We used to stay there when I was a boy.'

Massetti took a breath, and Spike blenched at the crackling noise that emerged from deep inside his chest. 'You know the police have arrested someone else in connection with Dr Capurro's murder?' Of course Massetti did. There was no other reason he would have come back.

Sure enough, the old man gave another of his ponderous nods.

'But you still need to go to the police. I could come with you, if you like?' Spike suddenly questioned if he was sober enough for another encounter with DI Isola. Probably, after a few espressos.

'I turned myself in as soon as I crossed the border,' Massetti replied. He scratched at his grey-flecked beard, and Spike saw a hospital tag looped around his wrist. 'They brought a lawyer in when they told me that they'd dropped the charges. She said the police have got hold of some new evidence in Esteban's case. Documents they think might exonerate him. She even thought I could bring a case for miscarriage of justice on my father's behalf.'

Spike wondered what might be motivating the RGP to be so helpful. In his experience, altruism wasn't high on their list of priorities – unlike a strong desire to minimise liability. 'I could help you find someone in London to fight the case? A QC with an expertise in Human Rights.'

'Maybe.' Massetti fingered the tag around his wrist. 'The doc says my liver's not so good. They've put me on the transplant list, but . . .' Massetti didn't finish his sentence, just hauled himself up from his chair. They walked together into the hallway. 'Your missus in bed then?' he asked.

'Asleep,' Spike replied. It was probably true. 'Good luck, Christopher.'

Massetti offered Spike his hand, then looked him in the eye. 'You were kind to me, Mr Sanguinetti. I won't forget that.'

Spike watched him walk away down the dark street. As he closed the door, he heard the chime of a new text message. He took out his phone and smiled. It was what he'd been waiting for. Sender: Jessica Navarro.

56

Spike whistled to himself as he made one last check of the papers for the Brusati conveyance, sticking index tabs beside the execution clauses his client would have to sign the next time he saw fit to visit Gibraltar. The delay had now been so prolonged that the seller was starting to get jumpy. Spike had already had his lawyer on the phone twice that week. On the most recent occasion, she'd threatened to renegotiate the sale price, so Spike had called Brusati and found him sipping negronis on his superyacht off Sotogrande. He'd laughed off Spike's concerns and told him to hold his nerve – he'd send the seller a case of Venetian spumante to take the edge off his indignation.

Slipping the Brusati file back into his cabinet, Spike's eye fell on the document that Ana Lopes had left on his desk earlier that day, and he felt his good mood evaporate. It was a printout of the web page for Kazan Kredit Bank. The bank's name was the only script in English, the rest an indecipherable Cyrillic.

'Is this it?' Spike had asked Ana, looking up at her as she tapped a ballpoint pen against her lower teeth.

'Afraid my Russian's a bit rusty, Spike,' Ana had replied. 'I hadn't realised it was part of the job description.' Then she'd lifted her hip from the side of his desk and picked her way between the piles of redline documents heaped on the floor as elegantly as a tight pencil skirt and a pair of red-soled stilettos would allow.

Spike got to his feet and walked into Peter's office before he could change his mind. Peter made him wait, as he usually did, so he just stood there with crossed arms as he watched his business partner sign off documents with his Mont Blanc. Finally, with one last ornate flourish, Peter sat back.

'You do know about CDD, right, Peter? AML? KYC?'

'So many acronyms! This early in the morning, Spike? Whatever's got into you?' Peter was enjoying this, Spike could tell. Not for the first time, he felt an overwhelming urge to smack the infuriating look off his partner's face, but instead he plucked a leather-bound Law Society tome from Peter's shelf and dropped it onto the desk, where it fell with a satisfying slap. 'We may not be Slaughter & May, Peter. But we're not some bucket shop. There are rules we have to follow. Anti-money-laundering directives. Know Your Client regulations. I made you go on courses, for Christ's sake! You might not have sat through them, but even you must realise that we can't accept client funds from a financial institution like this.'

Peter sat back, lazily massaging his round belly with one hand, entirely unmoved. 'Bonanza are a global business, Spike. They have substantial holdings in Russia. I imagine they have any number of local accounts.'

A small fly was buzzing around Spike's ear; he swatted it and it fell stunned onto Peter's mock Persian carpet. 'Do you even know if it's an authorised institution? We're talking about millions of euros, Peter. From a dodgy Russian bank.'

'It was a *charitable donation*,' Peter retorted as he swivelled his chair round to squint at his computer screen. With one click of his mouse, the printer started to spit out paper. 'Maybe I should have looked into it a little more, but it's immaterial now. Siri called earlier to say that Bonanza have withdrawn the donation. They can't afford to be associated with the Stanford scandal.' Peter reached into the printer tray and passed Spike a printout. The 3.5 million euros had already left the private client account.

'Happy now?' Peter said, holding out his hand for the sheet. 'And for the record, Spike' – he snatched it back – 'I don't appreciate you skulking about behind my back like some two-bit Perry Mason. If you have concerns about me or my ethics, then at least have the balls to come and talk to me about them. We're meant to be partners, after all.' He reached for his packet of cigarettes; finding it empty he crushed it in one fist and glowered up at Spike. 'Close the door on your way out.'

57

The altercation with Peter had made Spike late, so he was forced to jog to the hospital, and his face was shiny with sweat as he caught his first glimpse of Jessica through the sliding doors, rocking on the heels of her small orange trainers. Her dark hair was pulled back into a ponytail and her fringe had been cut straight across her forehead. Maybe it was just that it had been four days since he'd seen her last, but he thought that she'd never looked more lovely.

She turned to face him, and though she smiled, the chill in her eyes told him he'd not been forgiven. But Jessica could be generous in victory, so she offered him her cheek and let him kiss the cool skin. 'I missed you,' he whispered in her ear.

She gave no indication of having heard, just lowered herself into the plastic seat, clasping her maternity notes to her chest. Spike joined her in the adjacent chair and they sat together in silence. To an outside observer they must have looked like just another unhappy couple, Spike thought miserably, still divided as to whether they should have kept the baby.

'How's Charlie?' Jessica asked without looking up.

'Good,' Spike lied, realising that he'd barely seen the boy all week. 'Missing you, I think.'

'And your dad?'

'The same.'

Jessica nodded, eyes still trained on her feet.

'How are you feeling?' Spike asked.

'I haven't felt a kick in a while.' She looked into his eyes for the first time, and he could see that she was worried. 'I wanted to get it checked out.'

'Miss Jessica Navarro?'

They both started at the sound of the nurse's brisk voice. The usual midwife was waiting for them in the examination room, a fifty-something Sheffield expat who Spike found reassuring, but Jessica had never warmed to.

'And how are we today?' the midwife asked.

The 'we', Spike knew, was a courtesy. He was almost completely ignored during these appointments, which was fine by him.

'Not too bad.' Jessica eased herself onto the bed. 'I haven't felt much movement since yesterday.'

'Let's have a look then. Shall we?'

Spike braced himself as the midwife hoisted up Jessica's cotton dress and switched on the Doppler. No matter how many times they did this, there was always a moment while the midwife searched for the baby's heartbeat when Spike held his breath. He wondered if all fathers were afflicted with this anxiety, or if he felt it so keenly because his sister Juliet had been stillborn. But then there it was, *Ker-dum, ker-dum, ker-dum*, like distant horse hooves pounding the turf. Jessica's face relaxed; she even managed a small grin.

'When's your due date?' the midwife asked, manipulating Jessica's belly roughly with her thumbs.

'A week on Thursday,' Jessica gasped.

'Sounds about right.' The midwife reached into a mirror-fronted cupboard behind her and passed Jessica a specimen cup. 'Now if you could give us a quick sample, and . . .' She broke off to update Jessica's notes. As was often the case with her profession, the second half of the condition was left hanging.

'And yes, Dad,' the midwife resumed, addressing Spike for the first time as he helped Jessica up, 'Baby *is* fine.' She threw Jessica a wink. 'These men. All they think about is Baby. Bet he'll be wanting a boy, eh?'

58

As Spike paced outside the hospital lavatories, waiting for Jessica to emerge, a door down the corridor opened and a young police officer Spike vaguely recognised stepped out, chequered hat under one arm. If he spotted Spike, he didn't let on, just averted his eyes and continued towards the lifts.

Curiosity piqued, Spike peered through the glass panel into the private room. The patient lying in the bed was old and looked very ill. Though the man's face was grey and covered by an oxygen mask, Spike knew him at once. It was Sir Anthony Stanford. And slumped in a chair by the bed, head in hands, sat his son.

Spike knocked gently, and when Drew looked up, Spike saw that his eyes were swollen and pink. Drew squeezed his father's hand, then got to his feet and made his way to the door. Outside, he leant back against the corridor wall next to Spike. In his faded green polo shirt, hands shoved deep into the pockets of his chinos, he suddenly looked very young. Maybe all sons did when their fathers were gravely ill.

Spike placed a hand on his friend's arm and felt him flinch. Drew pulled away and rubbed the skin below his lower lip with the knuckle of his index finger. 'They think it was a massive stroke. Dad's been under a lot of pressure, of course. They've had him under police guard.' Drew's eyes roved around the corridor for the young police constable, and he gave a tight little smile. 'Most of the time.'

'I'm so sorry, Drew.'

'Are you, Spike?' Drew turned. 'Are you really?' He let out a mirthless laugh, and it was then Spike realised that he knew everything.

'I can see you're angry, Drew. But if you'd just let me explain . . .'

'I've been thinking a lot about you, Spike,' Drew cut him off. 'Sitting here with Dad, wondering if he was going to make it through the night. And the thing is . . .' Drew hesitated, as though searching for the most elegant way to articulate his thoughts. When he continued, it was in that measured, steely voice Spike knew he favoured when embarking upon a particularly aggressive cross-examination. 'The thing is, Spike, I don't think you'll ever make a great lawyer. It's not to do with intellect, really. You're just too emotional. Always caught up in this burning need to do the right thing.' He leant back against the wall again and crossed his ankles. 'But even *you* must have realised what it meant for my father when you turned that diary over to the police. And I've been wondering if it was really worth it. Selling out a good man to save a loser like Massetti. A drunk who stalked an elderly woman. Intimidated her so much that she was afraid to leave her home.' Drew glanced round at Spike, and the contempt in his eyes unnerved him. 'Where did you find it, anyway? Rifling through a dead woman's things?'

'The diary was sent to me.'

'By whom?'

'I don't know.'

That took Drew by surprise, and Spike could almost hear his mind running through the list of candidates who might have had the opportunity and motive to inflict such a damning blow on his father's reputation. Not a pleasant process of elimination, Spike imagined. He cleared his throat. 'It was evidence, Drew. I had a duty to hand it over.'

Though it was the truth, it seemed only to anger Drew further, and the carapace which he'd carefully constructed to get himself through weeks of strain finally cracked. He grabbed Spike by the shoulders and turned him bodily to face the glass. 'Look at him!'

Spike took in the tubes and wires, the slackness of one side of Sir Anthony's face.

'Are you seriously telling me that man could have murdered three people?' Drew hissed in Spike's ear. 'You know as well as I do this case will never make it to court. But that doesn't matter now, because you've already destroyed Dad's name. And you've ruined me.'

Spike pulled away.

'My father cared for you,' Drew went on, and they both heard his voice crack. 'He always told me there are two kinds of people in this world. Givers and takers. And you, Spike, are a taker. Who do you think got you that Government Scholarship?'

Spike was just processing that sobering piece of information when he heard an anxious voice behind him, 'Drew?' He turned to see Jessica hastening towards them, and when he looked back, it was just in time to see Drew swinging a punch. He dodged to the right and Drew's fist flashed past his face and hit the wall. As Drew careered back, nursing his bruised hand, he collided with Jessica, who stumbled back onto the linoleum.

'Christ!' Spike fell to his knees beside her, throwing Drew a furious look.

'You OK, DS Navarro?' The young police officer had reappeared, and was gripping Drew by the upper arm.

'I'm fine, Jason,' Jessica called up, as Spike helped her to her feet. Then she reached over and touched her colleague's sleeve. 'Really. No harm done.'

Drew glared down at the hand on his arm, then flicked up his eyes to the young officer with such disdain that the man coloured and let him go.

'Drew!' Spike called after him as he stalked away.

But Drew just shouldered his way through the door to the stairwell, with such force that it smashed against the wall with a gun-like crack.

'You sure you're OK, Jessie?' the police officer asked.

Jessica nodded, rubbing her coccyx. 'At least I didn't spill this.' They all looked down at the urine sample in her hands, and the police officer gave an uncomfortable laugh.

Outside the hospital, Spike hailed a cab. 'Catalan Bay,' he said to the driver.

Jessica threw him an enquiring look, and he smiled. 'I don't need to be back at the office for an hour or two. There's something I want you to see.'

Jessica settled back into her seat, gazing out of the window at a jumbo jet banking round to land on Gibraltar's tiny ex-military runway. 'You did the right thing, Spike.'

Spike pictured Sir Anthony slumped in his hospital bed; the hatred in Drew's eyes. 'Did I?'

For the first time in a while, he thought Jessica looked a little unsure of herself. 'I hope so.'

59

The taxi turned onto Catalan Bay Road, and Spike glanced across at Jessica. What if she didn't see what he had in the house? Or worse, if on a second viewing, it didn't live up to its early promise? Maybe this time even he would see only its flaws: the cracks in the walls, which might or might not be structural; the black mould colonising the grout in the bathrooms.

But as soon as Jessica caught her first glimpse of the house, he knew it was going to be all right. 'Is it on the market?' she asked, as he helped her out of the taxi.

'It will be. But if we can come up with a sensible offer, I think Old Davey will let us have it.'

If Jessica loved the house, its owner was equally appreciative of her charms. This time Davey Lavagna produced his toothless smile as soon as he opened the door and saw her, then Spike watched in amazement as he started scurrying about the house as fast as his old joints would allow, prising open rusted shutters and drawing Jessica's attention to the house's 'original features' with an exuberance that would have put Juan Felipe to shame.

But it was the view from the room Spike had earmarked as their bedroom that swung it. He'd known it would. 'Now this *is* something,' Jessica said, cheeks flushed with excitement as she stood on the balcony with her hands on her hips, looking down at the waves breaking on the sand. Buoyed by her smile, Spike grabbed her hand and led her into the box room at the end of the corridor. 'I thought we might have the nursery in here.'

The soothing sound of the surf filtered up. 'Yes,' Jessica said thoughtfully, eyes drawn to a long, jagged crack in the wall. She reached up and traced a finger down it. But then she turned back to the view, and Spike was relieved to see her smile again. 'So you're in?' he asked.

'I'm in.'

They found Davey dozing in his chair in front of the telly, the paper bag of pastries they'd brought him cradled on his lap. But as soon as he saw Jessica, he was back on his feet, brushing the crumbs from his cords. 'You like it!' he said, jabbing an accusing finger at her smiling face.

'We want to make you an offer,' Spike said.

Davey stuck his thumbs into his waistband and beamed. 'Well, well, well!'

'Subject to survey,' Jessica added.

Davey turned with a frown, the Genoese merchant in him suddenly suspicious. But it would have taken a tougher man than he to deny Jessica, so he just stuck out a hand. 'I'll wait to hear from you, then.'

60

On the cab ride home they talked about the house, Jessica looking more animated than Spike had seen her in months. Making plans, thinking about what they might do to the place after they moved in. Once they'd saved a bit of money, got Charlie and the baby settled.

'So you *are* coming home then?' Spike ventured. He still wasn't sure. Jessica nodded, and he had to force himself not to let out a sigh of relief. 'I'm sorry,' he said.

'I know you are,' she replied. It seemed a long time before she spoke again. 'And I get why you felt you had to do what you did. You and Drew have this strange Butch and Sundance thing going on.'

Spike winced. If that had ever been the case, it certainly wasn't now.

'I know you've always had a soft spot for Sir Anthony, so don't think I don't understand why you wanted to warn him that he was about to be arrested. But I shared that information with you in confidence, Spike. You were risking my career. Everything I've worked for all these years.'

Spike lowered his head, accepting his punishment. The cabby cast him a look of pity in the rear-view mirror, and he averted his eyes.

'You weighed up what it might cost me against your loyalty to the Stanfords, and you decided that my career could take the hit. And it's not the first time you've made me feel like this – as though our relationship is some kind of afterthought that can be sidelined, then picked up again, a bit bruised and battered, when you eventually remember it's important to you.' She sighed. 'But I can see it must have taken a lot for you to hand over the diary, knowing how damaging it would be for Sir Anthony's case.'

Spike was encouraged enough to hazard another question. 'What did the department say about disciplinary action?'

'They're attaching an official reprimand to my record. Other than that . . .'

Spike reached over and picked up her hand. 'I'll do better, I promise.'

The atmosphere lightened. Even the cab driver seemed to sense it, as he popped in the earpiece of his mobile phone and embarked on a colourful conversation with his bookie in *yanito*.

'Did Isola say anything else about the diary?' Spike asked.

Jessica raised an eyebrow. 'What is it that particularly interests you, Spike? The forensics?'

He gave a sheepish nod. She'd always been able to read his motives better than anyone else.

'The only prints on the diary were yours and Marcela's. You didn't receive the package until Tuesday, four days after Marcela was killed, so we were all working on the assumption that it was sent to you *after* she died. But it turns out that half the postal service were off celebrating Yom Kippur that week, so there was a backlog. It could have been posted on the Friday, but not delivered for several days.'

Spike rubbed his chin. He needed a shave. 'So Marcela could have sent it herself?'

'It's possible.'

'But why to me?'

Jessica shrugged. 'Maybe she was scared. She was sure Sir Anthony had killed Eloise Capurro, and was convinced he would come after her next. So she sent her diary to the one person she trusted. Her old friend, Spike Sanguinetti.' Jessica gave a roll of the eyes. 'God knows why.'

Spike accepted the insult without complaint. The driver chose that moment to overtake a construction lorry, narrowly missing a delivery truck coming the other way. Jessica glared at him, and he brought his telephone conversation to an abrupt end.

'You don't *really* think Sir Anthony could have done it?' Spike lowered his voice. 'Killed three people. At his age. In his condition.'

Jessica pulled a face that told him she thought it unlikely. 'Though . . .'

'What?'

'Sir Anthony's not the only person who might have wanted to keep the contents of that diary under wraps.'

Spike compiled a mental list of the members of the *Mil Cortes* and ticked them off one by one. 'Tito Peralta? He died twenty years ago.'

Jessica gave an impatient tut. '*Drew*, Spike. You saw how he was at the hospital. How fiercely he would protect his father's reputation.'

Spike wanted to laugh and tell her not to be ridiculous, but then he remembered the venom in Drew's tone as he'd accused Spike of ruining his career; the ferocity of the punch he'd swung. 'Or his own,' he murmured.

The taxi turned onto Winston Churchill Avenue. 'I can walk from here,' Spike said. 'Chicardo's Passage,' he called to the driver as he got out. 'Make sure she gets home safely.' He slapped a hand on the car roof and watched them drive away, relieved to see Jessica turn and offer him a smile through the rear window.

61

Spike felt the wind rising at his back as he walked past the marina on his way to the office. He paused for a moment to enjoy the melodic tinkle of the masts. Then, just as he was about to turn towards Main Street, he saw a familiar figure kneeling on the quayside, scrubbing down the side of a small fishing boat.

Christopher Massetti glanced up as Spike stepped over the low rope barrier. With that beard and his faded submariner jacket, he looked strangely at home in this setting, like a seasoned trawlerman preparing for the new season. He wiped his palms on his jeans, then offered Spike a hand. He'd lost more weight, Spike noted, but his grip was as firm as it always had been.

'You like the look of her?' Massetti gestured at the vessel.

Spike gave an unconvincing nod. What he knew about boats could be written on the back of a Royal Gibraltar postal stamp.

Massetti chuckled. 'I can't say I know much about sailing myself these days.' He hoisted one boot onto the gunwale. 'Mark christened her *Rebecca*. She's still registered in his name. Not been taken out since he died.'

Judging by the frayed fender ropes and the hull coated in barnacles and algae, Spike doubted she ever would be again. The stern was covered by a grey, guano-spattered tarpaulin, and as to what lay inside the wheelhouse, the glass was so encrusted with salt that it was anyone's guess.

'It wasn't always plain sailing between Mark and me, if you'll forgive the pun,' Massetti went on. 'I wasn't an easy man to get along with, and I wasn't his child. I suppose this is my way of making it up to him.'

And of keeping your mind off the booze, Spike imagined.

'Perhaps I'll take her out one day. All being well.' Massetti's grey eyes glinted.

'I hope it works out for you, Christopher.'

Massetti nudged the tub of filthy water with his boot. 'I'd better get on. It'll take more than a bit of spit and polish to get the *Rebecca* seaworthy, but once I'm done with her, at least she'll be clean.'

Spike nodded, remembering the order that Massetti had imposed upon the humble contents of his apartment. The man had a near-obsessive need for cleanliness. Something Spike could have benefited from in certain areas of his life, he knew. Especially his office. And Peter's . . . Suddenly a dark thought struck him, and it must have been obvious from his expression, as Massetti knitted his brows and tilted his head.

'Sorry, I've got to go.' Spike turned his back on the marina and walked quickly away. He couldn't believe he'd been so blind.

62

'Where's Peter?'

Ana Lopes plucked the bud of one headphone from her ear. 'Gone to Jury's. So I expect that's him for the day.' Her smile was affectionate rather than cruel, Spike thought. 'What do you need?' she asked.

'Don't worry, I can get it myself,' Spike called back.

As usual, Peter's office smelt of Creed cologne and stale cigarette smoke. A new case of Rioja had arrived, the pine-wood box already covered in ashtrays crammed with Silk Cut butts. For some reason, Spike had always half-expected to find one white tip rouged with lipstick, but it had never happened.

He pulled open a desk drawer. The bank statement was just where Peter had left it. He scribbled down the trans-action code and returned to the secretarial bay. 'Find out where these monies were sent when they left the client account, would you?'

Ana frowned as Spike gave her the Post-it note, but before she could protest, he'd already closed his office door. The MI5 file was still heaped on his desk, testament to all the time he'd wasted over the last few months, to how much he'd allowed himself to be distracted from what had been going on right under his nose. His phone rang almost imme-diately. '*En pala*?' he said, slipping into *yanito*, as he seemed to more and more these days in times of stress.

'Peter transferred the money to a Hambros account here in Gibraltar.' Ana paused. 'It's a legitimate account, Spike. In Ms Baxter's name on behalf of Bonanza Gaming.'

Spike set down the receiver. Well, that was it then. Feeling a sudden surge of rage, he swept the MI5 file off his desk, watching as the crinkled, wine-stained pages fanned out across the carpet. Then he took hold of the two bank statements, placed them side by side and sat for a moment, trying to clear his mind. To impose some order.

In August this year, the Galliano & Sanguinetti private client account had taken receipt of a BACS payment of 3.5 million euros from a Russian bank. The money had been intended for transfer to the Liberal Party coffers as a one-off donation, and in due course would have been reported to the Electoral Commission, and its provenance vetted. But then the Stanford scandal had hit, and Bonanza had cancelled the donation and presumably asked for their money back. But Peter hadn't returned the money to Kazan Kredit Bank. It had been wired to Bonanza's Hambros account in Gibraltar. And because the provenance was now Galliano & Sanguinetti, a trusted law firm known to Hambros, there was nothing in the transfer to concern the bank's Compliance Department. And there you had it – 3.5 million euros of freshly laundered money.

Spike propped his elbows on the desk and massaged his temples. It was the oldest trick in the book. He wasn't sure what upset him more: that Peter had done this thing, or that he'd considered Spike too distracted to notice.

The one part Spike couldn't get his head around was the Stanford scandal. Ostensibly, it had been Sir Anthony's arrest which had made Bonanza retract their campaign contribution, yet that had surely been an unforesee-able event. Had Peter planned to find some other excuse for Bonanza to pull the money? Or had he just used Sir Anthony's misfortune opportunistically? The latter possi-bility was the more galling, suggesting as it did that Peter had come up with the scheme himself and presented it to Siri Baxter. Spike still couldn't believe that of his partner, despite all the evidence to the contrary. The Peter he knew was egocentric, capricious and greedy. But he wasn't mali-cious, and he certainly wasn't stupid. Peter must have been blackmailed into it. Perhaps Siri Baxter had something over him. Spike was just pondering what that might be when he heard a rap at the door.

'I'm off,' Ana Lopes said. She turned to go, then changed her mind and stood there for a moment, as if lost for words. Very un-Ana-like. 'I don't know what's going on between you and Peter,' she continued. 'I like working here, and I like Peter, even if he can sail a bit close to the wind. But if there's something shady going on – with one of your clients, say – I just want you to know that I can't be involved.' She fixed him with her clever green eyes, and for the first time in their acquaintance Spike thought she looked vulnerable. 'I'm thirty-three next month, you see. I've already started over once in my life, and it wasn't easy. So I can't do it again.' With that, she quietly shut the door.

Spike sat there, both hands on his desk, staring at the space where Ana had stood, realising that his heart was beating very fast. One thing was certain: he was going to have to give careful consideration to what he did next.

63

Ana's delphic words of warning sat heavy in Spike's mind as he locked up the doors of Galliano & Sanguinetti. And as he walked past the lights of Jury's, he was struck by a renewed wave of anger. He could just imagine Peter inside, one elbow leaning on the bar, standing his cronies another bottle from the more expensive end of the wine list as they all revelled in the unexpected demise of Drew Stanford-Trench QC's glittering career.

By the time he got home, Spike was almost fizzing with righteous fury, so he paused on the front step and tried to shake himself out of it. Jessica had offered to cook them a special supper tonight, a proper family affair to get things back on track. Spike's worries about Peter and Drew would have to wait. Right now, his priority must be to do what he could to make her first night back a good one. So, face reset to a smile, he pushed open the front door.

Charlie was sitting at the kitchen table in his pyjamas, hunched in fascination over a perspex bowl covered in cling film. Spike kissed him hello, then peered at the dough inside: it had already risen so much it was pressing against the plastic.

'I may have slightly overdone the yeast,' Jessica called across from the stove. 'It got a bit out of control.'

Spike could hear the defensiveness in her tone. Jessica was a competent rather than confident chef, and cooking

302

under pressure had been known to make her angry. So he walked over and kissed the back of her neck. 'Smells delicious,' he said, looking down at the simmering pot of *salsa di pomodoro*. 'Can I do anything?'

'Maybe chop some olives?'

Spike found the jar at the back of the fridge and set about retrieving the olives from their watery graves.

'The surveyor called,' Jessica said. 'He's going to try and get to Catalan Bay tomorrow.' She threw him a glance. 'I mentioned the cracks in the walls.'

Spike bisected another olive. 'And?'

'He told me he'd check them out, but he wasn't surprised. Said every building in Gibraltar is subject to a certain amount of stress. Something to do with tectonic plates. I zoned out after that.'

Spike nodded in sympathy. Back in his schooldays, the peculiarities of Gibraltar's physical geography had been the subject of a thesis for a young Canadian who'd taught for a year at Bayside while completing her post-doctorate study. She'd lacked the deftness to pass onto her students the ardour she clearly felt for the topic, and Spike had wanted to lay his head down on his desk as he'd listened to her drone on about the fault line that lay between Africa and Europe. All he'd really taken away was a strong sense that the ground beneath their feet was far from stable. 'I still think we should pay the deposit,' he ventured.

He expected Jessica to reply that it would be wiser to wait for the survey, but she just turned to the sink and started straining the tomato sauce with a sieve. 'Why don't we clear the table?' She glanced around at Charlie with a tense smile. 'Then we can roll out the dough.'

64

Once Charlie was asleep, Spike poured himself a glass of wine and lay back on the futon as he waited for Jessica to finish her ablutions.

'Don't you think it's amazing how he can finish every sentence now,' Jessica called through from the bathroom.

'Dad's probably been reading him the same book every night,' Spike muttered, realising that he hadn't had time to read to Charlie in months. He took a large gulp of wine and closed his eyes. For most of the evening, he'd managed not to brood on Peter and his dark deeds, but the man was still there, lurking in one corner of his mind, rubbing his small hands together like some second-rate Mephistopheles. Spike knew he had to tell Jessica what Peter had done. But what if she advised him to take his suspicions to the FSC? Or to leave the practice altogether? Could he hack it as a lawyer practising alone? Probably not, he concluded darkly, remembering Drew's scathing assessment of his professional skills at the hospital.

'Sorry,' Jessica murmured, knotting her white waffle dressing-gown above her belly. She switched out the light and lay down next to him. Even at nine months pregnant, she somehow managed to make the manoeuvre look so easy.

'I need to tell you something, Jess.'

She turned her face to his. 'That sounds ominous.'

'It's to do with Peter.'

'Ah.'

'I found something at the office. Documentation that suggests a degree of financial impropriety on his part.' Jessica didn't reply, which was unusual, so he glanced over. 'Jess?'

She was lying motionless, but in the darkness he could see her eyes flitting from side to side, as though she was afraid to move any other part of her body. Spike sat up in alarm and flicked on the lights.

'I think my waters have broken.'

For a moment, Spike didn't move. Then he hurled himself onto his feet. 'Shall I call an ambulance?' He stumbled into his desk as he tried to pull on his trousers.

Despite everything, Jessica laughed. 'I told you you should've finished those antenatal classes. Just call a cab. Even you should be able to manage that.'

65

'What do you mean, *wait*?' Spike squared up to the five-foot-nothing midwife. 'She's in a lot of pain. Any fool can see that.'

The midwife ignored him and moved around the bed, where she guided Jessica's arm into a blood pressure cuff. '*She*'s not even 4 centimetres yet.'

The midwife raised her eyebrows, as though daring Spike to challenge her further. Feeling Jessica's hand squeeze his in warning, Spike resisted the urge to ask the girl if she was old enough to vote and instead looked about for reinforcements. Where was the matronly Sheffielder they usually dealt with?

'The longer you can do without pain relief the better,' the midwife went on, addressing her attentions to Jessica with a smile that Spike felt perfectly combined sympathy and sadism. 'But if you decide you *absolutely* need something, ask Dad to come and discuss it with me. Otherwise, I'll be back in an hour.'

The midwife turned on her heel and whipped the curtains around them in one brisk, violent movement. Moments later, Spike heard her offering a similar pitch to the couple in the adjacent bay – Moroccans, he'd concluded, though he hadn't seen them yet, just heard the man's basso mumblings interspersed by the occasional whimper of pain.

Jessica's grip on Spike's fingers tightened as another contraction hit. She fell silent as it reached its peak then, as the pain diminished, he saw tears slide down the side of her face. But it was the small cry of relief which was worse. 'What can I do?' he asked.

She didn't answer, just closed her eyes to ready herself for the next one, so Spike sat back in his chair, hearing the soft Arabic duet resume through the curtains. This wasn't working out as he'd hoped. He'd always thought that after the waters broke, the expectant mother would be rushed to the labour ward and within a few minutes a fragrant, bonny baby would be held aloft in triumph. The waiting had come as a surprise. He'd already expended most of his emotional energy and they weren't even in 'active' labour yet.

Suddenly Jessica's eyes flicked open, and Spike knew enough now to tell that the next contraction had arrived. This time she screamed, and when it was over, he stood up. 'There's got to be something they can give you.' He searched his mind for the right terms. 'Laughing gas or an epidural or something.' She didn't demur, so Spike pushed the damp hair out of her eyes. 'I'll be back in a minute.'

Out in the corridor, he scanned for the imperious, spray-tanned face of the young midwife, wondering if now might be a sensible time to start telling these people he was a litigator. But the woman was nowhere to be seen, so he walked over to the nurse at the front desk. She was on her phone, of course, so he tried what Jessica had called his most alluring smile, but the nurse just held up a hand and continued with her conversation.

Spike walked over to the water cooler, sinking two cups in fast succession as he stared up at the posters on the walls. More state-funded propaganda evangelising the near-magical benefits of breastfeeding – 'lactivism', he'd heard Jessica call it. Terrifying pictures counselling against the perils of meningitis. He thought back to that night at the police station when Marcela had been reported missing. Massetti's mugshot on the wall. It felt like a lifetime ago.

The doors of the maternity ward swung open, and a porter pushed a wheelchair past Spike towards the NICU. The woman in the chair wore a man's cardigan over her hospital gown and a pair of old slippers. Her eyes were red and raw; Spike averted his gaze and returned to the desk.

But by now the nurse was gone, so there was nothing to do but walk back to Jessica and admit defeat.

66

As soon as Spike re-entered the bay, he knew that something was wrong. The curtains around Jessica's bed were tightly drawn, and when he pulled them back, he saw the young midwife chewing on her cuticles. Robbed of its hauteur, her face suddenly looked childish and uncertain, and Spike could see the unease in her eyes as she watched a doctor analyse the printout that was spewing from the foetal heart-rate monitor. The man was remarkable only for the size of his paunch, the sort of person Spike wouldn't have looked twice at in the outside world.

The doctor held out a hand to the midwife, who meekly surrendered her notes. 'I'm concerned about these decelerations,' he said, skimming the chart with a frown that formed a pit in Spike's stomach. 'When did you last examine the mother?'

The midwife removed her fingers from her mouth, and Spike saw two spots of pink flush her cheeks. 'We're short-staffed tonight, Dr Sacco. Isn't it in the notes?'

Another contraction hit, and Jessica gripped the blue bed sheets, her face pale and contorted with pain. Spike couldn't trust himself to look at the midwife, so he turned instead to the doctor. 'Don't you think some kind of pain relief might be in order?'

But Dr Sacco wasn't listening; he was looking at the monitor, his face tense as he watched the green LCD digits plummet. An urgent beeping began, and the doctor reached out and slammed a hand against the call button.

A siren started to wail. Spike heard the sound of running footsteps, and suddenly the bay was full of focused professionals dressed in blue scrubs. Spike stepped out of their way, and as the doctor pulled back Jessica's blanket, they all saw the pool of blood soaking through her gown.

'Ready?' somebody said. Then they flipped Jessica onto a gurney, and everyone was running down the corridor towards the operating theatre.

67

'Just a few seconds,' Dr Sacco warned as he paused outside the theatre to let them say their goodbyes. Jessica's face was so pale now it frightened Spike to look at her. There wasn't time to say any of the things he wanted, so he just kissed her hand and told her that he loved her. Then the double doors swung closed, and there was nothing he could do but sit in the corridor and wait.

At some point, the call bell went off again, and Spike stood up and watched in dread as another team of medics sprinted past him up the corridor. Moments later, the doors burst open and Dr Sacco lumbered out of theatre, ripping off his latex gloves. Spike stared at the man in confusion, trying to understand why he was leaving if Jessica was still in surgery, and what that might mean.

As Dr Sacco passed, he squinted slightly, as though trying to recall who this poor chap was. Recognition hit as another nurse dodged around him, and though Sacco looked like he wanted to follow her, he found the compassion to place a hand on Spike's shoulder, applying just enough pressure to make him sit back down. Then he knelt beside Spike and looked up into his eyes. 'It's all right, Mr Navarro,' he said in a voice so clear and slow that it was as though he were talking to a child, or someone who didn't speak English very well. 'My consultant is in charge.'

Spike looked down at his feet, hoping that he wasn't going to be sick. Somewhere in the distance, he could hear the doctor still talking: 'Ms Attias is very capable. If it were my wife, I'd be glad to know she was in such safe hands.'

Spike moistened his mouth. 'Is Jessica going to die?'

Dr Sacco hesitated. 'We call it a placental abruption. That means the placenta has detached itself from the womb. There's a danger that we won't be able to stop the bleeding. There's also a risk to the baby – which is why we had to get your wife into theatre so quickly.'

'We're not married yet,' Spike murmured. It seemed important to get that across.

'This could have happened at any point in the pregnancy. Your partner . . .'

'Jessica . . .'

Dr Sacco gave a patient smile. '*Jessica* was lucky that this happened while she was in hospital, and the baby was at term. Speed is everything, you see, with this kind of event.' The doctor pressed his lips together, waiting for Spike to give the small nod which would show he'd understood.

Dr Sacco struggled to his feet. Somewhere in the distance, Spike realised that the emergency siren was still wailing, another man watching in terror as his wife was wheeled away. He forced himself to focus on the doctor's drooping brown eyes. 'We'll do everything we can,' he was saying, 'but Jessica has lost a great deal of blood. You ought to prepare yourself.' At the door, Dr Sacco turned. 'There's a chapel on the ground floor. If you wanted somewhere quiet.'

Then the doors swung closed again and the doctor was gone.

68

The minutes ticked past as Spike paced the strip-lit corridor. He'd spent too long in hospitals, too many hours waiting for a grim-faced medic to appear and lead him off to a private room where he or she could break the bad news. On the two worst occasions, his father had been with him: once as grieving widower, more recently as a patient. Part of Spike wished that Rufus were here now, and he felt for his phone. But then he decided that he couldn't face the task of putting what was happening into words. Not until he knew what they were up against.

To lose Jessica now would be unthinkable, just when they were so close to having everything that he'd only recently found out that he wanted. He'd wasted so much time, he realised, and the irony of it appalled him. He considered following Dr Sacco's advice and saying a prayer, but as he closed his eyes, all he could think of was a line by a poet whose name he could no longer remember. *I talk to God but the sky is empty . . .*

Suddenly the double doors swung open, and a woman pushing a clear plastic crib on wheels appeared. The nurse wiped her brow with the back of a latex-gloved hand, then grinned. 'Christ, it's hot in there.' She gestured down at the crib. 'Well, come on then. Meet your daughter!'

Spike felt his knees buckle slightly as he walked over and took a first look at the long-limbed purple creature inside.

'It's a . . . girl?' he said uncertainly, as he peered into the two knotted, bloodied eyes.

'So it would seem. And this one's a real beauty.' The nurse offered her little finger to the baby, and she grasped it as though she were holding on for dear life.

'Really?' Spike looked again into the crib. A short tuft of dark hair was growing from the back of the baby's wrinkled head, as though she were a small but aged member of some strange religious cult. 'Are you *sure* she's OK?'

'Ten fingers and toes. And her Apgar scores are terrific, considering.'

Spike felt his chin start to crumple. He fought it off. 'And the mother? Jessica? My fiancée?'

The nurse gave another toothy smile. 'She's lost a lot of blood. But Ms Attias is very pleased.'

69

Later, once they'd moved Jessica from the recovery ward to an amenity room, Dr Sacco agreed to let Spike see her. He found her awake, some kind of contraption feeding oxygen through her nose and a plastic tube looped over each ear. A midwife was fussing about with pillows, helping Jessica to sit up, and though her damp hair was sticking to her white cheeks, when she saw Spike the smile she gave was luminous.

The midwife dropped a straw into a plastic cup of water and held it to Jessica's mouth. 'Not too much,' she warned.

Jessica took an obedient sip, then sank back into the pillows. 'So you managed to get out of it after all,' she croaked, throwing the midwife a conspiratorial glance. 'My fiancé wasn't too taken with the business end of labour.'

The midwife scoffed as she bent down and picked up the baby. 'They never are.'

'Have you seen her yet?' Jessica whispered to Spike, eyes filling as she took the child in her arms. 'Isn't she beautiful?'

Spike gave what he hoped passed for an enthusiastic smile, and sat down on the edge of the bed. He reached over to touch his daughter's soft downy head as she started to feed.

'Look at that. She's a natural,' the midwife said in approval as she picked up a tiny pink wrist-tag from the side table. 'Baby Navarro, is it?'

'Juliet,' Jessica said without taking her eyes off the child's face. 'Juliet Navarro Sanguinetti.'

Spike felt his throat thicken. Juliet Sanguinetti. She'd given their daughter his sister's name.

And watching the midwife loop the plastic tag around Juliet's tiny wrist, he felt a tear roll down the side of his nose. For once in his life, he didn't brush it away. He just told himself to hold onto this moment. A single moment of unblemished happiness.

70

Stepping through the hospital doors, Spike was struck by a wall of sunlight, and felt himself stagger a little on the steps. A prosperous-looking woman in a suit swerved past him, heels clicking on the tiles, murmuring anxiously into her phone. Spike watched as the sliding doors swallowed her into the netherworld of the hospital, then turned and picked his way up Europort Avenue, disorientated by the rush of people. A whole night had passed since they had arrived at the hospital, he realised. And he half-expected everyone to stop in their tracks and stare at him, whispering in awe at what had just occurred. But they didn't, of course, because they couldn't have known, and even if they did, they probably wouldn't have been much moved by what seemed to him an astounding and unique experience, but in reality was just another part of the messy business of life. But as Spike watched these people bustle by, balancing their morning macchiatos and their brief-cases, clutching the hands of their snot-glazed children, he wondered how many of them had spent their own bleak night pacing the corridors of a hospital, waiting and hoping, trying to pray. Then he heard a noise and tried to place it. His phone.

'Son?' Rufus barked. 'Anyone there?' Beneath the veneer of impatience, Spike could hear the strain in his father's voice. He had to clear his throat before he trusted himself to speak. 'It's a girl, Dad.'

'Is she OK? Is Jessica OK?'

'They're both fine.'

A heaving sigh of relief. 'Charlie? *Char-lie*! He's coming to the phone now. Is there a name?'

'Juliet.'

His father emitted a thin, reedy noise from the back of his throat. Spike heard a rustle, then Charlie's high-pitched voice came onto the line, 'Papi?'

'You've got a sister, Charlie. She's called Juliet.'

A long pause. 'I made a Lego tower.'

Spike laughed. 'Is it a big one?'

'The biggest in the world. Ever.'

'Then maybe you could take a photo, and we can show it to Mama and the baby. What do you think?'

'OK.' Spike heard the sound of the phone hitting the kitchen floor, little feet slapping away.

'Hello?' came Rufus's voice.

'I'm on my way home, Dad. Just to get a change of clothes.'

'Well done, son.'

Spike tried to ignore the tightness in his throat. 'See you in a bit, Dad.' He slipped the phone back into his pocket. He was just mustering the courage to brave the crowds on Main Street when he heard another voice call out his name, and turned.

Danny Garcia looked a little taken aback by the enthusiasm of Spike's greeting. He retrieved his hand from Spike's grasp and massaged the fingers, as though hoping to restore circulation.

'Sorry, Danny. My fiancée just had a baby girl.'

A shadow crossed Garcia's face, but he quickly rallied. 'That's great news. All well, I trust?'

Spike nodded and smiled. Suddenly he couldn't stop smiling. 'How was the surfing course?'

'It was . . .' Garcia clicked his teeth. 'It was probably more Laura's thing than mine. But I think *she* enjoyed it. I heard Massetti kept you busy. A murder charge, no less.' Garcia gave a low whistle. 'But the man's got judgment, I'll give him that.'

'I don't follow.'

'When he asked for you, he chose the right brief.'

Spike looked Garcia in the eye. 'I thought the referral came from you, Danny.'

Garcia shook his head. 'Massetti requested you after he fired me. I told him you were more of a tax specialist these days, but he was adamant.'

Spike felt his euphoria fade. Garcia didn't seem to have noticed, just gingerly held out a hand for Spike to shake as they reached an unattractive prefab that some Pollyanna of an architect had seen fit to christen 'Regal House'. 'Well, this is me,' Garcia said. 'Congratulations again, Spike. On the birth. And the result.'

71

As he continued through the Old Town, Spike tried to reason with himself. Why shouldn't Massetti have asked for him by name? Spike Sanguinetti might not be the fixture in the Mags that he once had been, but he knew he still had something of a reputation as a criminal defence counsel. Yet the niggle remained: why would Massetti have acted as though Spike had been foisted upon him that day at the prison? As though he didn't give a damn what happened to him?

Spike reached the corner of Fishmarket Road. Uphill lay the route home; downhill, the sea. Maybe it was just the eerie chime of the masts, but something made him turn towards the marina. The first boat he passed was a cheap inflatable dinghy, unremarkable save for the oversized engine that told Spike it was used for more than just pleasure trips. Tobacco smuggling had long been part of life on the Rock – hardly surprising when cigarettes retailed at 25 euros a carton in Gibraltar and 40 in Spain. And as he stared down at the sun-bleached rubber, Spike was taken back to all those long summer nights he'd spent as a teenager with Joseph Guzman and Sebastian Alvarez. The hit of adrenaline as they'd powered a boat just like this one through the darkness towards the Spanish coast, cut the engine and drifted into the beach, where the boys from La Línea would wade through the blood-warm water to meet them with rolls of pesetas in plastic bags. Seba and Joe – what had happened to them? They'd had their children young; he'd barely seen them since.

A good-looking youth in a red polo shirt and matching shorts dozed on the deck of the next vessel, a sailor's cap tilted over his eyes. A tender, judging by the man's livery, and by the sleek stained-wood of the hull. Ocean Village had been conceived as bait to lure the chic yachting crowd, and looking at the well-heeled horde currently breakfasting at the 'internationally themed' restaurants on the harbour's pontoons, the plan had worked.

The *Rebecca* lay a few berths along. Her tarpaulin was down; Spike pulled out his handkerchief and leant over to scrub some of the muck from the windscreen. Through the glass, he could just make out the dials and gauges, cracked and dirty with disuse.

'She doesn't look like much, does she?'

Spike spun round and saw the youth standing on the quayside behind him, scratching his tanned stomach with a fingertip.

'I'm looking for Christopher Massetti.'

The youth knocked back his cap to light a cigarette, then waved the smoke out of his eyes. 'The old guy? I expect he'll be at the hospital. They want him there every day, he says.' He rolled his eyes in the way that men in their early twenties do when talking about the elderly and infirm. 'He hasn't stopped going on about it since I let him have some fuel.'

Spike inclined his head. 'Massetti's taken the *Rebecca* out?'

'You'd never think it to look at her, but she's sound enough. He's had her out on the water three . . . maybe four times these past weeks?'

'Vincent?' An autocratic female voice rang out, and they both turned to see a well-maintained woman of a certain age standing by the tender. She held a boxy white shopping-bag in each hand, and, had the filler in her face allowed it, she almost certainly would have been scowling. 'We did say ten o'clock, didn't we?'

Vincent crushed out his cigarette just a few seconds later than he might have done. 'We did, Mrs Fitzgerald. I'll be right with you.'

Spike watched them cast off, then turned back to the *Rebecca* and unhooked the first peg of the tarpaulin, wondering idly what kind of penalty he might expect to receive for trespassing on someone else's boat. But then he saw the crate on the deck filled with six-litre bottles of the bio-ethanol gel that Christopher Massetti used in his marine stove, and decided to take his chances.

He lifted the tarpaulin and stepped aboard, cursing beneath his breath as he stumbled over a boathook lying on the deck, its shaft polished and new. Hunching down the narrow steps towards the hold, he found the hatchway divided in two, a lock in the middle. The wood flexed a little as he pulled the handle towards him, but held fast.

He reached back up for the boathook and wedged it into the gap between the hatch doors. There was a splintering crack as he rammed the shaft down hard with the heel of his hand, then one half of the hatch flew open, releasing the overpowering stench of a chemical toilet. Spike reached inside and undid the internal bolt, grappling on the wall until he found a light switch. Then he walked over to the twin cabin beds at the end of the hold, eyes adjusting to the grimy sodium glow.

One bed had been neatly made up, the grey wool blanket pulled taut and tucked under with the kind of hospital corners that would have made a drill sergeant turn misty-eyed. The other had been stripped down; lying on the wooden frame was a pile of chess magazines. Spike sat down on Massetti's bed and picked up a well-thumbed copy of *Pergamon Chess*, imagining the old man lying there, debating the advantages of the Queen's Gambit over Fool's Mate as the waves lapped around him. His neck was aching again; he reached up to massage it, then heard paper rustle beneath him and slipped a hand under the blanket.

It was just a plain brown package. The envelope had been slit with a paper knife, and Spike reached inside and pulled out a wad of papers. It took him a moment to work out what he was looking at. Then he saw that the cover letter was headed 'Rosia Road Surgery'.

'Dear Mr Massetti,' Spike read. 'Further to your Subject Access Request (SAR), in accordance with the Data Protection Act 1998, please find enclosed a copy of your medical records dated from five years ago to the present day . . .'

Spike shuffled through the medical notes, feeling his breathing accelerate as he recognised the same sections he'd forced Eloise Capurro to read out in court carefully highlighted and annotated. He sat back and rubbed a palm across his face. When the evidence had been delivered to the courtroom, Spike had assumed it must have come from Danny

Garcia. It had never occurred to him that someone like Massetti could have been the source. But then he supposed that had been exactly what Massetti had wanted – for Spike to take him at face value, an old man with a grudge and a chronic drink problem. Someone to be pitied.

Spike stood up and smacked his head smartly against the fibreglass roof. Swearing, he spun around, eyes scanning the cramped interior. An Adidas holdall sat on the counter next to the marine stove; he zipped it open and pulled out handfuls of Y-fronts and a faded pair of paisley pyjamas. Massetti had used a sandwich bag to hold his wash things. It was a depressing sight, and in other circumstances Spike might have felt sorry for the man. But not today.

Heart shifting, Spike turned to the bed and ripped back the tightly made sheets. Then he wedged his fingers beneath the mattress and tipped it up. And there, in the cavity beneath, he found what he was looking for. Box file after box file of Massetti's carefully prepared research.

He opened the lid of the nearest file, jolting in shock as he saw a photograph of his younger, leaner self staring up at him. '*The Devil's Advocate*', the headline read; '*How far will one lawyer go for his client?*' A 'think' piece', the journalist had dubbed it, published in *Vox*, a now defunct local rag covering legal and political affairs. Five years ago, it had caused something of a stir amongst the legal community on the Rock, insinuating as it did that Spike's defence of his then client, Solomon Hassan, had exceeded the bounds of appropriate behaviour. Spike felt his mind drift back to all the professional and personal compromises he'd made over the past few years. If the author had known what had really gone on that summer in Morocco, he could have placed the article in a far more prestigious publication than *Vox*.

Underneath, he found a complete copy of the MI5 file on Esteban Reyes, Marcela Peralta's and John Capurro's names neatly underlined. He checked the postmark: Massetti had requested it three years ago, as soon as the information had been declassified.

The last box file was filled with notebooks. Spike recognised the blue hardback covers immediately, and felt his guts churn. He leant in and picked up the most recent of Marcela's diaries. The last entry was dated September 13, the day before Marcela had been reported missing.

Terrible argument last night with Tony at Dragon Trees. It was just like the old days, Tony telling me in that cold, logical way he has that he would manage the situation. But Eloise is <u>dead</u>. First Jack, and now Eloise, <u>who knew nothing</u>, who had nothing to do with what happened to Esteban. But I know we have no one to blame but ourselves . . .

The diary that had been posted anonymously to Spike was missing. In its place was a sheaf of photocopied sheets, carefully stapled in one corner. The evidence was undeniable. It was Massetti who had sent Marcela's diary to Spike. And the only person who could have taken it was the one who'd killed her.

Suddenly the stench of the place was too much. Spike lurched for the hatchway, knocking over a bin filled with empty tin cans as he gulped for cleaner air. He leapt off the boat onto the quayside and ran towards the Marine

Office. The hut was empty, so he reached behind the counter for the Mooring Ledger Book, trying to make sense of the scribbled entries. At 2 p.m. on 3rd September, he read, the *Rebecca* had left the marina. Then, on the morning of 5th September, she was back in her berth. Since then, she'd been marked as present at the marina every day.

Between those two days lay a date Spike was unlikely to forget: 4th September, the night of the fire that had killed Eloise Capurro.

Spike tore out the page and ran outside. As he reached the road, he realised that there was only one member of the *Mil Cortes* who was still alive. And he was at the hospital, too.

72

As Spike dialled the number for New Mole House, he saw that his hands were shaking. 'Put me through to DI Isola. Tell him it's an emergency . . .'

Even at a fast jog, it took Spike ten minutes to make it back across town to the hospital. All the way there, he kept trying to reassure himself that Sir Anthony couldn't be in any real danger. Massetti had kept Sir Anthony alive for a reason: to atone for the death of Esteban Reyes by taking the blame for the murders that his son had committed. Esteban had died knowing that he'd been falsely accused of killing two people, and Sir Anthony would suffer the same. An eye for an eye: Massetti would find a pleasing symmetry in that, Spike thought, remembering the copy of Dante's *Divine Comedy* that he'd seen in his apartment at Governor's Meadow Estate.

Nevertheless, by the time Spike reached the hospital, he found himself increasing his pace. He sprinted down the corridors of the first floor but found Sir Anthony's room empty. Lights out, bed stripped; for a moment Spike thought that nature might have done Massetti's work for him. He heard the squeak of unoiled wheels, and turned to see a hospital porter pushing an empty gurney down the corridor. 'What happened to the patient in here?'

'They discharged him yesterday,' the porter said. 'The police took him home.'

Spike exhaled in relief. If Massetti went looking for Sir Anthony at Dragon Trees, he'd find him recuperating under police guard.

'Funny thing,' the porter chuckled to himself, and Spike looked back up. 'The old man's on death's door for a week, and no one comes to see him but his son. Now he gets two visitors in the space of an hour.'

Spike caught the porter's sleeve as he turned to go. 'The other man. Did you see where he went?'

The man scrunched up his face as he tried to remember. 'He was after directions, I think.'

'To the Liver Ward?' Spike prompted.

'Well, he looked pretty yellow, I'll grant you that.' The porter tutted in sympathy, then snapped his fingers. 'I know. He said he knew someone who'd just had a baby.'

Spike felt his body tense up. Then he turned and sprinted for the lifts, hammering a fist on the button. He was about to abandon it for the stairs when the doors parted and he stepped inside, sensing the other passengers exchanging concerned glances behind him as he repeatedly punched the button for the fourth floor. At last the doors opened, and Spike dodged out sideways, swerving past porters and labouring women pacing the corridors, leaning on the arms of their partners.

He stopped a few yards from Jessica's room. All around he heard familiar sounds: nervous laughs, low moans of pain. More couples waiting for their lives to implode. Maybe it would be fine, he told himself. Perhaps he was just being paranoid.

Then Spike looked through the glass panel and saw Christopher Massetti sitting in a chair in the corner of Jessica's room. Cradled in his arms, wrapped in a white blanket, lay his daughter, Juliet.

73

Spike pushed open the door, and Massetti looked up with a frown. Then he raised a finger to his lips and beckoned Spike in. Juliet was asleep, Spike saw, the back of her head cupped in one of Massetti's huge palms. Spike glanced round at Jessica, searching for some indication of life, but her face was turned away from him and he didn't want to risk moving around the bed.

'Hello, Christopher,' Spike said, trying not to focus on the strong, callused fingers cradling his daughter's fragile skull. The bones were still unfused at birth, the midwife had said. One needed to be careful.

'She's dreaming,' Massetti murmured, and Spike forced a smile, feeling the muscles of his face ache with the effort. He made himself sit down on the chair by the empty cot. In the silence, he listened for Jessica's breathing, but all he could hear was the swish of nylon-covered thighs as a nurse bustled past the door.

Massetti pressed the baby to his chest, one hand stroking her back as he whispered sweet nothings into her tiny ear. He must have come straight from the marina, Spike thought. Above his docksider shoes, Spike could see his ankle bones, blue and sharp beneath the thin yellow skin.

'I saw you bring in Jessica yesterday,' Massetti said. 'Came to pay my respects. Looks like she's had a bit of a time of it.'

Juliet twitched beneath her blanket, and Spike felt a hot sensation prickle over his scalp. 'I'm not sure Jessica wants too many people handling the baby.' He made as if to get up, but Massetti glanced at him sharply, and he lowered himself back into the chair.

'The Marine Officer called,' Massetti resumed. 'Said someone had broken into my boat.'

Spike heard a faint noise, and looked down to see Juliet's mouth fixed around Massetti's little finger.

'Hungry, aren't we?' Massetti whispered. 'She's got a taste for life, this one.'

'I wish you'd give Juliet to me, Christopher.' Spike tried to keep his voice low and calm, hoping that Massetti wouldn't notice the crack in it. 'Her mother's hardly let me have a minute with her.'

Massetti nodded, but then they both heard the distant sound of sirens drifting in over the Europort, and he drew the baby closer. 'I never wanted a child, myself.' He gave Juliet a fond stroke of the head, and her blanket slipped down, revealing her tiny legs in their white romper suit, still kinked from their months in the womb. 'Only a fool would bring an innocent child into a world like this.' Massetti covered Juliet tenderly back up with the blanket. 'I knew you'd work it out in the end. Once you'd seen me at the marina. That was bad luck.'

Spike slid his hand into his jacket pocket, and Massetti narrowed his eyes. 'I took it from the Marina Office,' Spike said, as he laid the square of folded paper on the bed. 'No one has to know. You could just give Juliet to me and leave. Sail your boat back to Spain. Wait and see what happens with the transplant.'

The sirens grew louder, and Massetti gave a regretful smile. 'A man my age? An alcoholic? They don't put you at the top of the list, you know.'

Surely he wouldn't hurt her, Spike told himself. No one could hurt such a tiny baby. But then he thought of the infant he'd seen taken to a mortuary in Valletta all those years ago, and he remembered that monstrous things happened every day. And Massetti was a monster, he suddenly realised, because only a psychopath could have done the things he'd done to Eloise and Marcela.

Spike got to his feet and took a slow step towards Massetti. 'At least you managed to clear your father's name. No one can take that away from you.'

'That's what Eloise Capurro said.'

Spike froze. 'You didn't mean to kill her,' he coaxed. 'I know that now. You just wanted her to tell you who "Laurel" was.' It was a guess, and a terror paralysed Spike as he wondered if he'd gone too far. But Massetti just stroked a thumb down the side of Juliet's face. 'It was the only thing I didn't know,' he said. 'Not then. Not until I found the diary. And it took a long time for Dr Capurro to tell me it was Anthony Stanford. But by then the fire had taken hold.' Massetti looked back at Spike, and Spike saw condemnation in his eyes. 'I asked *you* to do it. That day in my flat. To talk to her. But you wouldn't. So I had to do it myself.'

Spike held out both hands. '*Please* give Juliet to me.' The baby whimpered under the pressure of Massetti's grip. 'It's hard for her to breathe, Christopher. When you hold her so tight.'

Massetti stared down at the child. Then his baggy face crumpled, and he let out a terrible, racking sob. Spike took another step forward, muscles tensed, preparing himself to run at the man. He could see the tears dripping down Massetti's yellow cheeks, catching in the bristles of his beard, grey eyes creased with pain. But then Massetti extended his arms, and Spike reached out and took his daughter, amazed even now at her lightness, hearing a gasp he didn't recognise as his own emerge from the back of his throat. When he looked back up, Massetti was gone.

'Spike?' Jessica rasped. She pushed herself up onto one elbow and gazed at him. 'Was that the doctor?'

Spike didn't answer, just clasped their daughter to his chest and kissed her soft warm cheek. Outside, the wail of the sirens grew more urgent.

Spike sat in the patrol car, watching DI Isola strut around the Ambulance Bay, yelling into his mobile phone. The detective's lantern jaw was tense with frustration, and Spike felt a vague sense of sympathy for whichever unlucky subordinate had drawn the short straw and been forced to call with what was evidently bad news. Reprimands delivered, Isola yanked open the car door and pitched himself into the driver's seat.

'So they lost him,' Spike said.

'Ceremony of the fucking Keys,' Isola spat. 'Massetti walked straight out of the hospital into a sea of Redcoats.'

Spike held his tongue as he waited for the man's fury to dissipate. He couldn't remember ever feeling so tired. 'Have you tried the boat yet?' he asked.

'What is it with the bloody boat?' Isola retorted. Spike raised an eyebrow, and Isola looked away with a grunt, which was as close as Spike would ever get to an apology, he supposed.

'Two officers were despatched to the marina as soon as we got your call,' Isola resumed. 'But there was no sign of Massetti. And we still don't have a warrant to go aboard.'

Spike reached up and massaged his aching neck. Then he took out the page he'd torn from the Marine Ledger and passed it to Isola. The detective looked at it for a moment, then back up at Spike, eyes widening as if to say, '*And*?'

Spike wondered if he had the energy to explain it all to Isola. Then he thought of his daughter cradled in Massetti's hands, and sat up. 'We were all working on the assumption that Massetti couldn't have killed Marcela because he'd fled to Spain.'

'And because there's no record of him crossing the border back to Gib,' Isola said defensively.

'That's because Massetti didn't cross the border *on foot*.' Spike tapped the Marine Ledger with his finger. 'He took the *Rebecca* out the day before the fire. Probably sailed her round the headland to Spain and moored at one of the fishing ports by La Línea. Then he walked back across the land border to Gib on the same day. You can check that, I suppose?'

Isola nodded.

'The next night, Massetti set the fire at the Capurro house. He hung around at the scene just long enough for someone to see him, then fled across the border to Spain.'

Isola looked down at the page again. 'And then he sailed the *Rebecca* back to the Rock that same night . . .'

'While the emergency services were all busy tackling the fire,' Spike completed. 'From then on, he stayed hidden on his boat. Kept out of sight during the day, then did what he needed to do at night.'

'Massetti had it all worked out,' Isola murmured, a certain amount of admiration in his voice.

Spike nodded. 'He even built in his own alibi. No one could ever have imagined he'd killed Marcela if they thought he was still on the run in Spain.'

'But what about Anthony Stanford?' Isola asked, and Spike could tell he was thinking about the CCTV footage.

'Massetti knew there was a camera outside the Capurro house,' Spike said. 'It came up during his trial. All he had to do was make sure that the only person captured on film was Sir Anthony.'

'That still doesn't explain why Stanford was there that night.'

Spike shrugged. 'Maybe Massetti summoned him. Sent him a text from Eloise Capurro's phone.' Spike looked away, trying not to think of what Massetti must have done to Eloise to make her give up Sir Anthony's name. 'The point is, Massetti had already started the fire by the time Anthony arrived. Then later, once Anthony was in the frame for Eloise's murder, Massetti sent me Marcela's diary to make sure that the police knew Anthony had a motive to kill the other members of the *Mil Cortes*.'

'All because of what they did to his father?'

Spike nodded, eyes on the Ambulance Bay outside, watching through the passenger window as the gates opened with a dull clank. The more he thought through everything that had happened since he'd agreed to take Massetti's case, the more he kept remembering details which troubled him. The business card Dr Martinez had found in Massetti's pocket which had led her to Spike's door. The newspaper articles about Esteban Reyes left so casually on Massetti's desk for Spike to see. The fact that Massetti had waited for his trial to end before revealing the note that John Capurro had sent summoning him to the hospital, making Spike believe he'd somehow won the old man's trust. A series of random events, Spike had assumed. But were they? What if they were all part of Massetti's plan? Mechanisms to arouse Spike's sympathy and ignite his interest in an ancient miscarriage of justice?

Isola pulled Spike back to the present, as he had a habit of doing. 'But where did Massetti get the morphine?'

Spike plucked at his lower lip between finger and thumb, then shook his head in defeat. Just one more thing to add to his long list of variables.

Isola's radio buzzed and he snatched it up. 'You got it? Then get aboard. I don't want to waste any more time.'

Spike watched as a young paramedic helped a stout, middle-aged woman out of the back of the ambulance, her head lolling. Then he looked back at Isola. 'I think I know where Massetti might be.'

75

Though the Ceremony of the Keys was over, the streets were still clogged with tourists, so Isola parked the patrol car on the corner of Bomb House Lane and they continued together on foot. As they walked up Convent Ramp, Spike made out the Moorish Castle rising from the flank of the Rock, the medieval prison where they'd hanged Esteban Reyes. A Union Jack hung limply from its ramparts.

'I meant to say,' Isola muttered. 'Congratulations on the baby.'

It was a grudging compliment. But Spike knew what it must have cost a man who'd once had Jessica within his romantic cross-hairs, so he was grateful. He was about to say so, but when he looked across at Isola, his eyes were focused on the road. So he just nodded.

Inside the wrought-iron gates of the Alameda Gardens, a family of English tourists were admiring the bust of General Eliott, the youngest straddling a black ceremonial cannon as her father anxiously tried to capture the spontaneity of the moment with a selfie stick.

Then, beneath the low boughs of the Judas tree, Spike saw what he'd expected to find. 'Over there,' he said, pointing at the figure slumped on the park bench. Lying on the gravel beneath the seat were two bottles of whiskey, one empty, the other with its seal unbroken.

Isola crouched down and laid two fingers on Christopher Massetti's neck. Then he turned to Spike and shook his head.

One of Massetti's arms was dangling over the side of the bench, like Marat in his bath. His yellowed eyes were fixed on the Judas tree, the skin of his face swollen with mosquito bites. There were flecks of vomit in his beard, and the smell of it took Spike back to that day in Massetti's flat, when he'd thought that the man was going to die, friendless and unmourned.

Spike looked down at his dead client and wondered what more he could have done. He took in the sunken cheeks, the dark patches of urine on his trousers. Then he turned and walked back towards the hospital.

PART SEVEN

76

Looking back, Spike found it hard to remember the days after Jessica had brought the baby home from the hospital, such was the grimness of the nights that followed. And he hoped he might someday be able to forget the stress of the inconveniently timed move into their new house. Yet now, sitting in an armchair in front of the wood-burning stove, with Juliet asleep in a Moses basket at his elbow, he couldn't help but feel content.

Not even the discomfiting presence of his business partner could entirely puncture the mood. Peter Galliano sat there like Henry VIII in one of his more benevolent humours, red lips pouting in approval as he cast his quick eyes around the sitting room. 'Well, I must say, Spike. You've done very well,' he boomed.

Spike glanced into the cot, and Peter produced a face of exaggerated contrition and continued sotto voce. 'The child's angelic, of course.' He waved a vague hand at the Moses basket. 'But the *house*. It's so light. And spacious. I mean, look at the size of that thing.' He pointed a fat finger at the Christmas tree, nose wrinkling at the glitter-covered baubles that Charlie had made at nursery, the crooked star askew on the top branch.

Spike shrugged. It was a little overdone, but secretly he rather liked it. Beneath the tree sat an enormous Fortnum

& Mason Christmas hamper that Peter had brought as a housewarming present. It bore all the hallmarks of the recycled corporate gift, Spike thought, and he hoped he wouldn't find a card inside from Siri Baxter that Peter had forgotten to remove. At any rate, it was loaded with delicacies that no breastfeeding mother would ever touch – foie gras, blue goat's cheese, dark chocolate liqueurs . . .

Spike looked back at the Moses basket and saw Juliet's eyelids flicker, then close again. She *was* beautiful, he'd decided. And even if that was just some atavistic urge that all fathers felt, no one could dispute that her skin was soft and smelled of something delicious. Even the alarming Mohican of black hair had given way to an unexpected covering of golden fuzz.

Peter cleared his throat. 'A longer commute into work, of course.' It took Spike a moment to recognise the inference – that his paternity leave was expected to end with the holidays. He watched as Peter pulled out his cigarettes and held them up enquiringly.

'You'll have to go out on the balcony. Come on. It's this way.'

Upstairs, the door to Rufus's bedroom was ajar, and Spike paused for a moment to watch his father at his easel, blurring the waves with the pad of a thumb. Sensing his son's presence, he looked round and smiled, and Spike wondered if his blue eyes weren't perhaps that little bit dimmer since he'd learned the news of Marcela's murder. Hearing a noise behind him, Spike turned to see Peter waiting on the landing, tapping one Italian-leather-shod foot.

He guided Peter between unopened packing boxes into their bedroom, then forced open the shutters. They stood in silence for a while on the balcony, watching the surf crash against the sand below. Then Peter canted his head and contemplated Spike though his long black eyelashes. 'I'm sorry about how we left it, Spike. That night when we discussed Siri's donation.' Peter blew out a smoke ring and watched it evaporate in the darkening light. 'It was a grave lapse of judgment on my part. I see that now. And I can only give you my word that it will never happen again.' His cigarette had burnt down; he dropped it onto the cracked tiles of Spike's balcony and crushed out the embers under his heel. 'I'm sure you've given a lot of thought, as have I, to what the right thing is to do under the circumstances. Whether an error of such magnitude merits investigation by the appropriate authorities.' He peered up at Spike, wet eyes filled with just the right amount of self-reproach. 'But looking around your beautiful home, seeing your *darling* daughter, I sense this may not be the ideal time to risk the fortunes of our little firm.' He dropped his gaze thoughtfully. 'Because it *is* a partnership, Spike. In the truest sense of the word. Galliano *&* Sanguinetti. Unlimited liability, as it were.' As if to labour the point, Peter lifted his walking cane and scraped the tip along a fissure that ran through the concrete. 'Nasty crack, that.'

The first peal of a cry came from downstairs. 'That's my cue,' Peter said, clasping his hands together and giving Spike his most bountiful smile. 'I've outstayed my welcome.' He laid a hand on Spike's shoulder and gave it a firm squeeze. 'I'm so glad we sorted all that out, old friend.'

77

The lamp posts on Main Street had been garlanded with Christmas lights, and Spike gazed up at them as he approached Marcela's, finding twinkling sleighs and angels, Christmas trees and bells. He paused for a moment outside the restaurant, watching through the frost-sprayed window as Sofia Peralta prepared for evening service. After Marcela's funeral, Sofia had talked about selling up and moving back to England. Perhaps she'd changed her mind. In that vintage black dress, with her glossy bob tucked behind her ears, Spike was struck again by her resemblance to Marcela, and he wondered what Sir Anthony might have thought to see her there, framed in the soft light of the window.

He started up the western face of the Rock, eyes drawn to its limestone summit. One day, he thought, some bright young thing trying to make a name in marketing would suggest they erect a giant star on its peak for Christmas. The press images would go global.

Turning onto the road to Dragon Trees, Spike recognised the same family of apes crouching on their outcrop, watching in silence as he rang the bell. A minute passed, then the door was opened by a slim, dark man in pink scrubs, holding a bumper festive edition of *¡Hola!* under one arm.

'I'm here to see Sir Anthony.'

The Spanish nurse bowed his head and beckoned Spike in with a long finger. '*Por aquí, señor.*'

Sir Anthony's beautiful glass cube was swathed in gauze. No magnificent views on display this afternoon, just a sombre half-light accentuated by the smell of antiseptic. The elegant art deco dining table had gone, replaced by a hospital bed, the multiple wires and leads that snaked across the glass floor suggesting a complex array of adjustable functions. On an occasional table in the corner sat a small artificial Christmas tree, decked with blue lights and a string of sad-looking tinsel. Remembering the scene he'd just left in Catalan Bay, Spike wondered if it might be the most depressing thing he'd ever seen.

Sir Anthony was propped up against an arrangement of thin pillows. His steel-grey hair was half-heartedly combed in a manner that revealed patches of alopecia Spike had never noticed before.

'Tea-coffee?' the nurse sang out.

Spike shook his head, and the man melted away. A high-backed dining chair had been positioned by the bed, and Spike sat down on it, averting his eyes from the palsied side of Sir Anthony's face, from the cloudy drool darkening the collar of his pyjamas.

Spike reached over and placed a gentle hand on the old man's shoulder. Sir Anthony shifted his head to the right, and Spike was relieved to find his good eye bright and alert. A bandaged arm emerged from the sheets, and Spike took his hand in his, feeling the coolness of the crêpey skin. 'Can I get you something, Anthony? Some water?'

'Maybe later,' Sir Anthony rasped, his voice slow but surprisingly clear. 'Sorry about the gloom. The sun hurts my eyes.'

Spike peered down at the white dressing wrapped tightly around the old man's wrist.

'It was a burn,' Sir Anthony finally admitted. 'From the night Eloise died.' He withdrew his arm beneath the sheets. 'I thought it had healed, but it seems I picked something up at the hospital.' Sir Anthony stared up at the gauze-covered glass. 'She was trapped on the top floor. The door was locked.' His voice grew hoarse as he remembered. 'I tried to reach her, but there was too much smoke.'

Sir Anthony said nothing for a while after that, and Spike was just about to stand up and leave. But then he spoke again, 'I had a letter from a friend in the Service last week,' he whispered, making an awkward movement with one shoulder. 'Nothing official; he just wanted to warn me that I'm to be stripped of my knighthood. Good of him, I suppose.'

'I'm sorry.' They both knew it was a platitude, but part of Spike meant it, and it pained him to see the old man twist his mouth into what remained to him of a smile. 'What's to be sorry about? Seventy odd years ago, I let an innocent man go to his death. To safeguard my own interests.'

'There were others involved,' Spike said. 'People whose lives would have been destroyed.'

Sir Anthony nodded. 'I've thought about it often over the years. And I suppose there's something in what you say. I might not have been the oldest of the *Mil Cortes*, but I was the most pragmatic. Perhaps I have my dissolute father to thank for that. Such things teach a boy to be resourceful.' His gaze flicked over to Spike, and he was left in no doubt of the subtext. 'John Capurro was a hot-headed fool. Tito was just a boy, almost catatonic with grief. And Marcela . . .' Sir

Anthony sighed. 'Well, Marcela was what I wanted most in the world.' He made a small motion with his forefinger, and Spike picked up the cup of water on the bed stand and held the straw to his mouth. 'But, of course, Marcela believed she loved Esteban in that way all teenage girls do. Especially when it's someone they can't have. And when Esteban died, and then his wife, I knew she could never forgive herself, let alone care for me. I had hoped we might be reconciled, but the guilt was too great. We never spoke when we crossed paths, never sought each other out. And, you know, John was just the same. Until he learnt he was dying, and decided that he had to see Esteban's son. To unburden himself.'

'Massetti's dead,' Spike said. 'Did you know?'

Spike caught the ghost of a smile on Sir Anthony's withered mouth. 'Drew's been keeping me informed.'

I'll bet he has, Spike thought. It wasn't as though he had much else to occupy his time. 'Can't get arrested' had been Peter's injudicious choice of phrase. 'The Attorney General's considering whether to charge Massetti posthumously,' Spike added.

Sir Anthony gave a quiet click of the tongue. 'Why don't they just leave the poor bastard alone?'

'He murdered three people, Anthony. In cold blood.'

'Perhaps.'

Spike remembered the conversation he'd had with Isola on the day that Juliet had been born, and leant in closer. 'Massetti couldn't have killed John Capurro. He didn't have access to the morphine.'

Sir Anthony managed a chuckle. 'It wasn't me, Spike, if that's what you're worried about. Though we did have the drug in the house. The morphine was prescribed many years ago. When the doctors said there was nothing more they could do for Angela.' His voice faltered. 'She was in a great deal of pain towards the end. A more devoted spouse might have used it to put her out of her misery.'

It took Spike a moment to work out what Sir Anthony was saying. Then it finally made sense. 'You think it was Eloise.'

Sir Anthony gave a non-committal grunt. 'I think that Dr Capurro loved her husband very much.'

Spike stared into Sir Anthony's good eye, watching the pupil dart about like a trapped insect, wondering if he could ask the question that had been preying on his mind; if the old man could muster the strength to answer. 'That night at the Dockyard, Anthony. Who was supposed to plant the bomb? Was it you?'

Sir Anthony closed his eyes. Spike assumed that marked the end of the conversation, but then he started to speak again, his voice low and strained. 'John,' he exhaled. 'John was meant to do it. None of us knew what was in the box when we brought it over the border, but as soon as John saw the bomb, he knew what Raúl expected of him. But when it came down to it, John's nerves failed him, as they always did. But Tito had been listening to everything Raúl said that night. Everything, of course, except how to work the timer.' Sir Anthony gave a sudden, hacking cough. 'Esteban and I were so close to stopping the bomb going off. But then we heard voices, so I grabbed hold of Tito and fled. But Esteban was made of sterner stuff.' Sir Anthony's strength was fading. 'After that, it was just a case of survival. Trying to keep the rest of us out of gaol. But Esteban never broke. He stayed loyal to his *Mil Cortes*. They strike medals for that sort of thing, you know.'

'I saw Drew at the hospital. He's very angry.'

Sir Anthony's hand emerged again from the blankets and took Spike's. 'It's easier for him to hold you responsible. That way he doesn't have to think about what I've done.'

In the corner of his eye, Spike saw the Spanish nurse hovering with a bowl of lavender-scented water and a sponge. He squeezed Sir Anthony's hand, then got to his feet as the nurse rolled the patient over and drew back the blankets. Spike turned away, but not before he'd seen the bedsores covering Sir Anthony's legs and buttocks. 'Tell him I said goodbye.'

'*Sí, sí,*' the nurse murmured as he worked.

In the hallway, Spike heard a key twist in the lock. There was only one person it could be. But Spike knew he couldn't put off the confrontation for ever, so he set down his briefcase and waited for the door to open.

78

Drew looked up at Spike with a scowl of surprise, his stubbled face puffy with fatigue. Then he stepped past Spike and folded his coat carefully over the banister. 'Seen enough?'

'Your father asked me to come. I think he had things he wanted to say.'

Drew sat down carefully on the third step of the staircase. 'So Jessica had the baby?'

Spike ventured an embarrassed smile. 'A girl. We called her Juliet.'

'That'll please Rufus.'

Spike nodded.

'Funny, isn't it?' Drew went on, but there was no amusement in his eyes. 'After all these years. Your life coming together perfectly, while mine . . .' He let out a bitter laugh and swept an arm in front of him. 'Well, mine is as you see it.' The heel of one shoe slipped on the step, and it was then that Spike realised that he was very drunk.

'I'm sorry about your father, Drew.'

'Which bit? The one where he has to lie in his own excrement? Or the fact that every accolade he's achieved in the course of a remarkable life will be forgotten because of some idiotic thing he did when he was sixteen.'

Spike moved towards the door. 'I should go. Jessica will worry.'

But Drew was swaying to his feet, upper lip curling. The sweetness of booze on his breath reminded Spike of Massetti in his pomp. 'You always thought you were better than everyone else, didn't you? Even when we were at Law School.' Drew's hooded eyes narrowed. 'So quietly pleased with yourself. So sure that only *you* could walk the righteous path.'

Spike tried to control his anger. But he hadn't had a good night's sleep in as long as he could remember, and after his recent encounters with Peter and Sir Anthony, his reserves of patience were low. 'Is that what's bothering you, Drew? The manner in which I choose to practise the Law?'

Drew grinned. 'Maybe it's just the irony of it. You with your lofty ambitions, while every lawyer on the Rock knows your partner is a crook.'

Spike shoulders stiffened, and he saw Drew's drunken eyes widen as he registered that he'd hit home. It had all been conjecture, Spike realised, until now. But the damage was done. 'You can tell yourself this is about my professional ethics if it gives you comfort, Drew. But we both know it's not about that at all. You got a taste of all those things you've always wanted. Influence. Status. Prestige. Then they were snatched away. And you blame me.' The expression on Drew's face was enough to tell Spike that he was right.

Spike reached for the door handle and heard Drew call out behind him, 'I could have done something for this place. I could have been useful.' Then Drew pushed past him and wrenched open the door. 'My father is going to die, Spike. And after that, you should know that I'm coming after you.' He gripped Spike's sleeve and leant in. 'You and your lousy partner.'

Spike pulled himself free and reeled out onto the road, hearing the door slam closed behind him. His head suddenly felt very heavy on his shoulders. High on the Rock, he saw that the apes were watching him. He turned his back on Dragon Trees and set off down the road towards home.

79

Spike was struck by a blast of spices as soon as he stepped into the house. Jessica stuck her head around the kitchen door, face glowing, hair tied back in a shiny ponytail. 'You need to see this. Your father's making Christmas pudding.'

'*Plum* pudding,' Spike heard his father correct over the sound of boiling water.

Spike knelt down by the baby bouncer, feeling the tension in his neck ease as he watched Juliet perform her gummy smile. Then he turned and saw Charlie standing behind him, arms dangling by his sides. 'What is it?' he asked gently.

The boy spun around and ran up the stairs, and Spike followed, hearing laughter echo behind him. Charlie's room was the neatest in the house, his favourite toys carefully arranged in a biscuit tin in the corner – an egg of desiccating Silly Putty, a robot from the Cathedral charity shop, a handful of stickle bricks he must have pocketed at nursery. The hoarding was some kind of defence technique, Jessica had concluded, in case Juliet suddenly sprang to her hindquarters and ran off with his treasures.

The little boy clambered onto his bed with a glance over one shoulder to confirm he had Spike's undivided attention. Then he pointed up at a long, thin crack on the wall. 'Look.'

'It's just a movement crack,' Spike said, aware that he was quoting a surveyor he'd never met, and hoping that further quizzing wouldn't reveal him to be a complete imbecile in an area where most fathers seemed to excel.

Charlie rose to his tiptoes and traced a finger down the fissure. 'Max Macfarlane . . .' he began.

It took Spike a moment to place the name. 'The ninja from nursery?'

'Max Macfarlane,' Charlie resumed, 'says Gibraltar has a hole in it. He says we're all going to fall inside.' The boy turned, demanding an answer, so Spike attempted a sage sort of nod, playing for time. 'I suppose Max is right, in a way.' He stood up and made a thorough examination of the crack. 'On one side we have Africa.' He tapped a finger to the left of the crack. 'And on the other' – a tap to the right – 'Europe. Two different' – he hesitated – 'plates. And Gibraltar sits in the gap between.'

The boy's frown deepened, and Spike assumed that his explanation of plate tectonics had been insufficient, probably because he didn't really understand it himself. But then Charlie pointed up, mirroring Spike's motions. 'Africa,' he said, tracing one finger over the fissure. 'And Europe.' He dug a nail into the crack. 'And us.'

'Exactly,' Spike said.

'But if we don't choose a side, will we not fall down the hole?'

'I think we'll be OK.'

'Promise?'

Spike nodded. 'Just as long as we all stick together.' He bent down and let the boy wrap his arms around his neck. As he held his child close, he thought about Marcela Peralta and Esteban Reyes. About Christopher Massetti taking his last breaths alone on a park bench with a bottle of whiskey and no socks. Of the expression in Sir Anthony Stanford's eyes as he awaited death on a state-of-the-art hospital bed in his beautiful mansion. Of what Peter had done for Siri Baxter, and how Spike had let him think he'd been beaten into submission, and of what Drew might make of that.

Then they both heard Jessica's impatient voice calling them from downstairs. 'Are you two coming to see this or not?'

Spike gave Charlie another squeeze and set him on his feet. 'Come on. Let's see if Grandpa's set fire to the kitchen yet.'

The little boy took his father's hand and dragged him down the stairs. Outside, Spike could feel the waves beating against the Rock, back and forth, back and forth, in time with their footsteps.

'We all stick together,' he heard Charlie whisper.

Yes, thought Spike. That's exactly what we'll do.

ACKNOWLEDGEMENTS

I'd like to thank Rodney French at the National Archives in Kew for helping me track down declassified MI5 files pertaining to actual espionage and sabotage cases in Gibraltar during the Second World War. Anyone wishing to delve further into this fascinating corner of history will find the NA – both online and in physical form – an invaluable resource.

ALSO AVAILABLE BY THOMAS MOGFORD

SHADOW OF THE ROCK

A SPIKE SANGUINETTI MYSTERY

A humid summer night in Gibraltar. Lawyer Spike Sanguinetti arrives home to find an old friend, Solomon Hassan, waiting on his doorstep.

Solomon is on the run. A Spanish girl has been found with her throat cut on a beach in Tangiers and he is accused of her murder. He has managed to skip across the Straits but the Moroccan authorities want him back.

Spike travels to Tangiers to try to delay Solomon's extradition, and there meets a beautiful Bedouin girl. Zahra is investigating the disappearance of her father, a trail which leads mysteriously back to Solomon. Questioning how well he really knows his friend, Spike finds himself drawn into a dangerous game of secrets, corruption and murderous lies.

'Evocative, engrossing and entertaining'
THE TIMES

ORDER YOUR COPY:

BY PHONE: +44 (0) 1256 302 699; BY EMAIL: DIRECT@MACMILLAN.CO.UK
DELIVERY IS USUALLY 3–5 WORKING DAYS. FREE POSTAGE AND PACKAGING FOR ORDERS OVER £20.
ONLINE: WWW.BLOOMSBURY.COM/BOOKSHOP
PRICES AND AVAILABILITY SUBJECT TO CHANGE WITHOUT NOTICE.

WWW.BLOOMSBURY.COM/THOMASMOGFORD

BLOOMSBURY

ALSO AVAILABLE BY THOMAS MOGFORD

SIGN OF THE CROSS

A SPIKE SANGUINETTI MYSTERY

A domestic dispute has escalated into a bloodbath.

When his uncle and aunt are found dead, Spike Sanguinetti must cross the Mediterranean to Malta for their funerals, leaving the courtroom behind. But the more he learns about their violent deaths, the more he is troubled by one thing: what could have prompted a mild-mannered art historian to stab his wife before turning the knife upon himself?

Reunited with his ex-girlfriend, Zahra, Spike embarks on a trail that leads from the island's squalid immigrant camps to the ornate palazzos of the legendary Knights of St John. In Malta, it seems, brutality, greed and danger lie nearer to the surface than might first appear.

'Excellent'
IRISH EXAMINER

BLOOMSBURY

ALSO AVAILABLE BY THOMAS MOGFORD

HOLLOW MOUNTAIN

A SPIKE SANGUINETTI MYSTERY

**At the heart of Gibraltar lies the Rock.
At the heart of the Rock lies darkness.**

The late-morning sun beats down on the Rock of Gibraltar as bored tourists photograph the Barbary apes. A child's scream pierces the silence as she sees a monkey cradling a macabre trophy. A man's severed arm.

In the narrow streets of the Old Town below, lawyer Spike Sanguinetti's friend and colleague is critically injured in a mysterious hit-and-run. Spike must drop everything and return home to Gibraltar, where he is drawn into a case defending a ruthless salvage company hunting for treasure in the Straits.

As Spike battles to save his business, he realises that his investigations have triggered a terrifying sequence of events, and that everything he holds dear is under threat.

'Tremendous atmosphere, rich characterisation and ideally complex plotting'
WILLIAM BOYD, *GUARDIAN*

ORDER YOUR COPY:

BY PHONE: +44 (0) 1256 302 699; **BY EMAIL:** DIRECT@MACMILLAN.CO.UK
DELIVERY IS USUALLY 3–5 WORKING DAYS. FREE POSTAGE AND PACKAGING FOR ORDERS OVER £20.
ONLINE: WWW.BLOOMSBURY.COM/BOOKSHOP
PRICES AND AVAILABILITY SUBJECT TO CHANGE WITHOUT NOTICE.

WWW.BLOOMSBURY.COM/THOMASMOGFORD

BLOOMSBURY

ALSO AVAILABLE BY THOMAS MOGFORD

SLEEPING DOGS

A SPIKE SANGUINETTI MYSTERY

An idyllic Greek island. A brutal murder. A dark secret unearthed.

An old friend persuades Gibraltarian lawyer Spike Sanguinetti to take a well-earned rest on Corfu's beautiful north-east coast. But when the bloodied body of a young Albanian is found and a local man accused of his murder, Spike reluctantly agrees to take the case. Beneath the island's veneer of wealth and privilege Spike uncovers truths so damaging that those involved will go to any lengths to protect them. And when a vulnerable young woman disappears, Spike knows that there are some sleeping dogs he cannot let lie ...

'Popular fiction at its best'
SUSAN HILL, *SPECTATOR*